7 BRIDES FOR 7 BODIES

by STEPHANIE BOND

a Body Movers mystery

CHAPTER ONE

"ARE YOU READY FOR THIS?" Wesley asked, his brow furrowed.

Carlotta Wren hooked her purse on her injured shoulder, wincing slightly when the weight of it landed on the padded dressing underneath her black wrap dress. She'd labored ridiculously over what to wear to visit their long-lost fugitive father in the Atlanta City Detention Center, where he was being held after Detective Jack Terry, her sometimes-lover, had arrested him yesterday at the townhome where she and Wesley lived. But she'd decided Diane von Fürstenberg was always appropriate.

"No," Carlotta admitted as she made her way down the steps of the front stoop. "Are you?"

"Sure I am." But her younger brother stabbed at his glasses—a telltale sign he wasn't sure at all.

At the end of their driveway sat a dark blue Atlanta Police cruiser, angled to block the entrance.

"To fend off reporters, I guess," Wes offered.

Jack's doing, Carlotta was sure. She sent him a mental thank you—the last thing they needed this morning was a media circus. The driver side window of the cruiser buzzed down and the uniformed officer asked if they were leaving. She confirmed they were and thanked the bleary-eyed man who waved, then started his engine and pulled away.

Carlotta's feet moved toward the garage, but her stomach churned like a washing machine, and she felt strangely detached from the moment. Part of her numbness she could blame on the painkillers she was taking for the slicing wound The Charmed Killer had inflicted on her before her father, Randolph

Wren, had materialized to save her. The prescription drugs had sent her on a fantastic trip across time the previous night in her dreams, the remnants of which still plucked at her. *What if's* and *should've been's* had plagued her most of her adult life. She desperately hoped their father's reappearance would help to put some of those doubts and anxieties to rest.

As the garage door raised, Carlotta glanced around to take in their unkempt yard and the shabby neighborhood, alert for interlopers now that their guard had left. But at nine o'clock on a muggy Wednesday morning in Lindbergh, an older section of Atlanta that squatted between the bling of Buckhead and the zing of Midtown, everyone was going about their business, seemingly oblivious that the world of the Wren children had just been turned upside down.

Again.

On the other hand, considering what she and Wesley had been through over the past ten years on their own, maybe their neighbors had gotten used to the commotion and were no longer paying attention.

And she was relieved Peter Ashford, the closest thing she had to a boy-friend, and Hannah Kizer, her dearest gal pal, and Cooper Craft, Wesley's endearing body-moving boss, had respected her request for space to allow her and Wesley to acclimate to a new normal.

Their father was back.

The realization still took her breath away.

But Randolph's sudden appearance to save her had unleashed a whole new set of questions—how had he known Carlotta's life was in danger? Where had he been for the past ten years? And where was their mother Valerie?

"Want me to drive?" Wes nodded to the two-door rental she'd been driv-ing since her blue Monte Carlo muscle car had been blown sky high by The Charmed Killer.

"You don't have a driver's license," she reminded him.

"You should rest your shoulder while you can."

He was right. And considering the momentous errand ahead of them, what was a piddling misdemeanor if they were stopped between here and the city lockup?

She handed him the keys. "No speeding."

He nodded solemnly. With a start she realized her lovable slacker brother seemed more grown up this morning, his normal smart-ass attitude shelved for the time being. He looked more mature, too, having traded his standard holey tee for a button-up shirt and jacket usually reserved for his body-moving jobs. But of course he wanted to look grown up for Randolph, who hadn't seen Wesley—as far as they knew—since he was a scrawny nine-year-old.

Wes unlocked the trunk and stowed his bicycle. Carlotta bit down on her tongue until her eyes watered. After the family reunion, her little brother would be off to do any number of things that were decidedly un-family-friendly, such as meet with his probation officer, report to his part-time computer-security job that was part of his community service for a hacking crime, or steal away to his secret side job of working undercover in a loan shark organization at the behest of the slimy D.A.—a job she wasn't supposed to know or talk about, according to Jack, who'd told her under duress.

Oh, and there was Wesley's freelance body-moving gig.

Damn Randolph for abandoning her, but double-damn him for abandoning Wesley. He had suffered from their parents' absence more than she had. She prayed their father would say the right things today, that he had some plausible explanation for skipping out on their lives. Granted, though, gentle-hearted Wesley, who believed their father was innocent of the white-collar crimes he'd been accused of, would not require much in terms of contrition. He would take whatever Randolph said at face value.

Notwithstanding the fact that Randolph had saved her from a madman, she wasn't inclined to be so forgiving.

Next to the rental car sat her beloved white Miata, incapacitated. Remembering the drug-induced "trip" she'd taken in the car the night before, Carlotta eyed the convertible warily as she opened the passenger door of the rental to swing inside.

Wes was already buckled in, seat and mirrors adjusted. He cranked the ignition. "Tell me again how Dad looks."

She gave him a little smile. "The same, only older. You'll see soon enough."

"What if he doesn't recognize me?"

"How could he not? You look just like him."

It was true—Wesley's light brown hair and fine-boned features were Randolph's, and model-worthy, although her brother didn't seem to be aware that his good looks turned heads.

Carlotta frowned when she thought of one head in particular. Liz Fischer, Randolph's attorney and former lover, had recently transferred her inappropriate attention onto Wesley. Carlotta wanted to throttle the woman, but Wes was an adult...as Jack had reminded her several times.

She frowned harder—Jack and Liz had history of their own.

"Is your shoulder hurting?"

"Hm?"

Wes backed the car out the garage. "You look like you're in pain."

"I'm fine," she murmured, giving herself a mental shake. She had too much on her mind to worry about where Jack Terry had left his DNA.

Wes maneuvered the car down the driveway, started to back out onto the street, then slammed on the brakes as a massive SUV blasted its horn and blew by close enough to shake their vehicle. Carlotta dug her nails into the armrest. Wes exhaled and pulled a hand down his face. "Sorry."

"Maybe I should drive."

"No, I got it," he said, then eased out onto the street.

"Do you know the way?"

Wes arched an eyebrow and Carlotta sighed. They both knew the way to the city jail by heart. And she couldn't blame her brother entirely—she'd seen the wrong side of cell bars herself. It was only for a few hours when she'd taken a tire iron to one of Wesley's loan sharks—totally justified. And there was the time she'd been arrested for murder—a big, fat mistake. But still, if one were keeping score in the spectator sport that was her life, she was sitting somewhere around minus ten points.

She settled back and tried to empty her mind of troubling thoughts—past, present...and future. Randolph's timely appearance had also interrupted her and Peter's impending trip to Las Vegas. It was supposed to have been an impromptu vacation, but she'd found a ring box in Peter's packed suitcase. She could only assume that between Cirque du Soleil and Celine Dion, he'd been planning to propose.

And wasn't a tiny part of her glad she had a reason to postpone that particular conversation?

The announcer on the radio delivered the traffic report—the rush hour in Atlanta usually averaged four hours—then heralded the day's headlines.

"In local news, police are reporting the capture of fugitive Randolph Wren, who famously skipped bail over ten years ago for investment fraud in a case where investors lost millions and nearly bankrupted the Buckhead firm where Wren was a partner. In a strange twist, Wren was apprehended during the arrest of a man accused of being The Charmed Killer. The GBI reports that Wren's name did emerge as a suspect in that case because of an alleged romantic relationship with one of the victims. It's not known what connection Wren has to the man in custody for a crime spree that resulted in the deaths of several Atlanta women. Stay tuned for more details on this developing story."

So much for trying to keep the sordid details from neighbors and coworkers.

Wesley leaned forward and swiped at the OFF button. "Assholes."

"They're just reporting what they were told," Carlotta murmured. "They have a job to do."

Her mind clicked to the voice message she'd received from Rainie Stephens, a reporter for the *Atlanta Journal-Constitution*. She and Rainie had worked together on a couple of cases and had fostered a mutual, if wary, respect. The short message had been personal and supportive in light of the news of Randolph's arrest...but Carlotta knew the underlying motive was to nab an exclusive from a victim of The Charmed Killer case who also happened to be the daughter of a federal fugitive. It was the kind of story that could catapult a local reporter to national exposure.

She checked her phone log to find several missed calls from Peter and Hannah, one from Coop, and a few calls from numbers she didn't recognize, although how strangers could've gotten her mobile number, she didn't know. Her voice mail message light blinked frantically. And there were a string of unanswered texts from Peter. *Are you ok?...Just ping me to let me know you're ok...Good night...Good morning...I miss you...Remember I love you.*

"Peter trying to reach you?" Wes asked.

She nodded. "He wanted me—us—to stay with him last night."

"I know—I overheard you talking at the hospital." He looked over. "Thanks for saying no. I wanted to be home."

Home. The cramped little townhouse where they resided was nothing like the palatial Buckhead home they'd grown up in. After their father had been fired from the investment firm that bore his name and they'd been forced to move out, Carlotta hadn't been back, hadn't been able to stomach seeing another family living there, overriding the Wren family memories. But last night in her time-travel dream, she had found herself walking through the threshold of their former home, and the relative grandeur of it was, sadly, still fresh in her mind. To her, the townhome would always represent a place their family had been banished to...but it made her happy to hear Wesley refer to it as home because it left her feeling as if maybe she hadn't done as sorry a job raising him as she usually believed.

She tucked away the phone, her mind swirling with the names of the people she needed to contact later—including her boss Lindy at Neiman Marcus to once again assure the woman that despite appearances to the contrary, she could still do her job.

As they neared the detention center, she and Wes maintained a tense silence. She chewed on her thumbnail, imagining her brother's thoughts to be as chaotic as her own. She cast about for something reassuring to say, but she was at a loss, her stomach rolling and pitching. Because the truth was, she didn't know how all of this was going to shake out.

Traffic eased and every red light turned green, as if the universe was hurrying her toward her father. After a decade of waiting and wondering and weeping, this was happening so fast...too fast. When she saw their destination looming ahead, she swallowed past a dry throat, wishing she'd brought a bottle of water.

And what if she burst into tears? She hadn't thought to bring a tissue. Or wear waterproof mascara. She gripped her purse harder—retro Gucci...

timeless, but not roomy. It wasn't big enough, for example, to hold photographs of all the things Randolph had missed over the years, assuming he'd even want to see them.

Wes shifted in his seat. "How long do you think we'll get to talk to Dad?"

"Jack told me we'd have twenty minutes."

Wes's mouth tightened. "Jerk."

"It's not his rule, Wes."

"Still...I bet he's gloating like hell to have brought down a big-name fugitive. He and the D.A. are probably still out celebrating."

"That's not really Jack's style."

"He has a style?"

She decided to let that one pass as Wes slowed the car to turn into the crowded visitor parking lot. The Atlanta City Detention Center was a popular place.

"What are you going to ask Dad first?" Wes's voice vibrated with nervous excitement.

She wet her lips. "I thought I would let him do the talking. Don't you think he owes us that much?"

Wes frowned as he maneuvered into a parking space on the back row. "Don't mess this up."

"What do you mean?"

"You sound angry."

Her chin went up. "I have a right to be angry."

His jaw clenched, then he shoved the gear shift into park and killed the engine. "Dad has a lot to deal with right now. He needs our support."

Carlotta gaped. "Support? Wes, he's the criminal here. We're the victims."

"He got caught saving your life," Wes said evenly. "He's in jail because of you. You should be grateful."

Fury rose in her chest like a tide. "Grateful? I should be grateful because Randolph walked out and left me with—" She broke off before she said something she couldn't take back.

"With me?" Wes's face was a mask of hurt.

"With his mess to clean up," she corrected. But the damage was done.

"Why didn't you turn me over to foster care?" Wes spat out. "I probably would've been better off."

Okay, that stung…and was probably true. She blinked back hot tears as he opened the door and flung himself out. The car shook when he slammed the door. He popped the trunk lid and hauled out his bike none too gently, then walked it to a nearby bike rack, as if to punctuate that he would be getting away from her as quickly as possible when they left.

She took a few calming breaths and reminded herself they were both emotionally raw at the moment, but they had been through worse.

Hopefully.

Carlotta opened the door and climbed out, relieved to see Wes was waiting for her at the entrance to the slightly formidable building. She never thought she would long for the relative coziness of the Midtown police precinct where Jack Terry worked and everyone knew her name.

As she approached, Wes held himself rigid and refused to look at her. The one moment when they should've been standing in solidarity, and she felt utterly alone. Despair welled in her chest as he swung open the heavy glass door.

"Wes—" she began.

"What the hell is *he* doing here?"

Carlotta looked up. A man in a sport coat waiting next to the security desk straightened, obviously waiting for them. Her heart went *kaboom*.

Jack.

CHAPTER TWO

AT THE SIGHT OF JACK TERRY, Carlotta's mind reeled with images from last night's dream in an alternate universe. In it, she had met the hulking detective all over again, under different circumstances…and their chemistry had been just as powerful.

"Did you ask him to come?" Wesley asked, his voice accusing.

"No, I didn't." But now that she thought about it, it made sense that Jack would be here, keeping an eye on his prize prisoner.

He strode up and nodded to her. "Hi."

After her disturbing dream, she was so happy he actually knew who she was, she felt positively giddy. "Hi."

Wesley elbowed her.

"I mean, I didn't expect to see you here."

"How's your shoulder?" Jack asked.

"Fine," she murmured.

"We're fine," Wesley added in a pointed voice.

Jack's gold-colored eyes were bloodshot and although his shirt was fresh, his rumpled jacket and tie told a different story: He hadn't slept since placing Randolph under arrest the previous day.

"What are you doing here?" Wes pressed.

"I thought you might be here early," Jack said, evading the question. "Are you sure you want to do this?"

He was talking to her, but Wes angled himself between them. "Get out of our way. If you hadn't wanted to be a big bad-ass hero, we could be catching up with Dad around our kitchen table right now."

Jack pursed his mouth. "I was only doing my job."

"Right," Wes said dryly, then jerked his head toward the door. "You can leave now."

"I want to be here for Carlotta."

Carlotta crossed her arms. The men had apparently forgotten she was there.

"This is a family affair," Wes said. "Are you looking to join the family, Detective?"

Okay, that made her smile a little. Wes knew one of Jack's pressure points—commitment. She enjoyed watching the big man squirm before she put him out of his misery.

"This was nice of you, Jack, but..." She trailed off because something behind her had caught his attention, and from the expression on his face, it wasn't glad tidings.

She turned to see GBI agents Wick and Green walking toward them, and immediately stiffened. The men had worked The Charmed Killer case and had not only grilled her mercilessly about her family's "connections" to the case, but when they had finally made an arrest, the agents had dismissed her declaration that they had the wrong person in custody. The pair made an odd couple visually—Wick, a tall, slim black man, and Green, a short, stocky white guy—but they seemed to play off each other to good—and irritating—advantage.

"Good morning," Agent Wick said, his smile tight.

"I see the gang's all here," Green added. "Hooray—that'll save me a few phone calls."

"What do you mean?" Jack asked, widening his stance.

"We've been asked to relocate Randolph Wren," Wick said, pulling a thick set of folded documents out of his jacket pocket and holding it up. "To USP."

Carlotta swung her gaze to Jack. "What does that mean?"

A muscle worked in his jaw. "They're moving your father to the United States Penitentiary across town."

"The federal pen?" she asked.

He nodded, then looked back to the agents. "When?"

Green checked his watch. "Let's see...uh—now."

"After his children have had a chance to talk to him," Jack added.

"Afraid not," Wick said, shaking his head. "They'll have to wait until he's settled at USP."

Panic spurred Carlotta forward a step. "But we've been *waiting* for over ten years."

Green gave a little shrug. "We have our orders. Your father belongs to the feds now."

Wes lunged forward, his hands balled into fists. "You assholes!"

Jack clamped his hand on Wes's shoulder. "Relax," he said in a low voice.

"You better watch your temper there," Green snapped. "Assaulting an agent will get you a jumpsuit to match your daddy's."

"We're good," Jack said cheerfully, but visibly tightened his grip on Wes.

Carlotta's stomach plummeted in abject disappointment that the family reunion might not happen, but her heart went out to Wesley, whose eyes glittered with angry tears. She'd at least had brief contact with Randolph in the past year—once he'd passed her a note that she'd found later, and once he'd engaged her in conversation while in disguise. And she'd seen him fleetingly yesterday when he'd saved her life. She had a face and a voice as proof her father was still alive, but Wes had nothing concrete to cling to.

"I would've thought you two would be busy dealing with The Charmed Killer," Carlotta said wryly, "seeing as how now you've got the right man and all."

Jack made a noise that could've been a cough or a laugh.

"We're trained to multi-task," Wick said, matching her tone.

Carlotta ground her teeth, but realized she needed to change tack. "Gentlemen, surely there's some way we can see Randolph before you transport him?" She wasn't beneath batting her eyelashes. *Flap, flap.*

Green made a clicking noise in his throat. "No can do, little lady. But we'll tell him you said hello."

Jack must've realized Carlotta wanted to punch the man in the face, because his other hand shot out to clasp her forearm and give her a warning squeeze.

"Yes," Jack said to the men. "Tell Randolph his children will see him at the federal detention center as soon as possible."

Wick's gaze bounced back and forth between the three of them. "Do you babysit in your free time, Terry?"

Jack gave a little laugh. "Funny. If you two jackasses don't move along, I'm going to turn these two loose and look the other way."

Green scowled. "You got a bad attitude, boy."

Jack's smile didn't waver. "So I've been told."

He maintained his hold on them until Wick and Green walked away, then released them with a grunt. Wes swiped at his eyes, his body shaking with fury. "I don't believe this!"

"But we can go now to USP, can't we?" Carlotta asked. "We'll follow them."

Jack shook his head. "It doesn't work like that. It'll take a while to process him, and then the feds will want their time with him." He sighed. "I know this sucks, but you've both waited a long time to talk to Randolph, and a couple of more days isn't going to kill you."

"Shut up." Wes stabbed his finger in the air for emphasis. "You're the one who arrested him, for God's sake. And if you hadn't stopped us just now, we would've already been back there, talking to our dad." He was near tears again. "Why don't you mind your own damn business?"

They were attracting attention from the security guards. Jack flashed his badge and gave them a signal that he had the situation under control.

Then he jammed his hands on his hips and looked at Carlotta. "Do you feel the same?"

She bit into her lower lip, her mind spinning. How did she feel about Jack being so involved in their lives? Her mind changed like the weather. Some days she wished their paths had never crossed…although the dream she'd had about the "other place" made her think they had been fated to meet, no matter what. And there was no arguing he'd saved her butt more than once, the confounding man. And the sex…well, the detective had skills not listable on LinkedIn.

Although Wes had a point that if Jack hadn't insisted on dragging Randolph away from the townhome, that if he'd only given them an hour as a family to talk before he slapped on the cuffs, they wouldn't be standing here right now, with Wes feeling as if he was never going to see his father with his own eyes.

"Carlotta?" Jack prompted.

"I feel…" Under his gaze and Wesley's, her voice faltered, then she tried again. "That is, maybe we *could* use a break from each other, Jack."

Jack's expression clouded, then he nodded. "Loud and clear." He turned toward the entrance, and she wanted to reach out to him, take back the words. Why was everything between them so tricky?

Suddenly he turned back. "Actually, why don't both of you take a walk with me to my car?"

"Gee, that didn't last long," Wes said sarcastically.

"One walk," Jack said. "Then I'll step back from the Wrens."

"Why should we?" Wes asked.

Jack massaged the bridge of his nose. "Trust me this once?" He swept his arm forward for Carlotta and Wes to precede him out the building.

Carlotta moved self-consciously, hoping this wasn't a ruse to place Wesley under arrest for something, like driving with a suspended license.

He led them to a special parking lot for law enforcement vehicles. When they reached his dark sedan, he gestured. "Get in."

Wes gave her a questioning glance, but she only shrugged. Jack held open the front passenger side door for her. She slid inside, thinking it had been a while since she'd ridden shotgun with him. Detective Maria Marquez had most recently occupied this spot. A pang of grief for the woman barbed through her heart. She had been jealous of the camaraderie the beautiful woman shared with Jack, but she was as shocked and saddened as everyone else when Maria had been killed.

It seemed as if Jack was destined to be alone.

Wes climbed in the back seat, his expression sullen and closed.

When Jack settled into the driver's seat and turned over the ignition, Wes popped up. "Where the hell are we going?"

Jack threw a frown over his shoulder. "You really should clean up your language."

"Fuck you."

"Nice," Jack said blandly. "I told you to trust me. And sink down so everyone can't see your fat head."

Wes flounced back in the seat, but did as he was told. Carlotta raised her eyebrows at Jack and he gave her a reassuring wink. He guided the car around the lot to a spot close to the building, and killed the engine. They sat in perplexed silence for a few minutes. When Carlotta tired of watching Jack play with the gadgets on his dashboard, she sighed and gave him a withering look. Then Jack lifted his hand and pointed to her right.

She turned her head to see Wick and Green appear around the corner of the building about fifty feet away.

And between them, handcuffed and dressed in a gray jumpsuit, was Randolph.

A lump of emotion sprang to her throat.

"This is total bullshit," Wes said, oblivious to what was happening.

"Wes." Her voice vibrated. "Look."

He looked out the window, then sprang up in his seat. "Dad! It's Dad!" He scrambled to open the door, which wasn't possible, of course, because Jack had locked them in.

"You can't get out," Jack said. "And he can't see in. Be quiet and enjoy the moment."

They did. Carlotta had her nose pressed against the window, drinking in the sight of her father. He was still tall and fit, but not as robust and tan as she remembered. He obviously wasn't getting in as much golf and tennis as he used to. And his hair had silvered around the temples and sideburns. He appeared to be healthy, though, and sure-footed. As the agents led him to a car, he tilted his face to look up at the sun, as if he might be afraid he'd never see it again.

She glanced back and saw that Wesley had his face and both hands planted against the window, his mouth slightly ajar. "It's really him," he whispered. "He really is alive."

Carlotta smiled, then turned and reached for Jack's hand to give it a grateful squeeze. He squeezed back.

Randolph glanced all around, as if he were looking for someone…looking for them? His gaze passed over the Jack's car, and for a few seconds, Carlotta felt as if he was looking directly at her. She held her breath.

Suddenly, Wes had lunged over the front seat between them, his hands aimed for the steering wheel, his feet off the floor. The horn blasted into the air. "We're here, Dad!" he shouted. "It's Wes and Carlotta—we're here!"

Several ear-splitting seconds had passed before Jack could shove Wes back into the seat. "Stay there," he bellowed.

The agents had both drawn their weapons, and Randolph was riveted to their car, his eyes and body alert. Wick hustled him into the rear seat of their car, and Green barreled toward Jack's sedan.

"This should be fun," Jack muttered. He glanced at Wesley. "If you try to draw attention to yourself again, I'll have to shoot you, and you'll never get to talk to your dad, got it?"

Carlotta pressed her lips together. Jack was bluffing, of course, but the part about not getting to talk to their dad must've hit home, because Wes frowned, but nodded.

Jack stepped out of the car and closed the door.

Carlotta shot Wes a reproving glance over the seat. "Jack was trying to do something nice."

Wes shrugged. "At least Dad knows we were here."

"Only if the agents tell him."

"We can tell him later it was us," Wes said, undaunted.

Outside, she saw Jack was getting a tongue-lashing from Green, punctuated with lots of air chops. She winced. Jack lifted his hands in a sign of mute surrender and the agent backed up, glaring until he reached his car and swung inside. The car sped away with more gusto than necessary, leaving a swirl of dust in its wake.

Jack climbed back into the car and sighed. "That was a dumb move, Wes."

Wes grinned. "I'm only nineteen—I do dumb things."

Jack gave Carlotta an exasperated look. She mouthed, "I'm sorry."

But Wes was bouncing in the backseat. "Did you see him, Sis? Doesn't he look great?"

His excitement was infectious and she laughed. "I did, and he does."

"Oh my freaking God," Wes said, still bouncing. "This is the best day of my life!"

"Easy on the springs back there," Jack said sourly as he started the car.

Carlotta laid a hand on his arm. "Thank you, Jack."

"Don't mention it—and I mean that. I'm already in enough trouble. Where are you parked?"

She told him the way, her pulse clicking higher as they approached her car. Wes was still talking to no one in particular about how awesome it was to see Randolph, and he couldn't wait to talk to him.

As soon as the car stopped, Wesley said, "Gotta run, Sis—I'll call you later."

"Wait outside for a minute, would you, Wes?" Jack asked. "I need a word."

Wes frowned. "Do I have a choice?"

"Nope."

He rolled his eyes. "Okay." Then he banged his way out of the car, and walked toward the bike rack.

Jack turned back to her. "Visiting or calling USP requires some paperwork and protocol. If you run into any snags, give Brooklyn a call."

Not him, but the lady who kept the Midtown precinct in order. Carlotta could already feel his detachment, and bitterly regretted her earlier words. "Jack…about what I said—"

"You're right," he said. "Now that Randolph is in custody, it's important that we maintain a certain amount of distance."

She nodded. "Okay. But I'm not happy about this."

"I'm sure Peter will be."

She decided not to respond.

"I assume your Vegas trip got postponed?"

"Yes."

His dark eyebrows climbed. "Well, then I've got something to be happy about, too."

She gave him a light punch in the arm, then sobered. "Jack, did Randolph say anything to you after you arrested him?"

"What do you mean?"

"Did he mention…our mother?"

A shadow fell over his eyes. "No. I'm sorry. I tried to draw him out, but he didn't say a word on the ride to the jail or while he was being booked. He wouldn't even make eye contact."

Although she wasn't surprised, her heart dragged with disappointment. She reached for the door handle. "I should go."

"So," he said with a little smile, "I guess I won't be seeing you around."

"I guess not," she said breezily.

His gaze caught hers and unreadable emotions flitted over his face. This man could make her feel so much…but was it because they were always enmeshed in a crisis? Adrenaline could be a powerful aphrodisiac…but would ultimately lead to a plunging crash.

Carlotta moistened her lips. Then before she did something crazy—like vault across the seat and straddle him—she lifted the door handle and escaped.

Plus ten points.

Then she frowned. No, wait—*minus* ten.

CHAPTER THREE

WES UNLOCKED HIS BIKE and expelled a sigh of relief when Carlotta emerged from Jack's car and retreated to her rental. He got nervous when those two were together—he was always afraid Carlotta was going to...leave.

Or be left.

He didn't worry as much when she was with Peter—he would do right by her. And so would Coop.

He walked his bike to the curb as Jack climbed out and walked toward him in his action-hero swagger. Wes smirked. Even a love-idiot like him could see that any woman who attached herself to this guy was going to pay for it tenfold in the long run. In his professional life, sure—Jack saved women and babies from burning buildings. But in his personal life, he was a little less noble.

Not that Wes had time to worry about it—he had his own problems. Just when he'd gotten clean from the Oxycontin and things were looking up with his coworker Meg Vincent, he'd gotten a call from Liz Fischer, his attorney and occasional booty call—

Although, come to think of it, maybe he was the booty since Liz did the calling?

Regardless of who or whom, there was a new development: Liz was pregnant.

With a baby.

When she'd told him on the phone, the memory of a busted condom has flashed in his mind and he'd promptly fainted. Mouse had brought him back around with a face full of pink lemonade Icee. And while he'd been trying to deal with that little earthquake, Carlotta had called with the news that had shifted his life another ninety degrees—Randolph was back.

Their dad was back.

He wiped a hand over his inadvertent grin—wow. It was surreal seeing his father again, like seeing a ghost. Sometimes he wondered if he actually remembered his parents, or if he'd simply memorized the photos. He was still pissed he hadn't gotten to talk to Randolph, to hear his voice and once and for all get his side of the story, but just the knowledge that he was alive and safe was a huge relief.

He took a deep breath. And Randolph's appearance had given him some clarity on what he needed to do where Liz was concerned.

Jack strode up to him. "That was a bonehead move back there. And you're welcome."

Wesley scoffed. "Don't expect a thank-you from me for that little sight-seeing trip. You're the one who caused this problem, remember?"

A muscle worked in Jack's jaw. "Randolph is one who caused this problem. Did it ever occur to you that I arrested him not to keep you and Carlotta away from him, but to make sure he couldn't take off again?"

"I thought you said you were doing your job?"

"I was. But I also wanted him confined to a place where he'd be forced to sit down and talk to you and your sister."

"And yet that hasn't happened."

Jack scratched his temple. "I didn't count on the feds to swoop in, at least not so soon."

"Yeah, well...I need to go." Wes jerked his thumb over his shoulder. "I have to be somewhere."

"It can wait a few minutes." Jack assumed his cop stance. "I want to talk you."

Wes scowled. "About what?"

"About how your fingerprints wound up on an anonymous note the APD received listing possible names of an unidentified headless corpse in the morgue."

Wes felt his face blanch—Liz had tipped him off that Jack had called her about it, but he hadn't had time to think of a cover story. He wasn't sure, but he suspected his buddy Mouse had offed the man since he'd made Wes pull the teeth out of the decapitated head as a rite of passage before being accepted into The Carver's loan shark organization. He owed Mouse a debt of thanks for helping him get off Oxy. The man didn't know he was working undercover for the APD to offset a charge of body tampering from when he—

Wes sighed. It was a long, sad story. And from the sour look on the detective's face, he wasn't in the mood to let Wes ruminate.

"If you witnessed something while working for The Carver," Jack said, "you don't have to make anonymous tips—just tell me. That's why I'm your liaison."

"Are you going to *liase* my body to Carlotta when I'm murdered for being a snitch?"

Jack frowned. "Don't bring your sister into this."

A red convertible Jaguar slid to a stop next to them, and Wes's stomach bottomed out. Liz Fischer, wearing big sunglasses and a scarf tied around her blond hair, smiled up at them. "Why, Jack, you wouldn't be questioning my client without me being present, would you?"

Jack looked perturbed. "Wouldn't think of it."

She lowered her sunglasses to reveal piercing blue eyes. "Good."

"What brings you to the city lockup, Liz?" Jack asked. "New client?"

"An old one," she said, sliding her gaze to Wesley. "I assume you're here to see Randolph, too?"

Wes nodded. "Didn't happen though—he was moved this morning."

She frowned and looked to Jack for clarification.

"Feds had him moved to USP."

She made a thoughtful noise. "Makes sense, although I'm sure D.A. Lucas is livid."

"He'll have to wait his turn," Jack said. "I guess the feds want a crack at Wren first."

She checked her watch. "I suppose I'd better head over there and see."

"Take me with you," Wes pleaded.

She shook her head. "They won't let him have visitors without the proper paperwork. They'll only let me in because they have to."

Wes swallowed his disappointment. "Will you tell him Carlotta and I tried to see him?"

"Of course," she said, her voice sounding motherly, which only further unnerved him. He wondered what else Liz and his father would talk about. Would they reminisce about their own affair? Would she tell him she was involved with Wes now? And that she was—his intestines cramped—pregnant?

"I hate to be a killjoy," Jack said, "but the three of us need to talk about Wesley's connection to a headless corpse in the morgue."

Liz waved off his concern. "A misunderstanding, I'm sure. I'll have my office call you later to set up an appointment for us to sit down and get it all straightened out."

Jack inclined his head in resignation.

She looked back to Wes. "Our last phone call dropped rather suddenly. Are you okay?"

He swallowed and nodded, not okay at all.

"You haven't returned my calls."

Sweat dripped down his back, and he was pretty sure he was about to have a stroke.

Jack cleared his throat. "I'm sure his father's return has taken precedence over everything else...right, Wes?"

"Uh...yeah." He managed to sling one leg over his bike. "I have to go see my probation officer."

"Oh, about that," Liz said. "I played interference for you. Call me later and let me know how it goes?"

His head bobbed like a Pez dispenser, then he hopped on his bike and pedaled like mad to get away from the situation. For now, anyway.

He glanced back to see Jack and Liz still talking, and hoped it wasn't about the anonymous note. After going to all the trouble of tracking down the dead man's possible identity through a tattoo, why hadn't he been more careful about leaving fingerprints on the paper?

And damn, from one bad situation to another, he thought a few minutes later as the building where his probation officer worked loomed in front of him. Last week he'd been required to submit to a blood test to check for drugs. The "blocker" his friend Chance had given him hid his Oxy use in urine samples. But as he'd watched his polluted blood fill the vial, he'd known he was busted.

But that was before Mouse had tossed him in a warehouse to detox, the hard way. It had been hell, but he'd lived. He prayed his P.O. was in a charitable mood today.

On the other hand, he thought with a laugh as he cooled his heels in the waiting room, if she violated his probation and he went to jail for hacking into the courthouse database, maybe he'd get to see his father in the mess hall or in the rec yard.

"Something funny, Wren?" the lady at the window barked.

He shook his head. "Nope...not a thing."

"You're up."

He pushed to his feet and made his way to E. Jones's office. He was glad he'd worn a jacket—hopefully it made him look more mature. He certainly felt more mature than a mere week ago. In that time he'd gone through rehab, found out he was going to be a father, and discovered his own long-lost father had returned.

It had been an epic few days.

He rapped on the closed door and waited, straightening his collar.

"Come in," a woman's voice called.

He walked in and his spirits lifted involuntarily at the sight of E. Jones seated at her desk, her pretty head bent over a file in a way that had her dark red hair falling forward. She looked up and the light in her green eyes faded.

Uh-oh.

"Hello, Wesley."

"Hi."

"Sit down."

He did. "I—"

"Don't speak."

He swallowed his words.

She studied him, her hands steepled over the open file. "You've put me in a heck of a spot here."

He pressed his lips together.

"You know, of course, that you failed last week's drug test."

He nodded miserably.

"Your attorney called and told me you got clean over the weekend?"

Another nod.

"How do you kick an Oxycontin habit in three days?"

He wet his lips. "Am I allowed to speak now?"

"Yes."

"Cold turkey."

"Cold turkey, huh? So you think you've kicked your addiction just because it's out of your system. Have you dealt with what caused it in the first place?"

"I guess so. I starting taking it for pain, and the pain is gone."

"What kind of pain?"

He shrugged out of his jacket, then rolled up his shirt sleeve to reveal the crude red scars on his arms. "You asked me last time what caused these marks."

She gave him a wry smile. "As I recall, you told me they were paper cuts."

"I lied. A loan shark known as The Carver started cutting his name into my arm." He traced the puckered skin. "He got as far as 'C-A-R.'"

From her wide-eyed look of horror, he'd gotten her attention. "Because you owed him money?"

That wasn't the full story, but he nodded. "We got behind on our bills at home, and I borrowed the money to catch us up." Also a stretch of the truth, but his freedom was on the line.

"And you couldn't pay it back?"

"Right. I thought by charging friends for fixing speeding tickets in the courthouse database, I could buy my way out of trouble."

"But instead, you were arrested."

He splayed his hands. "And here I am."

She lifted one winged eyebrow. "It didn't occur to you to get an actual job?"

"In this economy? Where could I get a job making the kind of money I needed?"

She sighed. "Wes, there are people everywhere who are behind on their bills, but they don't break the law to get the money they need."

"I know, and if I had to do it over again, I would do things differently." He wiped at his eye and poked it to whip up a few tears. "All I'm asking is to have my blood drawn again and tested. And you can take it every week from now on if you want. But I can't go to jail, not now."

She took the bait. "Why not now?"

"You haven't heard? My father is back."

"Your fugitive father? Hasn't he been gone for—"

"Over ten years, yeah. But my sister was being attacked by The Charmed Killer, and he saved her."

She pursed her mouth. "Carlotta was being attacked by a serial killer, and your dad just happened to appear and save her?"

"Yep."

She studied him, then sighed. "If I didn't know your history and your sister's penchant for trouble, I'd swear you were making this up."

"Call Detective Jack Terry at the Midtown precinct. He'll back me up."

"I will—later. Meanwhile, have you spoken to your father?"

"No. I tried to this morning, but the feds had him moved to another facility."

"USP?"

"That's it." Then he grinned. "But I did get to see him when they walked him out."

She smiled. "That had to be a nice moment for you."

"You have no idea." He conjured up a contrite expression. "So you see, I can't go to jail now. E., please give me another chance."

She narrowed her eyes, but he could tell she was wavering. He held her gaze and didn't blink to allow the moisture to build up in his eyes.

Finally, she sighed. "Well, since you already have your sleeve rolled up..."

He beamed.

She punched in a number on her desk phone. "Don't make me regret this."

Wes shook his head, then noticed the engagement ring on her left finger. She hadn't been wearing it last week and had seemed upset. But apparently, she and her fiancé Leonard were back together. Which meant she still didn't know Leonard was a drug runner. He itched to tell E., but then he'd have to say how he knew, and that would get his buddy Chance in trouble.

Plus Leonard had threatened to put him in a coma if he told, so mum was the word. He had enough problems without borrowing more.

After the blood was drawn, E. asked her normal battery of questions.

"How is your community service job?"

"Fine," he said. Except Meg was on vacation and had taken the sunshine with her. He felt sick when he thought of what she would think of him when she found out he'd gotten his attorney pregnant.

"And your courier job?"

His cover for working in The Carver's organization as a collections agent with Mouse. "Great. It's helping me pay down my debt." That part, at least, was true.

"And you're not gambling?"

"Absolutely not." Not today anyway. So far.

"And how do you think your life will change now that your father is home?"

He blinked. "I…don't know. I guess I still don't have my head wrapped around it."

"That's understandable. Call me if there's anything I can do."

"Okay. Thanks."

She closed the file folder. "And assuming your blood test comes back clean, I'll see you next week."

Wes made his getaway, feeling marginally better than when he arrived, yet knowing the week ahead was going to be a rollercoaster. Hopefully he'd get to see his dad soon. But Meg would be back from vacation Monday, and he dreaded that conversation.

He was massaging his sore arm in the parking lot when his phone rang. He pulled it out of his backpack and stared at the screen. *Meg Vincent*. His heart squeezed. He wanted to hear her voice, wanted to tell her the news about his dad, wanted to know if she missed him as much as he missed her.

Instead he hit "decline" and stuffed the phone to the bottom of his bag.

CHAPTER FOUR

CARLOTTA FOUGHT TEARS of frustration on the long drive back to the townhouse. This morning when she'd opened her eyes, she'd had such high hopes for the day. Finally, she and Wesley would have answers to the questions that had undermined every move they made, every day. Instead, now Randolph was right under their noses…and totally out of reach.

From the console, her phone vibrated. She picked it up and smiled when she saw Hannah's name on the screen. In last night's travel dream, Hannah hadn't known her—at first. But soon they had been fast friends again, and partners in crime-solving. Their friendship was meant to be.

Carlotta connected the call. "Hiya."

"How the hell is dear old Dad?" Hannah asked, her voice brimming with excitement.

Carlotta sighed. "We didn't get to talk to him. Two agents came and moved him to the U.S. Penitentiary."

"You're shitting me."

"Nope. The universe is conspiring against me having a conversation with my own father."

"How did Wes take it?"

"Not well. But we did at least get to see Randolph when he was taken from the building, so Wes got to set eyes on him."

"God, I'm sorry. What now?"

"Jack said communicating with Randolph at USP will require some paper-work, so I'll look into it as soon as I get home."

"Does your father still have an attorney?"

Carlotta thought of Liz and winced. "I suppose...but I kind of hate her."

"Still, she should be able to help."

Carlotta groaned. "You're right. I'll call her." The thought of dealing with the woman who had seduced both Wren men made her sick to her stomach.

"How's your shoulder?"

"Hurting...but healing."

"Chance told me to ask if you need some meds."

She frowned, still getting used to the idea of Hannah sleeping with Wes's best friend Chance Hollander, a fat trust-fund brat who dabbled in illegal contraband. "Uh, I'm good, thanks."

"Okay—let me know if you change your mind. You're not going into work today, are you?"

"Officially, I'm still on vacation. I'm supposed to be in Vegas, remember?"

"Right—with Richie Rich. Count yourself lucky that a serial killer attack got you out of that one."

"Very funny."

"I'm working a banquet at the East Lake Golf Club tonight—want to crash? It might take your mind off things."

"I don't think so," Carlotta said. "I didn't get much sleep last night, so I'll probably turn in early. But thanks."

"Sure. Have you heard from Coop?"

Carlotta smiled. Hannah's crush on Dr. Cooper Craft preceded knocking boots with Chance Hollander. "He left me a voice message, said he was sorry about Bruce Abrams." Also, Coop had said he thought it best if he kept a "friendly" distance for a while.

"It wasn't Coop's fault that the man was so threatened by him that he went bat-shit crazy and started killing people."

"I know. He's just sorry I got caught in the middle."

"Do you think Coop will get his job back at the morgue?"

Carlotta flashed back to meeting Coop in the "other place"—there he had been the chief medical examiner, but seemingly on the same self-destructive path he'd followed in this world. "I don't know if that's possible...or if he'd even want the job."

"So he'll go back to body-moving?" Hannah sounded hopeful.

"I'll try to find out if I talk to him," she promised. She didn't add that it could be a while.

"Okay. Well, keep me posted on everything. And let me know when you're ready to get out."

"Thanks, Hannah."

She disconnected the call just as she pulled into the driveway. When she saw Peter's SUV sitting in front of the garage, that familiar unsettled feeling pooled in her stomach. She was grateful to Peter for being there for her lately, but she knew he had an underlying motive, and at times, she felt smothered.

On the other hand, Peter worked at Mashburn & Tully, the investment firm where Randolph had once been a partner. Randolph had once reached out to Peter in a phone call, and had advised Carlotta to stay close to Peter. So even if her heart wasn't yet recommitted to him, her life was still bound up in his.

And he'd been nice enough to allow her to live at his big house in Buckhead while The Charmed Killer had been on the loose. And nice enough to overlook the fact that she'd totaled his Porsche. And nice enough to offer Wes refuge as he recovered after going off drugs cold turkey.

Peter Ashford was a very...*nice* man.

He was out of his vehicle before she brought her rental car to a stop. He was dressed for the office in an impeccable dark suit, but considering the time of day, he either hadn't gone in yet or was taking a very early lunch. Peter offered her a comforting smile, but his tall body was ramrod stiff, as if to say he wasn't going to be blown off again.

Fair enough.

She took a deep breath and alighted from the car, lifting her face to extend a smile and a light kiss to his mouth. "Hi."

He seemed to relax. "Hi. I was worried when you weren't answering your phone."

And since he'd given her the phone and was paying for the service, there was an implied entitlement to her availability. "I'm sorry. Everyone wants a piece of me today. I had to turn off the ringer."

He looked hurt. "So I'm 'everyone'?"

"No," she murmured, tamping down her irritation. "I was going to call you as soon as I settled in." She touched her pinging shoulder. "I need to take another pain pill...and I didn't get much rest last night. And—" To her horror, she burst into tears.

"Shh," he said, pulling her face against his chest. "You should've stayed with me."

Although if she had stayed with Peter, she wouldn't have taken the mind-boggling trip that had given her a glimpse into what it would be like to be married to him. As it turned out, in the "other place," Mrs. Carlotta Ashford was leading an enviable and pretty darn happy life.

Well, except for the fact that she'd been planning to murder someone. But Carlotta had circumvented that little plot and set herself on the right path before departing, leaving *that* Carlotta and Peter to live happily ever after.

As for *this* Carlotta and Peter...

"Let's get you inside," he said, taking her keys and steering her toward the door.

She let him take charge because it was easier than pushing back. And it felt good to turn everything over to someone else, if only for a few minutes.

Out of the corner of her eye, Carlotta spotted movement in the yard next door. She turned her head to see their neighbor Mrs. Winningham scoop up her ugly dog Toofers and sprint toward the door of her own little house. The nosy woman had been chloroformed by The Charmed Killer to keep her quiet while he'd attempted to relieve Carlotta of her life. Apparently she had recovered—thank goodness—but it appeared she had also reached the end of her patience for the abandoned Wren children, who attracted trouble to the neighborhood like bugs to a roach motel.

Carlotta raised her hand in a guilty wave. "Hello, Mrs. Winningham!"

The woman responded by slamming her front door shut with a force that shook the windows.

Carlotta winced. "Okay, she officially hates us."

Peter scoffed. "She can't blame you for what a madman did—you could've died, for God's sake."

"We haven't exactly been the best neighbors."

"Well, maybe you won't have to live here much longer," he said in a hopeful voice.

She managed a smile, glad she hadn't revealed to Peter that before the attack, she had decided to move in with him and give their relationship the attention it deserved. Because now everything had changed. How perfect that as soon as she'd made a decision about the direction of her life, her prodigal father had returned and upended everything.

When Peter pushed open the door, embarrassment washed over her. The townhouse was shabby, and Wesley's recent installation of a security system had left holes and patches in the walls. A sagging tinsel Christmas tree sat in the corner, complete with gifts underneath, just as it had been when Randolph and Valerie had taken off all those years ago. Wesley had refused to let her take it down or open the gifts until their parents returned. She wondered if Randolph had noticed the sad, tarnished little relic when he'd stormed inside to save her.

And if that reunion Wesley dreamed of would ever happen.

"Pardon the mess," she said as she punched in a code on a keypad next to the door to disable the alarm. "It's worse than usual."

"Glad to see Wes installed a security system," Peter said. "When I think of what that maniac almost did to you—" His face darkened.

"But he didn't," she said, moving toward the kitchen.

"Thanks to Randolph."

She nodded.

"So how was it, seeing him this morning?"

Carlotta relayed the anticlimactic encounter as she downed a tablet for the pain in her shoulder.

"I'm sorry," he said, picking up her hand. He glanced at her dress appreciatively. "He missed out."

She tried to smile, but she suddenly felt antsy with all the loose ends dangling in front of her. "Did you go into the office today?"

He nodded.

"I assume everyone had heard that Randolph is back?"

Another nod. "The office was buzzing. Ray Mashburn, Walt Tully and Brody Jones barricaded themselves in Ray's office all morning."

Randolph's two former partners, and the chief legal counsel for the firm. Curious. "Wonder what that was all about."

"I don't know. I ran into Walt in the men's room and said hello, but he didn't respond, acted like he was in a trance."

"You'd think they'd be celebrating since Randolph allegedly embezzled money."

"You would think."

"Will you keep your ears open?"

"Of course. But I didn't plan to go back to the office. I was hoping we could spend the day together. I'm supposed to be on vacation, you know." His blue eyes shone with wry humor.

"I know," she murmured. "Our plans keep getting waylaid."

"I'm trying not to take it personally."

"There will be other times," she assured him. "Under the circumstances, though, it might be helpful if you go back to the office today and keep an eye on everyone there."

Peter frowned. "If something underhanded is going on, I don't think those guys are going to let down their guard when I'm around."

"Because of our relationship?"

He nodded.

Carlotta pressed her lips together. "Actually, I've been giving that some thought."

"Uh-oh."

She raised her hand. "Hear me out. I'm thinking that, maybe for now, we should pretend that we're...estranged."

"Estranged?"

"It's for your protection," she added quickly. "So the partners won't be worried you have a conflict of interest where I'm concerned. And maybe they'll let something slip that will help Dad's case." She brightened. "It's win-win."

He frowned. "Except we have to pretend we're not a couple."

She rearranged her mouth into a pout. "Except for that part."

He looked unconvinced. "What am I supposed to say prompted our breakup?"

"Randolph's reappearance, of course. Tell the partners you realized you had to choose between the Wren family and your work family, and you decided your loyalty lies with Mashburn & Tully."

He wiped his hand over his mouth. "I see you've given this some thought."

"If you mean I've thought about what kind of problems Randolph's return might cause for you at the firm, then yes. You've worked too hard to build a reputation there for it to be jeopardized now."

"But what if there's no information for the partners to let slip? What if Randolph—"

"Really did cheat his clients and steal money from the firm?"

He gave a curt nod.

"Then all the more reason for you to distance yourself from the Wrens," she said lightly.

He shook his head slowly, but she could tell she was starting to sway him, which told her that Peter had been nursing some of the same concerns about how this turn of events might affect his career.

Rightly so, she chided herself before she could feel offended.

"It will look like I abandoned you." His Adam's apple bobbed. "Again."

"Don't worry about that," Carlotta said, reaching for his hand. "You and I will know the truth. And once this situation is resolved—one way or the other—we can resume our...relationship."

Frustration creased his face. "Carly, I've made no secret about my feelings for you, and I thought we were on a good path. In fact, I was hoping our trip to Las Vegas would cement our relationship...formally."

"I know, Peter. Your suitcase was open on your bed and when I went to zip it, I found the engagement ring."

"Ah. Well, I'll take the fact that you were still willing to go as a good sign."

"I was looking forward to spending time with you," she murmured, "but I'm not ready to wear your ring."

His eyes clouded, but he nodded in acceptance. "Then I'll make you a deal. I'll go along with this little breakup idea of yours, if you promise to take this time apart to consider wearing my ring."

Well played, she thought, her estimation of the man before her rising a notch. If she'd ever doubted that Peter had the ability to swim with the sharks of Mashburn & Tully, those fears were somewhat mitigated. Peter Ashford knew how to go after what he wanted.

"It's a deal," she agreed.

He smiled, then looked suspicious. "I hope Detective Terry isn't going to be your beard?"

Her eyebrows went up. "Jack…my beard?"

"Your pretend boyfriend while I'm out of the picture."

She bit back a smile at the thought of Jack being anyone's boyfriend, pretend or otherwise, then shook her head. "In fact, Jack and I agreed it was a good idea for us to establish some distance, too. He was the arresting officer, after all, and will likely be involved in investigating Randolph's case."

"Right," Peter said, seeming much relieved. "Good idea." Then he narrowed his eyes. "And Craft?"

"Coop is also giving me a wide berth. He feels guilty, thinks Abrams attacked me because of him."

"He has a point," Peter said, his mood seeming to improve further. "Hanging around him has put you in harm's way more than once."

Time to change the subject…and to get rid of Peter before he changed his mind about their plan. "Thank you, Peter, for agreeing to do this for…us." Then she touched her forehead. "I'm sorry to cut our visit short, but I need to call Randolph's attorney."

"Before the painkiller kicks in?"

"Before it wears off."

He laughed and stood. "Okay, I'll get back to the office and start spreading vicious lies about us."

"Remember, it's for a good cause." She walked him to the door. "Call me if anything interesting happens."

"Good to know I can at least call you," he said, then lowered a really good kiss on her mouth.

She leaned into him and enjoyed the sensual exchange, remembering the way they had consummated their relationship in her dream. It gave her hope that if she and Peter could get back to the emotional place they'd been at when they were younger, the physical part would rebound, too.

He lifted his head and groaned. "And on that note, I'm off to tell everyone we're totally wrong for each other."

She smiled and waved him off, then closed the door and hugged herself.

Jack, Coop, and Peter had all retreated to their respective corners, giving her space to deal with the new man in her life: Randolph.

Recycled tears filled her eyes…tears cried a thousand times over for parents who had simply disappeared, seemingly uncaring of the two broken-hearted children they'd left behind with a tainted last name.

In her dream last night, no doubt triggered by years of wondering what her and Wesley's lives would've been like if their parents hadn't left, she had gotten a glimpse of what might've been. It wasn't perfect, but their problems had been external…solvable.

Carlotta shook herself—the painkillers were starting to bleed through her system, leadening her limbs. She picked up the phone, found Liz Fischer's phone number and connected the call. Prepared to leave a voice message, she was surprised when Liz answered.

"Hello, Carlotta."

"Hi, Liz. I guess you know why I'm calling."

"About Randolph, I assume."

"Have you seen him?"

"I just left USP, and yes, we talked briefly."

Carlotta gripped the phone harder and tried to keep her voice level. "And how is he?"

"Physically, he looks to be fine."

"And otherwise?"

"I'm afraid that's about all I can say. But he was concerned about your injury, and asked me to tell you and Wes that he loves you very much."

Her throat constricted. "And did he happen to mention our mother?"

"I can't say. I'm sorry."

She closed her eyes and exhaled. "What can you tell me?"

"Nothing," Liz said. "We shouldn't even be talking except I wanted to give you and Wesley some peace of mind."

She bit her tongue to keep from saying she knew what Liz was giving her little brother. "When can we see him?"

"That's...problematic."

Carlotta frowned. "Jack said there was some paperwork involved?"

"Yes, but the paperwork has to be initiated by Randolph."

"Can you be more specific?"

"He has to send a form to the person he wants to visit him, then the recipient has to fill it out and return it before being granted visitation rights."

She could see the red tape revolving in her head. "How long will that take?"

"Days, maybe weeks. But the first step is up to Randolph."

Meaning he could stall the process indefinitely. Carlotta pushed down a rising tide of frustration. "What about phone calls? Or email?"

"He would still have to initiate...and you should know that email and phone calls are monitored closely."

Meaning she had recommended her client not use them.

Liz sighed. "Carlotta, I'm sorry I don't have better news. Randolph is under a lot of scrutiny right now. The next several days will be consumed with interviews by different federal and state agencies. Let him get all this behind him. My best advice to you is to be patient and try to stay busy. I have another call coming in. I'll be in touch when I can."

The call was disconnected. Carlotta stared at the phone, shot through with disbelief. Randolph was mere miles away, but for all intents and purposes, he might as well be on the moon.

She stood and paced, chewing on a thumbnail, choking back sobs, alternately sad, helpless, and furious. She glanced all around the townhouse and felt the walls closing in. One thing was certain...she couldn't simply stay here and go mad.

Massaging her aching shoulder, she picked up the phone again to call her boss Lindy at Neiman Marcus.

"How are you?" Lindy asked, her voice low with concern. "I read about the attack in the newspaper...and about your father."

Carlotta winced. "I'm fine…better. Actually, since my trip was postponed, I was wondering if I could come in tomorrow for a shift."

"I understood you were injured."

"I might have to stick to light duties," Carlotta conceded.

"We're in the middle of inventory," Lindy reminded her. "You know how strenuous that can be."

"I really need to be busy right now," Carlotta said honestly. "So if there's any area where I could be helpful, I would appreciate the distraction—er, the work."

A thoughtful noise came over the line. "Now that I think about it, there's a short-term job offsite that might be a good fit for you."

Instantly, Carlotta's mood bounced. "I'll take it." Anything to get her mind off the absent men in her life.

CHAPTER FIVE

WELCOME TO THE WEDDING WORLD EXPO—Your Ultimate Destination for Planning the Happiest Day of Your Life!

At the sight of the white banner flapping over the entrance to the Georgia World Congress Center, Carlotta puffed out her cheeks in an exhale. When she'd wished for something to take her mind off the men in her life, she should've been more specific.

On the other hand, seven days being surrounded by white wedding gowns, multi-tiered cakes, and china patterns would probably make her want to either embrace the inevitability of coupledom, or swear off men altogether.

And there was one upside to attending the event: famed wedding dress designer Jarold Jett was supposed to put in an appearance. She'd packed her autograph book in the hopes she could snag his signature.

Carlotta checked her lanyard for the address of the display area Neiman's had reserved in the enormous convention center, and stepped over the threshold into a flurry of activity and noise.

The cavernous hall was jammed with booths and soaring displays as far as she could see. White was the prevailing color: curtains, table skirts, bunting, balloons, columns, and archways. Accented with lots of gold and silver and pops of pastels, the booths showcased flowers, food, makeup, photography, videography, music, housewares, travel, luggage, lingerie, tuxedos, jewelry, and gowns, gowns, gowns overflowing into the aisles.

Everything was sparkly, spangly, shiny, and shimmery. Scents of sugary treats, fresh blossoms, and perfume rode the air. Chamber music and dance tunes boomed from different directions. Carlotta moved down a center corridor feeling as if she was under assault. Even for someone who was accustomed to the over-the-top merchandising of retail sales, it was sensory overload.

The Atlanta location of Neiman's didn't feature an in-store bridal boutique like the renowned Dallas location, but they saw their share of brides in the formalwear department, in the jewelry department, and in gift registry. And the NM café was a popular venue for bridal parties and showers. It made sense they would have a presence at the Expo...but still, the spectacle put Carlotta on edge.

Which spoke volumes about her state of mind, she realized.

They hadn't heard a word from Randolph, and Wesley was communicating in monosyllables. Being denied access to their father was reason enough for her brother to be surly, but she had a feeling something else was bothering him.

And it could be *so* many things.

Meanwhile, the voice mail inbox on her cell phone and their home phone continued to fill with messages from people who wanted to talk to her, check on her, interview her, or—in a couple of creepy cases—simply meet her. Between being the last intended victim of The Charmed Killer and the daughter of Randolph "The Bird" Wren, she was in demand.

Carlotta wound her way through the exuberant exhibition until she located the expansive and unexpectedly dark-hued booth the store was cosponsoring. The theme of the exhibit was projected onto the tall background wall: *Your Perfect Man.*

Carlotta pushed her tongue into her check. Seriously?

Admittedly, among a sea of booths brimming with white, frilly femininity, having a groom-based booth was a standout idea. The display area was populated with a multitude of products in rich, masculine vignettes, separated into four distinct sections for four different male archetypes—the warrior, the king, the lover, the magician.

Hm.

The cosponsors' products were intermingled, but Neiman's clothing and accessories dominated the lifestyle displays that included furniture, luggage, sports gear, and electronics.

The booth already had a few lookers, so Carlotta stepped forward to introduce herself to a hostess who was smoothing a gray throw over the back of a leather club chair. "Hello, I'm—"

The woman turned and her familiar face erupted in surprise. "Carlotta! I didn't know you'd be here! I thought you were on vacation."

Carlotta maintained her smile for Patricia Alexander, her prim but energetic coworker at Neiman's. The blonde was like an annoying puppy yapping at her ankles, and just when she started to tolerate the woman, Patricia would reveal a witchy side.

"My trip was cancelled," Carlotta said. "I thought you were doing inventory back at the store."

"So did I. But someone working the show called in sick and I happened to be standing there, so Lindy asked me to fill in." She beamed. "I guess she knew I'd be interested in weddings." She thrust out her left hand and wiggled the sparkling ring on her finger. "Leo and I got engaged!"

Carlotta's eyebrows rose. "Wow. I thought you broke up with him."

"I did, because I felt like he was keeping something from me. And he was—he has a daughter, and he thought I wouldn't accept it. He apologized and told me everything and then he proposed!"

"When did all this happen?"

"Last week—the night of the full moon. It was so romantic. He took me to Stone Mountain and proposed during the outdoor laser show."

"That's...super."

"Isn't it? And you'll get to see Leo again—he's going to be in the celebrity fashion show on the last day." Patricia clasped her hands together. "How great is it that you and I will be working together all week?"

"Great," Carlotta agreed.

Then Patricia gasped. "But are you okay?" She leaned in and lowered her voice. "I heard you were *stabbed* by The Charmed Killer?"

"Er...yes." Carlotta inadvertently touched her shoulder. "But I'll be fine."

"What a relief that maniac is behind bars."

"Yes."

Patricia's eyes widened. "And your *father* is back in town?"

The woman's family had deep roots in Buckhead society, and she knew the entire sordid story of the Wrens' ruin. Carlotta tried to smile. "That's right."

"He just showed up, out of the blue?"

She felt compelled to defend Randolph, especially since Patricia would likely retell the story. "He saved my life, actually. Somehow, he knew I was in trouble."

Her jaw dropped. "He's been watching you all this time?"

"I don't know."

Patricia's neck turned blotchy. "But he's been...close by?"

"Uh..." Carlotta gestured to a couple of customers who looked as if they had questions. "We probably should get busy. What can I do?"

Patricia straightened, as if she suddenly remembered where they were. "Just answer questions. And if customers find something they like, offer to help place an order online." She indicated two kiosks equipped with flat screen monitors and keyboards.

"Anything else?" Carlotta asked, noticing Patricia seemed distracted.

"We, um...get commission on any Neiman's merchandise we sell. Too bad we don't have any wedding gowns on display—I bet we could've made a bundle." Her throat convulsed. "So...your father's in jail?"

Carlotta nodded, puzzled over Patricia's sudden unease. Maybe she was afraid Randolph had been stalking Carlotta and her coworkers at the store?

"Good," Patricia said, then caught herself. "I mean, I'm glad he's back...for your sake, of course."

"Thank you."

"Oh, and one of us is supposed to help with the fashion show this afternoon," Patricia continued, her voice stronger. "Neiman's is supplying all the menswear. It's going to take place in the rear of the hall—they're still putting together the runway. And don't forget to download the Wedding Expo app to your phone..."

Carlotta nodded, allowing the woman to drone on, steeling herself for a long, boring day standing on her feet. But it was better than bouncing off the walls of the townhouse. She spent the next few minutes familiarizing herself with items in the expansive booth and assisting browsing customers. She passed the first sluggish hour handing out coupons for free shipping on website orders, then smothered a yawn.

When had retail gotten so godawful boring?

Across the aisle, a woman screamed. Carlotta wheeled, all senses on alert for danger. Thief? Stalker? Rapist?

But instead of fighting off an assault, the woman was holding up a frothy white dress, her face lit up with the discovery that had elicited the loud response. Carlotta exhaled and shook herself—she had to stop looking for intrigue in every situation.

She glanced around at the smiling, hopeful faces of the women pouring into the exhibition hall, chattering excitedly. There was nothing here but happy people planning happy occasions, set to embark on happy lives.

She sighed. Everyone, it seemed, was happy...except her. She glanced back to the squealing bride, tempted to approach her and ask her how her life had gotten to such a happy place. But when she saw the woman's companion, she froze.

Tracey Tully—now Mrs. Dr. Lowenstein. A friendly acquaintance of Carlotta's back when they'd attended private high school together, and daughter of Walt Tully, Randolph's former partner at the firm.

In Carlotta's vivid dream that had swept her to an alternate universe, she and Tracey had been best friends because their lives there had traveled along similar paths...but in this world, she and Tracey were on less affable footing. She took a step backward to evade detection and bumped a piece of luggage that toppled with a loud thud.

To her chagrin, Tracey looked up, then made a beeline for her through the crowd. "Carlotta Wren, what are *you* doing here?"

Carlotta straightened and extended her good arm to indicate the masculine-themed booth behind her like a game-show hostess. "I'm working...with Patricia," she said, including the blonde in her vague gesture. The two women knew each other, still moved in some of the same circles.

"Oh," Tracey said with a sniff. "Well, I knew you weren't here planning a wedding. I heard you and Peter broke up."

Well, at least Peter had gotten the word out—no doubt Walt Tully had told his daughter posthaste.

"You and Peter broke up?" Patricia asked. "Is that why you cancelled your vacation?"

"Among other reasons," Carlotta murmured.

"Oh, right—your felon father is back," Tracey said with a tight smile. "Did he happen to say where he's been all this time?"

Carlotta's face burned. "Actually, I haven't talked to Randolph. He was taken into custody."

"Your mother wasn't with him?"

"No."

"So she's somewhere living high on the money your father stole from clients?"

"That was never proven," Carlotta said, lifting her chin.

"Because he didn't stand trial," Tracey snapped. "My father personally paid back a portion of some of the money clients lost, but the partners couldn't fix everything. People lost their homes because of your father." Then she swung her gaze to Patricia. "Didn't they, Patricia?"

Carlotta looked to Patricia. "What is she talking about?"

But Patricia wouldn't make eye contact.

"You didn't know?" Tracey continued. "Patricia's parents were two of Randolph's biggest clients. He stole a small fortune from the Alexanders."

From the look on Patricia's face, Carlotta knew it was true—no wonder Patricia had been acting strange about Randolph's return. Dismay flooded her chest. Patricia had made occasional comments since they'd worked together about money being tight, but Carlotta thought the woman was worried about buying an extra pair of Louboutin shoes, not referencing her family's overall financial well-being.

Patricia squirmed. "Mom and Dad were hanging in there until the real estate market tumbled."

Carlotta thought she was going to be sick. She mentally retracted every bad thought she'd ever had about the woman. By all rights, Patricia should hate her.

Patricia nodded toward a customer. "Excuse me. It was nice to see you, Tracey."

"You, too, Patricia." Then Tracey turned her smug mug on Carlotta. "Are you starting to realize the kind of damage your father did?"

Carlotta blinked. She'd assumed the individuals who'd suffered losses blamed on Randolph were tycoons or institutional investors…she hadn't thought about the actual faces on the other side of the scandal. She'd been too young and too busy trying to feed herself and Wesley.

"And why," Tracey continued in the silence, "Peter can't be associated with you?"

Carlotta finally found her voice. "Yes. I wouldn't want Peter to be punished for someone else's sins." Then she glanced around. "But this isn't the time or the place for this discussion. I have customers waiting." Carlotta started to turn away, loath to let Tracey know her words had found their mark.

"Maybe you can help my friend," Tracey said quickly. When Carlotta turned back, the woman who'd screamed over the dress walked up. "This is Iris Kline. She's looking for a gift for her fiancé. Iris, this is Carlotta. She's my favorite salesclerk."

Ignoring the barb, Carlotta extended a smile to the woman. "Hello. Do you have something in mind?"

Iris shook her head. "Not really. It's just a little make-up gift." She blushed. "Greg and I had a little argument. Planning a wedding is murder on a relationship."

"I can imagine," Carlotta soothed. "Does he have any hobbies?"

"He golfs…but he has every kind of golf gadget you can imagine. I'd like to get him something more personal."

"Absolutely," Carlotta said, morphing into sales mode. "If you had to choose, which one of these labels best describes your fiancé?"

The woman scanned the displays. "Warrior…king…lover…magician." She laughed. "I'm not sure."

"Is this some kind of riddle?" Tracey asked, annoyed.

"Just a fun way to identify a man's personality," Carlotta said cheerfully.

"Like, what's an example of each?" Iris asked, circling the displays.

Carlotta wasn't expecting to have to supply an explanation. She surveyed some of the items presented in the first section—leather couch, rugged casual wear and boots, a no-nonsense black suit and red tie, fishing gear and a water-proof smart phone. "I'm no expert, but I suppose a warrior could describe an alpha guy, like a military man or a...cop." *Like Jack.*

"And a king?"

Carlotta scanned the second section—club chair, preppie clothes, modern slim-fit suit, golf equipment, humidor, and ultra thin laptop. "Maybe someone who is a natural-born leader, or who has a good pedigree." *Like Peter.*

"And a lover?"

A suede chaise, trendy clothes, surf board, leather-bound books, globe, and electronic tablet filled out the third section. A hot flush began to climb Carlotta's neck. "I would say that's a man who...is fun and sweet and...cerebral." *Like Coop.*

"And a magician?"

The last display featured a convertible leather sofa, black clothes head to toe, a poker table and deck of cards, expensive sunglasses, and several electronic gadgets. "Um...someone who can transform himself...and make you believe anything is possible?" *Like Randolph.*

Iris looked troubled. "I'm starting to think I don't know Greg very well."

Ever eager to salvage a sale, Carlotta plucked an item from a table and held it up. "How about this stainless steel comb? It's on-trend, very sculptural, and heirloom quality. Luxurious, but useful."

The woman smiled. "He is a little vain. I'll take it."

"I told you," Tracey said to her friend. "Carlotta is simply the best little salesgirl ever."

Carlotta gritted her teeth and rang up the sale with practiced civility. When they left, she gave Tracey a cheerful wave, resisting the urge to accentuate with her middle finger. How ironic that under different circumstances, the two of them might've been close.

She straightened items around the displays, marveling over the fact that the men in her life so exactly matched the four archetypes. Was that why she'd had so much trouble sorting through her feelings for Jack, Peter, and Coop—because they were so different, and because they each appealed to a different part of her?

And all three of them different still from Randolph. Which was a good thing…wasn't it?

She glanced at Patricia, who was at a kiosk with a customer, hopefully racking up a big, fat commission. Humiliation and anger rolled through her that Randolph had done something to affect the life of someone she knew. It made her that much more antsy to talk to him…to confront him and ask if he'd actually stolen money from people who trusted him.

The theme projected across the back of the booth mocked her. *Your perfect man.*

If only such a creature existed.

"Hello, there."

At the sound of a familiar deep voice, Carlotta winced, then lifted her gaze.

Jack.

Perfect timing.

CHAPTER SIX

"STANDING HERE THINKING about me, I see," Jack said, nodding to the *Your Perfect Man* proclamation on the booth background.

Carlotta angled her head at him. "You have self-esteem issues, Jack—you have way too much of it."

Unfazed, he shrugged his wide shoulders.

"What are you doing here?" she asked. "Planning a wedding?"

"Right," he said dryly.

"What then?"

He put his hands in his pockets and shifted uncomfortably. "After my run-in with the state boys at the jail, and...some other things, my captain thought I needed a few days off. So I put in for security work, and this ridiculous event was my draw."

Indeed, the orange lanyard around his neck proclaimed SECURITY OFFICER.

The thought of him in the middle of this feminine fracas made her smile. "What exactly are you supposed to be keeping secure?"

He squirmed. "A muckety-muck celebrity thinks he needs a bodyguard from his adoring fans."

"Jarold Jett?" she asked hopefully.

"Sounds right." He pulled a piece of paper from his pocket, then nodded. "Yeah. What is he, a reality TV star?"

"Close. He's a wedding dress designer, and he's a judge on a competition design show."

"Great."

"I've heard he suffers from anxiety attacks—he doesn't like crowds. That's probably why he wants a bodyguard."

Jack looked heavenward. "I should've gone fishing."

She grinned. "Actually, I'm hoping to get his autograph."

He stuffed the paper back into his jacket. "Is that why you're here?"

"Not exactly."

"Don't tell *you're* planning a wedding?" His gold-colored eyes were suddenly serious.

Patricia walked close, then reached between them to pluck a sterling silver flask from a shelf. "Not Carlotta," the blonde offered triumphantly. "She and her boyfriend broke up." Then she sailed away to show the item to a customer.

Carlotta glanced after the woman. *Minus ten points, Patricia.*

Jack's eyebrows rose. "Broke up, huh? Did Ashford take his letterman jacket back?"

She frowned. "I'm working, Jack."

He frowned back. "Shouldn't you be taking care of your shoulder?"

"I'm being careful. I need to keep busy, and my boss thought this would be more light duty."

He conceded with a nod. "Have you made contact with your father?"

"You mean has he made contact with us? No. Liz explained the visitation process and it seems that once again, Randolph is holding all the cards."

His mouth tightened. "I'm not taking up for him, but the feds are probably keeping him under wraps."

"Why?"

"Maybe they're afraid you or Wes will help him hide or destroy evidence."

Unbidden, a conversation she'd had with the doctor who'd treated her broken arm a few months ago came back to her. Doctor Eames told her he'd been a tennis partner of Randolph's, and that Randolph had once confided he thought someone in his firm was trying to frame him. He'd asked if he could bring an unnamed item to Eames for safekeeping. But before the exchange could take place, Randolph had been arrested, then had disappeared.

But assuming such evidence ever existed, Carlotta certainly didn't know of its whereabouts. She scoffed. "Wes and I just want to have a conversation with our dad."

"I know. But if and when you do, be aware that your communication will be monitored."

"Liz told me. I don't understand what's going on—why do the feds even want him?"

"Securities fraud falls under the jurisdiction of the Secret Service and the FBI. They might eventually pass the case back to the county D.A., but my guess is they want to see if the case is juicy enough to hang on to. Randolph wasn't connected to The Charmed Killer case, except where you're concerned, but they don't know that yet."

"Are you going to get to question him?"

Jack dropped his gaze for a few seconds, then looked back to her. "No."

"But you've been working Randolph's case, and you were the arresting officer."

"I've…um…been warned to stay away."

"Because of what you did for us at the penitentiary?"

"Maybe. Whatever the reason, I had to hand over the case files, and I was told only the feds are allowed to talk to him."

She made a frustrated noise.

"I know it's hard, but sit tight, and everything will eventually work out."

She nodded, trying to believe him, then gestured to a customer. "I really should get back to work."

"Me, too. After all, I did agree to stay away from you." He looked her up and down, taking in her pale yellow silk blouse, slim turquoise skirt, and strappy pink sandals. "Remind me why I did that?"

Carlotta's skin tingled from the electricity pinging between them. "Because you arrested my fugitive father, and things could get messy?"

"Oh, right." He worked his mouth from side to side. "Do you think we could suspend our agreement for a while?"

She narrowed her eyes. "Why?"

"I'm on my way to meet the hoity-toity dressmaker, and I could use a translator."

"Jarold Jett is American, Jack. He speaks English."

"But I don't speak designer. I need a buffer."

She laughed. "Okay. If I can bring my autograph book."

"Get it."

Carlotta walked over to Patricia. "Can you handle things here on your own for a while?"

"And keep all the commissions for myself? No problem."

She balked, remembering the money the Alexanders had lost. "Patricia, I had no idea your parents were—"

"In fact, if you want to cover the fashion show later," Patricia cut in, "that would be fine with me."

At the woman's matter-of-fact change of subject, Carlotta bit down on her tongue. "Okay." Patricia had a right not to want to discuss the matter, not to accept her apology.

"Edward from the men's department will be there. Check in with him."

"I will. See you later."

When she fell into step next to Jack, he asked, "Is something wrong?"

She gave a humorless laugh. "You mean something else? I found out this morning my coworker's parents lost their home because of Randolph."

"They invested with him?"

"Right."

He sighed. "It's not your fault, Carlotta."

"It sure feels like it is."

As they threaded their way back through the booths, the noise and flurry was cacophonous.

Jack winced. "I didn't know things like this existed—a trade show just for weddings?"

"It's big business."

"A big scam, more like it."

A woman wearing a voluminous white wedding gown and holding a tray offered them a taste of a wedding cake with edible gold leaf. They declined.

"Like I said," Jack muttered, then gestured to a booth featuring caged cooing white rock doves available for release at ceremonies. "Do people actually do this stuff?"

"And more," Carlotta said. "It's the day most women think about their entire lives, so they want to make it special."

"Special is one thing—spectacle is another."

"Tomato, to-mah-to."

He frowned. "Is that something you've always wanted—a big wedding?"

She shrugged. "I never really thought about it. When all the girls I grew up with were getting married, I was being a mom to Wesley." And she hadn't been invited to any of their elaborate weddings...had only sold them dresses for their bridal parties, and read about the galas after the fact in the society section of the newspaper. To lighten the mood, she teased, "Don't you think everyone should get married at least once, Jack?"

"I'm not against marriage," he said, surprising her. "I just think some people are more excited about the ceremony than about the person they're marrying."

"I agree it can get over the top. But some people think it's important to have a lavish ceremony to make a statement, to include their family and friends, to make it mean something."

"With a cop's salary, I guess that leaves me out of the marrying business."

"Whew," Carlotta mocked.

He laughed. "So...you and Ashford parted ways, huh?"

She didn't want to lie, so she sidestepped. "It makes sense, doesn't it? Randolph's reappearance is bound to cause Peter problems at the firm."

"I suppose it could be awkward," he agreed.

"Besides, right now I need to be available for my family...such as it is. Wesley isn't taking this situation with Dad very well."

"Wes has a lot on his mind."

"How much longer will he be working undercover in the loan shark's organization?"

He gave her a pointed look. "Which you aren't supposed to know about, remember. And that's up to the D.A."

"The man who has it in for my family."

"Don't forget that Kelvin Lucas owes you for helping to close The Charmed Killer case."

"You mean for not becoming his last victim? Actually, Lucas owes Randolph for that...and you."

His face went hard. "I might not have arrived in time to save you. And don't think I haven't replayed that scenario in my mind a hundred times. After what happened to Maria, I don't think—" He broke off, his voice hoarse.

Alarmed at his tone, she reached over to touch his arm. "Don't go there, Jack. I'm fine." But she understood why his captain had suggested he take some time off. She had a feeling the GBI agents weren't the only people Jack had been short with lately. He needed to decompress after the shocking loss of his partner.

They exited the convention hall and walked across the plaza to a turn-around where taxis dropped off passengers. From the expression on Jack's face, she knew he was still far away, picturing the scene where Maria had been found drowned in her bathtub, they'd later learned, at the hands of her violent ex-husband. Carlotta wet her lips, wanting to offer Jack some kind of comfort where his former partner was concerned.

"Jack, a couple of nights ago, I...went somewhere."

"Where?"

"Um...to a place where we're all living slightly different lives. If it's any consolation, Maria was fine there...and I gave you information that would keep her safe."

He gave her a dubious look. "Are you high?"

"No. Although I might have taken one too many pain pills the night I went to this...place. And I know it sounds crazy, but trust me, it happened. Wes was there, and my parents."

"Your parents, huh?"

"I got to see what my life would've been like if they hadn't left."

Jack arched an eyebrow. "And?"

"And...it wasn't as perfect as I'd fantasized, just different than my life now. I, um, was married to Peter."

"Really? And how was that?"

"Fine."

"Just fine? Hm."

She ignored his teasing. "And you were there…and Coop…and Hannah. We didn't know each other at first, but we did by the time I left."

"Left?"

"To come back here, of course."

"Of course. Through a wormhole in the space-time continuum."

"Laugh if you will, but it happened. I just thought you'd like to know that somewhere, Maria is fine."

He looked unconvinced. "If you say so."

She gripped his hand and locked gazes with him. "I do say so."

He startled at her seriousness, then squeezed her hand. "Okay."

"You believe me?"

His smile was sad. "I want to."

It was the most he'd ever revealed himself to her. Ironic, considering he'd recently promised to take a step back from her…and considering he'd just arrested her father. Wesley's suspicions about Jack reared in her head. Was he being vulnerable…or manipulative? After all, he knew how to play good cop *and* bad cop.

A black limousine pulling to the curb dragged her attention away from Jack. When the driver opened the rear door, a well-dressed man with salt-and-pepper hair alighted, managing not to touch anything. He was handsome, stocky and tanned, and glanced around with an air of "I have arrived."

"That's your man," Carlotta said, then glanced at Jack with an unsettling sense of distrust. *And you always get your man.*

CHAPTER SEVEN

"HELLO, MR. JETT," Carlotta said, stepping forward with a smile. "I'm Carlotta—I work for Neiman's. And this is Jack Terry, he's with event security."

Jarold gave Jack a once over glance. "Good. You look like you can keep the riffraff away from me."

Carlotta swallowed her judgment over the man's declaration—maybe he'd been stalked or assaulted in the past.

"My personal assistant couldn't get on my flight," he continued, "so she won't arrive until tomorrow."

Jack offered the man a curt nod. "I'm supposed to tell you your trunks arrived."

"I certainly hope so," the man said, then made a face. "Traffic was hideous."

"I know," Carlotta said sympathetically. "That's Atlanta. The good news is traffic inside the Wedding Expo is heavy, too. It's a great crowd."

He ran a finger around the inside of his shirt collar. "Goodness, is it always this humid?"

"Yes. But it's great for the skin, so cleansing."

He seemed disarmed by her good cheer, then gave a begrudging smile. "I can see that from *your* lovely complexion."

She grinned and extended her arm toward the entrance. "Shall we go inside where it's cool?"

"By all means," he said agreeably, then called back to Jack. "You, there— bring my bag."

Jack rolled his eyes, but picked up the man's Louis Vuitton suitcase which, from the way he strained, wasn't packed with wedding veils. He dutifully followed them inside and trailed patiently while she and Jarold Jett strolled past booths, making their way to the newly constructed runway in the rear of the hall. Along the way, several people shouted the designer's name and waved and some people rushed up to gush, touching his arm and shoulder.

"I'm wearing one of your dresses on my wedding day!"

"I never miss your show!"

"I love your perfume!"

The man visibly recoiled from the contact, and when one over-eager fan moved in for a hug, Jack stepped in and asked her to give Mr. Jett some space.

Jett was cordial to the fans, though, and Carlotta could tell he enjoyed the attention. Still, he moved ahead with his hands curled close to his body.

"Brides can be a little intense," Carlotta offered in an attempt to calm him.

He nodded. "Have you ever been married?"

When she thought of how young and naïve she'd been when she'd been engaged to Peter, her face warmed. "No. I'm single."

"As beautiful as you are? That's a tragedy."

She laughed. "Thank you. And…it's complicated."

"Does it have something to do with the behemoth carrying my suitcase?"

Her surprise must have shown because he scoffed.

"I saw you holding hands when the car pulled up, and I saw the way he looked at you."

"Oh…Jack and I are just…friends."

The man cocked an eyebrow. "Has anyone told him?"

She chanced a glance back to Jack who couldn't hear what they were saying. He gave her a wry wink.

Push…pull…push…pull…

"I'm planning my own wedding," Jarold offered.

"I know," she murmured. "I'm a fan of *Designer Wars*. I was watching when you announced your engagement to Sabrina Bauers. Congratulations."

A loving look came over his face. "She's too good for me."

Carlotta managed a smile back. From what she had heard of the super-model's diva behavior, she was sure the woman would agree.

When they reached the fashion show area of the convention hall, Jarold nodded with surprise and approval. "Yes, this will do nicely."

Indeed, the coordinators had done a beautiful job of setting up a T-shaped runway with voluminous bunting and bows and soaring silver-colored curtains all around. Enormous flower arrangements adorned the stage and sparkling chandeliers studded the floating ceiling. It was as spectacular as any movie set.

"There are two things the South does to wonderful excess," Carlotta offered. "Funerals…and weddings." Even though the fashion show was more than an hour away, the audience seats had already begun to fill.

"I confess I had my doubts about coming," Jarold said. "But now, I'm quite looking forward to the week's events."

Behind them, Jack coughed. "You're going to be here all week?"

"Yes." Then Jarold looked concerned. "And I hope you aren't getting a cold."

Jack wiped his hand over his mouth as if to erase what he wanted to say.

Carlotta fought a smile and withdrew her autograph book. "Mr. Jett, if it isn't a terrible imposition, may I have your autograph?"

"Absolutely." His mouth quirked. "A paper autograph book? You don't see these anymore. Now everyone wants a selfie."

"It's old school," she conceded.

He shuddered. "Lately I've been signing tablets and smartphone screens with those nasty little stylus pens or, worse, my finger."

She nodded with understanding. "I assume you have your own pen?"

"Of course," he chirped, removing a slim black pen from his inside jacket pocket. "Waterman—also old school."

He inscribed a message and his name with a flourish, then drew a wedding dress doodle to fill the page.

Carlotta turned it around to read. *To Carlotta, May you have your own happily ever after with your perfect man. Wondrous wedding wishes, Jarold Jett.*

"Thank you." She gave in to a little thrill at the thought of having a personal memento to take home, something she would relish again and again. "I will cherish it."

She escorted Jarold to the secured area behind the runway where make-shift changing tents had been erected. The space was a whirlwind of commotion, with coordinators and helpers running around, pushing racks of gowns and tuxedos under plastic and pallets of shoes and accessories.

Carlotta made sure Jarold was delivered to the tent that contained his trunks of merchandise. An assistant was already steaming the luxurious creations. Carlotta handed him off and said goodbye, assuring Jarold she would be watching the show.

Jack set the man's suitcase where he was directed, averted his gaze from the half-dressed models donning wedding gowns, then cleared his throat. "Where should I wait for you, sir?"

"Take this." Jarold Jett handed him a clear plastic bag containing a flat black disc the size of a coaster.

"What is it?" Jack asked.

"I'll buzz you after the fashion show. It also lights up."

Jack scowled down at the large beeper. "I'm not TGI Friday's."

"Tomorrow when my assistant arrives, she'll provide you with an app so you can track my whereabouts via my mobile phone. This will do until then."

Carlotta waited for Jack to throw the buzzer back at the man, but to her amazement, Jack simply looked away, seemed to resign himself, then looked back. "How am I supposed to know where you are when this thing goes off?"

The designer gave him a haughty smile. "Look for the crowd of people gathered around me."

Jack's mouth tightened and he nodded, then left the tent.

Carlotta followed, surprised he had given in to the man's demands with such little resistance. Outside she caught up with him.

"Hey...what was that?"

His eyebrows climbed. "What was what?"

She gave him a light punch in the arm. "You, rolling over like a puppy."

"Just trying to get through this assignment." He looked away. "The extra cash will come in handy."

Carlotta frowned. That was the second time today Jack had insinuated he didn't make enough money. Was he having financial problems?

"You must have a big mortgage," she said in a teasing voice. She'd never seen where Jack lived, and he'd never talked about it.

"Nope. But I haven't exactly been saving for a rainy day, either."

"Are you expecting one?"

He blinked. "Expecting what?"

"A rainy day."

"Oh. Who knows what the future holds?"

Carlotta arched an eyebrow. "Are you okay?"

"Fine. Did you get your autograph?"

She nodded and withdrew the book to show him the inscription.

His mouth quirked. "Perfect man, huh? That's a lot of pressure."

She surveyed the sexily imperfect man before her. "It's a figure of speech, Jack."

He gestured toward the exhibition hall. "Since Mr. Big Shot doesn't need me at the moment, I think I'll make some rounds and check in with the other security officers."

"Okay. Will you be back to watch the fashion show?"

He made a face. "That's not really my scene, but I guess I'd better stay close to Jett."

Something in his tone made her squint. "Has he received threats?"

"Allegedly. Could be a promotional stunt, though."

"Hm...I haven't heard about it in the tabloids."

Jack gave her a pointed look.

"Not that I read the tabloids," she rushed to say.

He looked dubious.

"Well...maybe a quick scan at the grocery checkout, but who doesn't do that?"

"Me." He quirked a brow, then strode away.

Carlotta watched him, her senses on alert. Was it her imagination or was Jack's body language tense? His shoulders seemed pulled in, his chin lower than usual. And although he was never quick to smile, he seemed more withdrawn.

And there was the money thing.

Carlotta worried her lower lip. Granted, losing a work partner and closing a grueling serial killer case was bound to take its toll, even on a man with Jack's fortitude. And maybe the loss of Maria had made him feel a little less invincible, had forced him to think about the future and financial security.

She sighed…it seemed everyone she knew was more burdened these days. Was this how adulthood progressed? Mounting pressure until one's body finally gave out?

She pushed aside that cheerful thought and went in search of her Neiman's contact. She was supposed to be working, after all.

And keeping her distance—mentally and physically—from Jack.

CHAPTER EIGHT

CARLOTTA FOUND EDWARD KING, her Neiman's contact, in one of the tents, fussing with the shirt collar of a male model dressed in a sleek charcoal gray suit. The handsome forty-something black man was totally old school, always well groomed and dressed to the max. He was a Neiman's veteran, had worked nearly every department, and was widely rumored as the person who would someday have Lindy Russell's job if and when the woman ever stepped down or moved on.

"This is a nice surprise," Edward said, offering an air kiss to her cheek in deference to having his hands full of pins and tape. "I thought I was going to get stuck with that Patricia girl."

"Patricia's not so bad," Carlotta murmured guiltily.

"Well, look at you, being all generous," Edward said with a grin. "I guess I'll have to get to know her better. Hey—what are you even doing here? Weren't you stabbed or something?"

"A flesh wound," she said with a wave.

He shook his head. "Lately, you've been on the news more than the mayor."

She squirmed. Edward was from New York, so hopefully he wasn't privy to the entire sordid story of Randolph "The Bird" Wren flying the coop and his subsequent return. "Put me to work. What can I do?"

Edward gestured at the dozen or so male models wearing exquisite tuxes and suits, horsing around, and rolled his eyes. "Help me corral these young bucks. They have to be fitted, their hair combed, and lined up with their brides in thirty minutes. It's like taking a bunch of toddlers on a field trip." Indeed, they were destroying a cart of fruit and pastries sitting nearby, oblivious to the crumbs and powdered sugar falling onto lapels

Edward's jaw hardened. "Who brought in that food cart? Get it out!" He looked back to her and shook his head as two men wheeled it outside even as they stuffed donuts in their mouths. "Who thought finger food around two-thousand-dollar tuxes was a good idea?"

She grinned. "Do you have the order they're supposed to line up?"

He nodded toward a sheet of paper taped to the end of a rolling shelf. "That's the most I have to go on. This isn't the most organized event."

"It'll be fine," she soothed. "People just want to be entertained."

Edward frowned. "So that's why that blowhard Jarold Jett is here?"

She detected a note of testiness in his voice that hinted of familiarity. "Do you know him?"

"I worked for him years ago in New York. The man is a tyrant."

"Really? He seemed a little uppity, but then so do most celebrities."

"Jarold Jett is *not* a celebrity."

"Sorry—designer."

"*Please.* Our tailor at Neiman's has more talent."

Carlotta laughed. "I walked in with him, and his tent is practically next door, so you're bound to run into him."

"I'm safe," Edward said with a wave of his hand. "Mr. Jett-Setter won't remember a lowly pattern cutter from twenty years ago."

Raucous laughter blasted from the young men carousing in the tent, and a playful shoving match broke out. Edward scowled. "Watch the clothing, please!"

Carlotta clapped her hands. "Can I have your attention, gentlemen?"

All eyes swung in her direction. "You can have anything of mine you want!" a handsome, cocky guy crowed.

More laughter ensued as Carlotta gave them a wry smile. "What I want is for you to line up in the order I call for Edward to make last-minute adjustments."

"Where are our brides?" one of the models asked, rubbing his hands together.

"Next tent over," she said, then plucked the sheet of paper from the rack. "Now, I need Darren, Lewis, Jeremy, Ben, Luke, Jonathon, Thom, Danny, Sam, and Tony to line up here." She pointed to an imaginary spot and the men started moving toward it in various degrees of leisureliness. They were all slender and chiseled in that effortless way of young men, handsome and full of themselves, with good skin and straight teeth.

"Isn't this bad luck?" one of the men—Jeremy, if they were in the correct order—asked.

"What do you mean?" she asked.

He seemed nervous as he pulled at his stiff white collar, and he was working a big wad of chewing gum. He had a pretty-boy, sullen look about him. Carlotta pegged him as a former prep school athlete—entitled and obviously underemployed. "Wearing a tux before your actual wedding day." He slurred his words a little. He was either hung over or high. "Is it bad luck?"

"Yeah, it means you'll have to get married someday," the guy behind him—Ben?—said with a laugh.

"I *am* getting married," Jeremy said miserably. "Next month."

"For real?" Ben asked, horrified. "Why?"

"Have to...my girlfriend's pregnant."

"Whoa," Ben said, taking a step back, as if fatherhood might be contagious. "Bummer, dude."

"Tell me about it." Jeremy swung his head back to Carlotta. "So I guess this'll be my dry run, huh?"

She tried to smile, but nursed a barb of sympathy for the baby this man-child had fathered, and hoped Jeremy would rise to the occasion. Her mouth watered to tell him that fathers could make or break a child.

"Next," Edward said, waving impatiently for Jeremy to step up for his jacket to be pinned.

Carlotta swallowed the words, chiding herself not to project her personal problems onto other people. Jeremy might turn out to be a world-class dad.

Or at least a dad who sticks around.

She spent the next several minutes tying bowties and smoothing creases and giving stiff shoes a quick shine with a tissue while good-naturedly deflecting the young men's frisky comments. Their youthful enthusiasm was a distraction from her problems.

She shepherded them outside the tent just as beautiful women emerged from Jarold Jett's tent wearing stunning creations of white, ivory, and—the newest bridal trend—pale pink. All the brides wore red wigs. A nod, she assumed, to Jarold's fiancée Sabrina Bauers, who was famously ginger. And some designers used identical styling to ensure the attention was on the clothing, not the individual models.

With an eye on his watch, Edward tried to organize the group by height and style. He chastised Jeremy for the gum, and Jeremy grudgingly took it out. Only to pop it back in as soon as Edward turned his back.

Carlotta sighed—the child was going to have a child.

Minus ten points.

"Look alive, people," Edward called. "You're on in five minutes."

Indeed, in the background they could hear the emcee over the P.A. system welcoming the crowd to the fashion show, and a smattering of applause.

Jarold Jett materialized. "I'll take it from here," he announced to Edward, dismissing him without a second glance.

Edward gave her a sour "told you so" look and came to stand next to her while the guest designer reshuffled the order of the couples until he was satisfied.

"And I get to introduce the prima donna," Edward muttered. "Thanks for your help. Are you sticking around to watch the show?"

She nodded. "I'll come back here afterward to give you a hand."

Edward moved toward the stage door. Carlotta headed in the opposite direction to watch from the audience just as music began to play. Clumps of tiny girls walked down a carpeted runway wearing bright dresses with big skirts, scattering flower petals behind them—and tasting a choice few. The audience *ahhed* and laughed at their adorableness. The seats were full, so Carlotta moved to the back of the room to stand against a wall.

She smiled at the show's delightful opening, but acknowledged the headache that was needling its way to the surface—a by-product, no doubt, of the little grenade in the back of her mind fighting for her attention, threatening to detonate any second and take her down. Next to what was happening in her life, the frivolity of the bridal show seemed surreal.

She clapped with the audience at the miniature models, but when her hands idled, her mind began to run wide open. What was happening to Randolph right now? Did their mother know yet he'd been arrested? How was Wesley holding up?

Restless, she pulled her phone from her small purse to check for messages. Peter and Hannah had each texted twice, and she had voice mail messages from numbers she didn't recognize. Hoping one of them was from Randolph, she dialed in to listen, her hand over one ear.

One message was Rainie Stephens again, asking if they could talk. And the other was from D.A. Kelvin Lucas himself, commanding her to call his office and arrange an interview regarding The Charmed Killer case "as soon as humanly possible."

"Wow, what a face," Jack murmured, stopping to stand next to her.

She stabbed a button to delete the voice message and stashed her phone. "Kelvin Lucas has summoned me to his office for an interview."

"About what?"

"He said it was about The Charmed Killer case, but I have a feeling he wants to talk about Randolph."

"I'd say that's a safe bet. Abrams signed a confession, so hopefully there won't be a trial, but Lucas still needs a follow-up statement from you describing the attack. When are you going?"

"I'll call back to make an appointment."

He wet his lips, then said, "Liz should probably go with you."

Carlotta rolled her eyes up at him.

"I know you don't like her—"

"I hate her."

"Liz isn't all bad."

Carlotta gave a harsh laugh that caused some people sitting in the back row to turn and shoot daggers with their eyes. She mouthed an apology, then lowered her voice. "Please do not try to sell me a bill of goods about the woman who slept with my father *and* my brother." She bit her tongue to keep from adding "and you." No need for Jack to know she still smarted over the fact that at one time he'd enjoyed Liz's bed, too.

"I'm just saying she can be an ally against Lucas."

"I'll think about it. So...anything exciting happen on your rounds? Any misbehaving brides about?"

He gave her a bored look. "You know it's bad when you hope Mr. La-tee-dah buzzes you with a faux emergency."

"Did you just use the word 'faux'?"

He grimaced. "This is going to be a long damn week."

She swallowed a smile, nursing a pang of sympathy for Jack that he'd been relegated to the little boys' table of police work, in part for trying to do something nice for her and Wesley.

On the runway, a pint-sized, dark-haired boy in black tuxedo tails was "escorting" a little blond girl in a yellow dress down the aisle, staring at her with worshipful eyes. But she was having nothing to do with him. Her mouth was screwed up in a tight little bow and every time he tried to take her arm, she yanked it away. The crowd loved it. Carlotta laughed, thinking that the push and pull between men and women started in the womb. "They're adorable."

When Jack didn't say anything, she turned her head to find him staring at her.

"What?" she asked.

"I didn't know you liked kids."

She shrugged. "I don't *dis*like kids. I raised Wes, remember. You don't like kids, Jack?"

He shifted from foot to foot. "I like kids...I guess."

Carlotta squinted, confused at the turn of the conversation, but decided Jack was in a foul mood and wanted to be elsewhere—at the precinct, no doubt.

Edward appeared on the stage and despite his earlier description of Jarold Jett, he smiled and gave the man a rousing introduction. But Carlotta noticed the tense body language of the men when Edward passed the microphone to his former boss.

"Every woman dreams of her wedding day," Jarold said, "and I've made it my mission to create gorgeous gowns to make her dreams come true. I hope you enjoy my new collection."

The crowd offered an exuberant welcome to the celebrity designer, then the lights dimmed, and the first couple emerged.

The bride's gown was elaborate, with a voluminous train. The groom was the miserably betrothed Jeremy, and although his smile was strained, she was happy to note he did the Neiman's formal black suit justice. And even though she knew he and the female model had probably met only moments beforehand, they were a convincingly beautiful couple.

And Carlotta had to admit there was something about seeing the proverbial bride and groom in all their dressed-up glory that made her heart swell in...anticipation? Hope? Optimism?

"Do you like it?" Jack murmured.

She started, then took in his mocking smile. "The gown? It's lovely, but my taste is a bit more simple."

"Oh? You've already picked out your wedding dress?"

She angled her head. "That would be ridiculous, don't you think, since I'm not even engaged?"

He conceded with a nod, then his expression changed. "Carlotta—"

A gasp from the crowd interrupted him. Carlotta turned to see that Jeremy had collapsed on the runway. His body jerked with seizures. His "bride" was screeching and running in place.

Jack was already jogging toward the stage, talking into his phone. Carlotta ran after him. He shouted for a doctor or a nurse and leapt to the stage. The young man stopped seizing and lay limp and unmoving. Carlotta's heart squeezed in panic. She stepped up onto the runway to quiet the bride and pull her back.

"What happened?" she asked the crying woman.

"He was fine, then he just suddenly f-fell."

"Before you came out, did he say he was feeling ill?"

"No...he asked for my number." The young woman dissolved into sobs.

At the end of the runway, Jack put his fingers against the man's neck, but Carlotta could tell from his expression that he felt no pulse. A woman in the audience identified herself as a nurse and Jack waved her over. The lights came up, and in the harsh illumination Jeremy looked deathly pale.

Jarold Jett came rushing out and shrieked with impressive showmanship. Carlotta handed off the hysterical bride to him and Edward, and noticed as they led her away that Jarold recovered enough to gently remind her not to get runny mascara on his gown.

Jack shouted for everyone to stay back, and some in the audience headed for the exit. The nurse began chest compressions and was still administering them when the paramedics arrived a few minutes later. But when Jack made eye contact with Carlotta, he gave an almost imperceptible shake of his head and she realized with horror that the groom was dead. A paramedic covered the body with a sheet.

The next few minutes were a blur as Jack attempted to clear the area. "Everybody—out!" he ordered, waving toward the exit.

An attractive blond woman wearing a pink pantsuit approached Jack, looking distraught. "I'm Melissa Friedman, director of the Wedding World Expo. I can't believe this has happened. How long will it take to remove the body?"

"Maybe hours. I suggest you shut down the show."

The woman looked horrified. "The entire Expo?"

"For the rest of the day, yes."

She straightened. "And who are you, exactly?"

He produced his badge, which seemed to give her pause. "You're closing down my show?"

"No. I'm strongly suggesting that *you* close it down, out of respect."

Melissa Friedman's mouth tightened. "All right. Just know that you are single-handedly crushing the dreams of countless women."

He gave her a flat smile. "So I've been told before. Now, if you don't mind, we really need to clear this area for the medical examiner."

The woman trotted away, grim-faced.

Jack glanced her way. "You, too, Carlotta—out."

She hated to be banished from the action. "But I talked to the vic just a few minutes ago."

One eyebrow climbed. "The vic? You've been watching *Law & Order* reruns again?"

Her chin went up. "I'm just trying to help."

"Okay. Do you know his name?"

From her bag, she pulled the list of the models' names and scanned it. "Jeremy Atwater. By the way, he was slurring his words when we talked."

"He was drunk?"

"Or maybe high. I didn't smell any alcohol. The woman he was walking with told me he seemed fine, then he just fell."

"Do you mind if I ask the questions around here?"

"Not at all, Jack."

He frowned. "Thank you. Now—out."

"But—"

"No but's, Carlotta. This isn't a crime scene, so there's nothing to stick your pretty nose into, no molehill to make a mountain out of."

She pulled back at his harsh tone, then he looked contrite.

"It's a horrible tragedy, but unfortunately, these things happen."

"But how can you be sure a crime wasn't committed?"

The P.A. system squawked, then a voice she recognized as Melissa Friedman sounded over hidden speakers. "Ladies and gentleman, due to unforeseen circumstances, I regret to inform you the Expo is closing for the day. But we'll be open tomorrow through Wednesday to help you plan every minute of your special day. We look forward to seeing you again!"

Jack gave Carlotta a pointed look and jerked his thumb toward the door.

"Spoil sport," she muttered.

"Don't forget 'dream crusher.' Now beat it." His expression eased a bit. "Go home and take a nap and let your shoulder heal."

She frowned and slowly moved toward the exit. At the sight of the familiar medical examiner's jacket threading through the crowd, Carlotta's pulse picked up at the hope of seeing Cooper Craft—he would let her snoop. Instead,

Assistant M.E. Prettyman appeared, and Carlotta was shot through with disappointment that she was out of angles to investigate the incident.

Then she sighed—how pathetic that she needed a distraction from her life so badly she was hoping something sinister was afoot with a young man's sudden death?

Carlotta remembered Jeremy's nervous question to her about whether wearing the tuxedo before his own wedding was bad luck. She obviously needed to brush up on wedding superstitions.

CHAPTER NINE

"THANKS FOR MEETING ME," Liz said.

Wesley nodded, afraid to speak. In the recent past he'd been tied to a chair, sliced up by a psychopath, robbed at gunpoint, and shot at on more than one occasion...yet this was the most scared he'd ever been in his life.

Liz looked pretty and pale in her black pantsuit and silk blouse, sitting across from him at a Midtown coffee shop. She sipped some kind of girly tea. He'd tossed back his espresso shot while waiting for her and now his leg was jumping under the table.

"How are you, Wes?"

He gritted his teeth. "I've been better."

A small smile lifted her red mouth. "This must be a confusing time for you."

"How's my dad?"

Her eyes flickered with warmth. "He's been better."

Wesley grunted with frustration. "Jesus, Liz, tell me about him. Where has he been? Where's Mom?"

"He's fine," she said quickly. "Just frustrated, like you. And unfortunately, I can't tell you where your mother is."

"Why not?"

"Because he hasn't told me."

"But she's okay?"

"He hasn't said otherwise."

"When do we get to see him?"

"I explained to Carlotta—"

"Yeah, she told me about the paperwork, but that's nuts. He's right across town and we can't see him!"

"I'm sorry, Wes, but it's your father's decision."

He pounded the table with his fist and sat back in the booth.

Liz cleared her throat. "We have other things to discuss."

His stomach cramped.

"How did your meeting go yesterday with your probation officer?"

He relaxed an iota. "Oh, that—it's cool. She let me take another drug test."

"And you're sure it'll be clean?"

"Yeah."

"Good. And the drugs are behind you?"

"Yeah."

Liz took a drink of her tea and Wes wiped at the perspiration on his upper lip.

"What about the other thing?" he blurted. "The thing you told me about on the phone?"

One winged eyebrow arched. "Oh, that."

"Yeah, that. Are you still...?"

"Pregnant? Yes."

He swallowed hard past a dry throat. "Is it mine?"

She hesitated. One heartbeat...two...three...

At four he thought maybe his heart had stopped altogether. His lungs also seemed to stall, trapping stale air in his brain.

"I believe so."

His intestines cramped before her words sank in—there was a chance it wasn't his. Then he frowned—how many other guys was Liz balling? But before his pride could be wounded fatally, self-preservation kicked in—hopefully, a lot.

"And you're going to have it?" he asked.

She nodded. "That's why I went away for a few days—to think it over. And I decided maybe this is a blessing in disguise."

He begged to differ, but he wasn't in her shoes.

"After all, I'm not getting any younger."

He avoided that minefield. "What are the chances it's mine?"

She pressed her lips together, obviously unwilling to share the number of her bed partners. "The timing says it's yours, but I'm confused because you and I were always careful."

Misery gathered in his chest and he wanted to cry. "There was a busted condom I didn't tell you about...but it was just once."

She closed her eyes briefly and puffed out her cheeks in an exhale. "Once is all it takes. Mystery solved."

He leaned over and puked in the floor. Customers scattered, chairs scraping and groans sounding. He wiped his mouth with a napkin and mumbled, "Sorry."

Liz sat frozen for a few seconds, then covered her mouth with her hand and leaned over to do the same. More groans sounded and customers began a mass exodus.

"Hey!" the barista shouted, bounding out from behind the counter with a roll of paper towels. "You two take your hangovers somewhere else!"

Liz stood and, holding a napkin to her mouth, tossed a ten dollar bill on the table, presumably as a tip for the cleanup. Wes followed her out to the sidewalk. "You okay?"

She nodded, her face as white as skim milk. "Just some latent morning sickness."

He gestured vaguely to her stomach. "So...what do we do now?"

She put a hand to her head. "Let me get back to you on that." She started to turn, then added, "By the way, we have an appointment to sit down with Detective Terry Monday morning to discuss how your prints got on that anonymous tip letter regarding the decapitated body in the morgue."

Yet another shit storm he was going to have to navigate. "Okay."

"Which means you have until then to think of a plausible story."

"Okay. Liz?"

"Uh-huh?"

"When will you see my dad again?"

"I'm not sure. Maybe later today if the schedules align."

"Will you tell him I've always believed in his innocence?"

A smile softened her mouth, then she nodded. "I'll be in touch."

Wes watched Liz walk toward a parking garage and felt utterly overwhelmed. He unlocked his bicycle from a rack with shaking hands and pictured a car seat strapped to the handlebars.

Jesus God.

He had no real ride, no real job, no real family, and no real prospects for anything real good happening anytime real soon. He could barely keep his own life between the lines, he certainly had no business being a father to anyone.

And what would his own father say when he found out?

And what would Carlotta say? (Okay, this he could guess.)

And—*gulp*—what would Meg say?

The sweet escape of an Oxy hit flitted through his mind—it would be so freaking nice to float away and forget about everything for a few hours…

But since the excruciating, near-death pain of withdrawal was still fresh in his mind, he pushed aside the traitorous thought.

When he jumped on his bike, though, he had the urge to do something else—flee. Leave all his problems behind. Ride his bike to a train station, take the train to the Greyhound station, jump on a bus to the West Coast…maybe Vegas. He could get a job in a casino, build up his poker-playing credentials, and make a name for himself. Who would miss him?

Carlotta? Only when it came to meal time, since he did most of the cooking.

Liz? Unlikely. She might even be glad he was out of the picture.

Meg? Maybe at first. Then she would concede that her father was right about Wes, that he was an unsavory sort who couldn't be trusted.

His dad?

The thought of not getting to talk to his father gave him pause. On the other hand, if anyone understood the impulse to run from his problems, it would be Randolph.

He stilled. Was this how his father had felt all those years ago, overcome with problems that seemed insurmountable to the point that the best solution was to disappear?

A horn blasted into the air, jolting him out of his reverie.

"Get out of the road!" a driver yelled from a mini-SUV that had stopped inches from Wes's rear bike tire.

Wes realized he was sitting like a statue in the lane next to the curb. He gave the driver an apologetic wave and pushed off, pedaling toward the agreed-upon meeting place with Mouse.

Mouse was one of The Carver's henchmen who had smoothed the way for Wesley to be folded into the loan shark's organization under the guise of paying off his own gambling debt. Unaware that Wes had agreed to infiltrate the group to gather information on The Carver's drug-running son Dillon, the big man had taken Wes under his wing, had even taken it upon himself to kidnap Wes and force him to go through drug detox in one weekend.

But that didn't mean Mouse wouldn't tie a cinder block to Wes's dick and drop him in the Chattahoochee River if he found out he was the one who'd sent the anonymous tip to the police about the headless body.

At Grindhouse Killer Burgers, the black Town Car was already sitting in the parking lot. The driver side window zoomed down to reveal Mouse wearing a makeshift bib of several napkins and wrecking a massive cheeseburger.

"I thought you were on a diet," Wes said.

The big man held up the burger. "It's on a potato bun—that's a vegetable."

"I stand corrected. You look skinny already."

Mouse popped the trunk. "Get in, smartass."

Wes circled around to stow his bike, and paused—once he'd found a severed finger inside.

And just like that—a memory smacked him up the side of the head.

The severed finger had belonged to the man who had also become separated from his head...and the finger had been wrapped in *his* jacket Mouse had yanked off him once when he was trying to get away. Mouse had warned him they were keeping the blood-soaked jacket, which conveniently had Wes's monogram on the inside pocket (thanks, Carlotta) in case Wes decided to sell them out.

Christ, if he told Jack what he knew, the finger, literally, would be pointing back to him.

Wes's heart was jumping as he lifted the trunk lid, but the only item in the carpeted interior was a big honking golf club.

"Bring the driver with you," Mouse called.

He removed the club, then stored his bike. "New hobby?" he asked as he swung into the passenger seat of the Town Car.

"Nah," Mouse said through a mouthful of burger. "I broke my old club over the head of a deadbeat sports gambler. Had to buy a new one."

Wes fingered the TaylorMade SLDR driver. "This is a pretty nice club to be swinging at someone's head."

"That's what the salesman told me. So I signed up for lessons."

Wes blinked. "Really?"

"Thought golf might help me lose a few pounds."

"Only if you actually learn how to hit that little white ball."

"You play?"

"Used to, when I was a kid." Wesley stroked the shaft of the shiny driver. "My dad took me."

Mouse polished off the last of the burger and ripped off the bib to swipe at his mouth. "Is your old man dead?"

"No. He was just gone for a while. But he's back now."

Mouse frowned. "How long was he gone?"

"Ten years, give or take."

From the intense expression on Mouse's thick face, he could tell the big man was doing math in his head. "So you were just a pup when he left."

"I guess."

"Where's he been?"

"I don't know. He was a fugitive."

Mouse stared. "No shit?"

"No shit."

"Was he captured?"

"Not really—he's been outsmarting the police for years. But my sister was in trouble, so he came out of hiding to save her life, and got caught."

Mouse gaped. "For real?"

"For real."

"Where is he now?"

"They're holding him at the federal pen across town."

Mouse winced. "Federal, huh? That's no good. Why'd he run in the first place?"

"They say he stole a bunch of money from a bunch of rich people. He was an investment broker."

"Wow...so you're the son of a con man?"

Wes scowled. "He didn't do those things."

Mouse nodded, but looked unconvinced. Then his eyes widened. "Does this have something to do with the bug we found in your wall?"

"Maybe. I don't know yet. The feds won't let me see him."

"I know a couple of guys on the inside if you want me to find out if he's okay."

Wes perked up. "Yeah, Mouse, that would be great. His name is Randolph Wren."

"Hm...sounds familiar. Wait." He snapped his fingers. "Wren—of course. I read about him in the newspaper and didn't make the connection. They call him 'The Bird.' "

Wes's chest puffed up. "That's right. The Carver isn't the only criminal to have a nickname." Then he blanched. "Not that my dad is a criminal...or The Carver either, for that matter."

"I'll make a couple of phone calls today, and ask my contacts to find out what they can."

"Can you make sure he knows it's me asking?"

"Sure thing," Mouse said, then wrinkled his nose. "You smell like throw-up."

Wes looked down at his splattered shirt. "Sorry—something didn't sit well on my stomach."

"Are you still sick from the withdrawal?"

"Nah. I guess it's my nerves—my dad being back and all."

Mouse grunted. "I've been a little nervous myself, wondering if you had anything to do with sending that anonymous letter about our dead guy to the police."

Wes swallowed hard. "I told you I don't even know who the guy is."

"Good." Mouse leaned over, removed an aerosol can of air freshener from the glove compartment and doused Wesley.

"Hey, watch the eyes!"

When the cloud cleared, Mouse steered the car away from downtown.

"Where are we going?" Wes asked.

"Driving range in the 'burbs. The two late-paying butt-cracks we're collecting from are on the Georgia State golf team, and their roommate said they're out improving their swing."

"Ergo the golf club."

"What the fuck does air-go mean? Is that a golf term?"

Wes cracked a smile. "Yeah, Mouse."

They headed north on Georgia 400—and instantly hit a wall of slow-moving cars spanning every lane.

"Man, this traffic sucks," Wes said. "I would kill myself if I had to deal with this commute every day."

"You get used to it."

Wes's head snapped around. "You live up here?"

"What can I say? The schools are good."

"You have kids?"

"Boy and a girl."

Wesley really didn't want to know that much about the man's personal life, but now he was intrigued. "So...how do you like that?"

"Like what?"

"Being a dad."

Mouse smiled. "It's the best. My daughter is a dancer, and my son plays baseball. I don't want to miss out on anything they do." Then his smile vanished. "Sorry, Little Man, I wasn't thinking. I mean, I'm sure your dad—"

"It's okay," Wes cut in. "It's cool that you enjoy being a dad."

But he knew what the man was thinking—how could Randolph Wren abandon his kids?

Maybe because Randolph didn't feel as if he'd be missing out on anything.

Carlotta had been almost an adult when their parents had left—they had gotten to see her grow up, and probably assumed she would marry Peter and be fine.

But what about him?

Wesley bit down on his tongue and turned his head toward the window lest Mouse see the offhand comment had gotten to him.

Randolph had been a good athlete, and Wes always felt as if his virile dad was disappointed with his bony bespectacled son who was more comfortable with a book in his hands than sports equipment. Maybe Randolph had thought Wesley didn't need him.

And vice versa.

Wesley's thoughts fast-forwarded to his own impending fatherhood. What kind of father would he be? It wasn't as if he'd had an example.

"You okay over there?" Mouse asked.

"Yeah," Wes said, straightening in his seat.

"Hey, what's going on with that girl you have a crush on—Maggie?"

"Meg," Wes corrected, realizing too late he'd walked right into that little confession.

"Meg, right. So you two are an item?"

"Uh...no. That's not going to work out."

Mouse frowned. "Why not?"

"We're just too different," Wes said.

Which was true. Meg was the kind of girl who had the world by the balls... and he was the kind of guy the rest of the world had by the balls.

"So what's the plan?" Wes asked to change the subject, pointing to the sign ahead for the driving range.

Mouse handed him a creased flyer featuring the smiling Georgia State men's golf team. Two of the headshots had been circled with a red crayon. "The plan is for you to strike up a pleasant convo with these two big spenders—Darrell Plank and Tom Morrow—and collect at least a fiver from each."

"Or?"

Mouse nodded to the driver Wes held. "Break it in for me."

Wes hefted the club, indulging in thoughts of spending weekends on the golf course with his dad once all their problems were behind them. He really did need to practice his swing. His dad didn't need to know how he'd developed his technique.

CHAPTER TEN

"PETER, IT'S FINE," Carlotta assured him over the phone as she walked on the sidewalk toward the exhibition hall. "The young man's death was tragic, but there was nothing sinister about it."

She should know—hadn't she tried to turn it into a homicide?

"Still, I don't like it," Peter said. "You're supposed to be resting and giving your shoulder a chance to heal. What if the guy had some sort of virus and you catch it?"

"If that were the case, I'm sure the CDC would be all over it."

He made a frustrated noise. "I worry about you."

"Don't," she said, then realized her tone was a little sharp. "I'm fine," she soothed. "How are things at the office?"

"A little strange. The partners have been scarce, and when they come in, they sequester themselves."

"Has anyone mentioned Randolph to you?"

"Only Brody Jones. Walt told him you and I had gone our separate ways."

"And?"

"And...he said he thought it was a good career decision."

She knew that—but still, it stung. "Anything else?"

"He wanted to know if you had spoken to Randolph before he was arrested."

She frowned. "What did you tell him?"

"I told him you were injured, and you'd only exchanged a few words before being taken to the hospital. That seemed to satisfy him."

Why would Brody Jones care if Randolph Wren had had a conversation with his daughter before he'd been arrested? "Anything else?"

"Not really. He just reiterated that Randolph had done a lot of damage to the firm's reputation they'd had to repair, and they were afraid his reappearance would be bad for business."

"That's understandable, I suppose. Actually, Peter, there is something you can do for me."

"Name it."

"Can you get me a list of my father's clients who lost money?"

"I...sure. It might take me a day or two. Why do you need it?"

A tiny red flag rose in her head. Why did he need to know why she needed it?

"If you don't mind me asking," he added.

"Not at all. I found out the parents of one of my coworkers lost money. I just want to know if any other acquaintances are on the list."

"I understand. Who is the coworker?"

Another red flag rose. "Um...Patricia Alexander."

"Yes...her parents are Hess and Laura. They were two of Randolph's best clients."

She closed her eyes briefly. "Thanks for your help, Peter."

"So...have you spoken to Randolph yet?"

Carlotta hesitated. Why was she reluctant to share with Peter the fact that she hadn't heard from her father?

Because on some level she feared he might feel compelled to share information she gave him with the partners in the firm...and play both sides of the fence.

It hit her like a gong—she didn't trust Peter...which wasn't fair because he hadn't told the police about Randolph calling him at the office.

Unless it was out of self-preservation, so the partners wouldn't think he was helping Randolph.

Someone fell into step next to her. "Good morning, early bird."

Carlotta looked up to see Jack striding along, sipping coffee, as if they walked to work together every morning.

"Carly, are you there?" Peter asked.

"Yes, I'm here."

"Is someone with you?"

"I'm at the Expo, so I have to go."

"Okay," he said reluctantly. "Call me?"

"I will," she promised, then disconnected the call.

"No need to hang up on my account," Jack said amiably.

"Unless I don't want you to eavesdrop on my conversation," she said dryly.

"Keeping secrets, huh?"

She smiled. "Don't we all, Jack?"

Instead of answering, he turned his head in the direction of three large groups of protestors who had gathered near the sidewalk, holding up handmade posters and pumping their fists in the air, shouting cheers and jeers together and at each other.

"What are they protesting?" Jack asked.

"That group supports same-sex marriage," Carlotta said, pointing. "That group supports multi-partner marriage, and that group wants to abolish marriage altogether." She angled a smile at Jack. "I bet I can guess which camp you're in."

He held up his hands. "No comment, not applicable."

"Oh, come on, Jack—you've never come close to getting married?"

"No," he said vehemently. Then almost under his breath he added, "Not yet."

She gasped. "So you haven't ruled out the possibility entirely?"

He stopped, then reached into his pocket and pulled out the flashing bull's eye beeper. "Duty calls. Jett kept me out until one this morning. I was hoping I'd get here early enough to enjoy a cup of coffee before he arrived."

"He's supposed to sign copies of his new book this morning at the media booth. It's just inside the entrance, to the left."

He gave her a grateful wave, but watching him stride away, Carlotta was left with the feeling that Jack had been relieved for an excuse to get away from her and their conversation.

But then again, hadn't they promised to maintain a proper distance from each other?

Someone walked by and shoved a brochure into her hand announcing an art exhibit titled "After the Dress." *This visually stunning and thought-provoking show features wedding gowns of bygone decades and live narrative from the women who wore them regarding what they learned about themselves during marriage and after divorce.*

Carlotta pursed her mouth. Apparently the Wedding Expo was the catalyst for stirring up all kinds of opinions on marriage—the good, the bad, and the ugly.

She stuffed the brochure into her bag and hurried inside. Jarold Jett had done her a favor by summoning Jack to keep him occupied. She had arrived before the Expo opened to the public with her all-access worker-bee lanyard in the hopes of going back to the runway and tent area to snoop around a bit—assuming everything hadn't been dismantled.

She casually made her way back to the walled-off area where a "Do Not Enter" sign was posted across a curtain that spanned the doorway. Carlotta rolled her eyes—really? A lousy sign and a curtain? She would have to talk to Jack about the lax security…after she got in and out, of course.

After a quick scan of the area, she slipped through the curtain, prepared to say she'd left something in one of the changing tents if anyone stopped her.

But thankfully, the area was deserted…eerily so. Carlotta walked to the end of the waist-high runway and took in the mashed, strewn white flower petals that had fallen from the bouquet carried by the woman who'd been walking next to Jeremy. One of the petals looked dark and wet, as if it was stuck to something. She carefully picked it up to find a flat wad of chewing gum, tinged with blood. Jeremy had been chewing gum—it was probably his, dislodged when he'd collapsed.

A noise behind her startled her. She curled the flower petal in her hand and turned around guiltily to see a man in janitorial garb holding a push broom.

"Uh, nobody's supposed to be in here, ma'am."

She gave him a huge smile, and held up her handy lanyard. "I'm an exhibitor—I work for Neiman Marcus. We cosponsored the fashion show yesterday, and everything ended so quickly, I left a few things in the changing area." She gestured vaguely to the white tents behind the stage. "Do you mind if I get them before someone makes off with them?"

The guy glanced at her legs, then nodded. "I guess that would be okay...if you hurry."

She blasted him with another smile. "Thank you." Then she moved toward the tent, folding the gummy flower petal into a side pocket of her purse to discard later. She wasn't watching where she was going and tripped, catching herself at the last minute. On the carpeted floor lay one of the red wigs the brides had been wearing in the fashion show. She scooped it up and carried it with her to the changing tent where the young men had dressed in their groom's garb.

The tent was empty. All the clothing and accessory racks had been removed, leaving only a few folding chairs, a looted snack cart littered with dead flies and empty water bottles, and a bank of temporary plastic lockers, most of which stood open. Carlotta went through them one by one, but didn't find anything...and truthfully, didn't know what she was looking for.

Trouble, Jack would say.

She conceded defeat with a laugh, left the men's tent and stepped next door into the women's tent to return the red wig. The brides' tent was also empty, but even more trashed, with remnants of flowers, sequins, straight pins, and elastic hair ties cluttering the floor. One lone flip-flop lay forsaken, as if someone had literally walked out of it and kept going. She could only imagine the pandemonium of getting the women out of their dresses and away from the terrible scene. The fact that the wig she held sported strands of dark hair gave her a sense that the wearer had ripped it off mid-stride. Clumps of tissues overflowing a small garbage can spoke of the tears that had been shed in the aftermath.

It was a terrible thing to witness someone's death, to see a person alive and happy one moment, and the next, dead and, well...*unhappy.*

Except Jeremy hadn't exactly been happy about being a groom, had he?

Had his discontent led him to ingest a lethal mix of drugs and alcohol? Had the stress of his impending wedding triggered an aneurysm?

Regardless, it all seemed so unnecessary and random, it was mind-numbing.

Shaken, Carlotta laid the disheveled wig on a table and left. Another couple of workers had joined the first guy, along with Melissa Friedman, who was barking orders to get the place cleaned up and reconfigured in time for the noon flower arranging contest, *chop, chop!* Carlotta ducked her head and slunk outside the curtain.

And was instantly propelled back into the land of happy.

The Wedding World Expo had reopened with a vengeance. Between it being Friday, and the extra punch of publicity generated from the news reports, the betrothed women of Atlanta had shown up in impressive numbers. The crowd was rolling toward the booths at the rear of the exhibition hall like a big, colorful tide.

Carlotta picked up her pace and hurried to the *Your Perfect Man* booth. No surprise, Patricia Alexander was already there, looking as bright and shiny as a first-grader.

"I wanted to get a jump on commissions since yesterday was cut short," Patricia said.

"Good idea," Carlotta agreed.

"Gosh, that was just awful what happened yesterday. Did you see it?"

"Yes. Actually, I had a brief conversation with the young man beforehand. Such a tragedy."

Patricia angled her head. "Bodies seem to turn up wherever you are."

Carlotta straightened. "That's not true." All of the time.

"Still. You have to admit it's kind of weird. It's like you have this *thing* around you...like a black cloud."

Carlotta swallowed a retort, remembering that Patricia had reason to take pot shots at her, and her family. And besides...she wasn't exactly wrong about the body count.

"I can see why you would think so," she murmured. Then she conjured up a smile. "So...have you and Leo set a date?" She'd met the guy once—he played for the Gwinnett Braves farm team. She hadn't been bowled over by him, but Patricia was completely smitten, which was all that mattered.

The blonde lit up. "We're thinking a fall wedding, you know, after his playing season ends."

"That sounds nice."

"Something small and elegant," Patricia said. "We're saving our pennies for a new house." She could guess what Patricia made in a year, and Leo wasn't in the major leagues yet...plus he had a daughter to support, so a big elaborate wedding probably wasn't in the budget.

And because of Randolph, Patricia's father couldn't foot the bill. "That sounds lovely," Carlotta said with a smile. "Very classy."

"Maybe someday you'll have a wedding of your own," Patricia said. "Peter isn't the only fish in the sea."

"Right."

"Although he is one of the most handsome."

"Yes."

"And one of the richest."

"Er...yes."

"Why did you break up again?"

"Um...it's complicated."

"Does it have something to do with that detective that's always hanging around?"

Carlotta squirmed. "No."

"Because I think he has a thing for you."

Her cheeks warmed as she thought of the specific "thing" Jack had for her. "Detective Terry is a bona fide bachelor."

Patricia scoffed. "Every man's mind can be changed by the right woman."

Carlotta squinted. Was Patricia implying that Carlotta wasn't the kind of woman who could change a man's mind? "Then obviously Leo has found the right woman in you."

Patricia nodded happily, then pivoted away to help a customer. Carlotta exhaled, feeling a headache coming on. If things were awkward between her and Patricia now, how much more tense would things become if Randolph went to trial? How many of her acquaintances and customers would be in the court gallery, demanding their pound of flesh from her father?

And could she blame them?

In her small Tory Burch crossbody bag, her phone vibrated. Her heart lurched hopefully—stupidly—that it was some word from Randolph. Or Wesley calling to say hello and he was sorry for acting like a jerk since their foiled visit to the jail two days ago. Instead it was Hannah returning an earlier text.

Got a weeklong catering gig, catch up with you soon.

Carlotta battled a stab of disappointment. Between Hannah's erratic job and spending all her free time with Chance, she'd been scarce lately. But it wasn't her friend's fault her life was crumbling at the corners.

Carlotta texted back *Okay, talk soon.*

She checked to make sure she hadn't missed a phone call from the U.S. Penitentiary, then reluctantly dialed Liz's phone number. The woman answered on the first ring.

"What is it, Carlotta? I'm busy."

Carlotta swallowed a foul word. "Too busy to go with me Monday to sit down with Kelvin Lucas?"

A beat of silence passed. "What's this about?"

"I assume he wants to take my report on The Charmed Killer case, but I'm afraid he'll use it as an excuse to dig for information about Randolph."

From the throaty noise Liz made, she could tell the woman agreed. "What time?"

They synced details, then ended the call without ceremony. Carlotta stowed her phone with gritted teeth—she was so tired of Randolph occupying space in her brain!

With a mental shake, she busied herself helping customers, trying not to think about anything except selling men's clothes and accessories. It was, at least, fun to help women decide if their man was a warrior, a king, a lover, or a magician. She had to give kudos to the booth designer—it was an interesting way to connect with shoppers and engage them in conversation. She drew on the high energy of the show and before she knew it, Melissa Friedman was announcing over the loudspeaker that the flower arrangement competition would begin soon in the runway area, and seats were filling fast.

Carlotta sighed. Yesterday a young man had died on that runway, and today the world marched on with its frivolous pastimes…but it was how things had to be.

Still, it made a person feel inconsequential.

"Hello, Carlotta."

At the sound of the vaguely familiar female voice, she turned and blinked in surprise at the curvy redhead who had stopped next to the booth. "Hi, Rainie." Guilt suffused her chest. "I'm sorry I haven't returned your calls. I've been…busy."

Rainie Stephens smiled. "I understand. You have a lot going on right now. How is your injury?"

"Better, thanks."

"It must be if you're working." She nodded to the display. "The four male archetypes—very clever."

"I can't take credit for it, but yes. What brings you to the show? Are you planning a wedding?"

Rainie laughed and shook her head. "No. I'm writing a general interest piece for the paper. I'm sure you heard about the young man who collapsed and died yesterday?"

"Yes. I was there when it happened—very sad."

"Is there a story there?"

Carlotta shook her head. "It was awful, but innocent enough. The poor guy had a baby on the way, was going to be married soon."

Rainie made a mournful noise, then glanced at her watch. "Do you have time now to chat? I'll buy you lunch."

"I'm really not up for an interview, Rainie."

The woman fingered a black leather Tom Ford wallet. "Maybe you can help me find a gift, then?"

Carlotta was wary. "Okay. Someone special?"

"Cooper, as a matter of fact. His birthday is next week."

Rainie and Coop had some relationship history, but Carlotta didn't know the details. A tiny ripple of jealousy pinged through her chest that the woman knew more about Coop than she did. "Right."

"So which one of these archetypes do you think best matches Coop?"

She didn't want to say, but her gaze involuntarily went to one particular display.

Rainie's eyebrows rose. "The lover, huh?"

"Um…I…wouldn't really know."

The redhead circled the display, then nodded. "No, you're right…he's a lover."

Carlotta pressed her lips together. "If you say so."

"Can you recommend something?"

"How about this?" She held up a straw fedora with a black band.

"Yes, I think it would suit him nicely. I'll take it."

Carlotta stepped to a register to ring up the sale, still on her guard.

Rainie leaned into the counter. "So how about some questions to satisfy my own curiosity? Off the record."

Carlotta hesitated, then remembered the times Rainie had helped her. "Okay…off the record."

"When Bruce Abrams attacked you, did he tell you why he killed all those women?"

"He implied he was doing it to set up Coop."

Rainie's eyes clouded in concern. "Did he say why?"

"I got the impression he felt as if he was operating in Coop's shadow."

"Makes sense, I suppose. Coop was a popular chief M.E."

A part of Coop's life that transpired before Carlotta knew him. "I'm sure he was."

"God, I'm so relieved Abrams is locked up and Coop's nightmare is over."

The way she said it made Carlotta think Rainie was helping Coop pick up the pieces…which was great. He deserved to be happy. "We're all relieved." She wrapped the hat in tissue and placed it in a shopping bag. Coop was the kind of guy who could wear a fedora. He was…cool.

Rainie handed over her credit card. "How is your father?"

Carlotta gave a careful shrug. "I wouldn't know. I haven't talked to him."

"Why not?"

"Are we still off the record?"

Rainie's eyes softened and she nodded.

"The feds are keeping him under wraps."

"I heard he'd been moved to USP. You must be going crazy."

Carlotta managed a smile. "Crazy is starting to feel normal." She handed back the credit card, receipt, and shopping bag. "Coop will love it."

"I hope so," Rainie said happily as she tucked away her wallet. "Carlotta, when you're ready to talk on the record about everything that's happened, call me. It can be cathartic, you know, to tell your side of the story." She started walking away.

Carlotta was tempted to call her back—to grant her an exposé into the life of the children of fugitives, to make public the way she and Wesley had been ostracized and had scraped by. They had been victims as much as the people who'd lost money they'd invested with Randolph. It would serve him and Valerie right for what they'd done, and for what Randolph was still doing to them.

"Rainie—wait."

The woman turned back. "Yes?"

Except Wesley would never forgive her. And at the moment, the ground he stood on was shaky enough.

"Enjoy celebrating Coop's birthday."

The woman smiled wide. "We will. Thanks."

The rest of the day dragged, marked by hourly announcements on the P.A. system for whatever activity was taking place in the presentation area—a tasting, a class, a demonstration. Jack walked by once and waved, but didn't stop, seemingly resolute to keep their pact. As the clock crept toward closing time, Carlotta became more and more antsy to get home to check the mailbox, although she knew the chance it would contain some sort of correspondence from her father was slim. And unless Wesley decided to put in an appearance to make dinner, she was looking at a bagged salad to keep her company.

Stifling a yawn, she was on her way to the vending area for a shot of caffeine when she spotted someone who looked familiar. She did a double-take. The tall, polished woman wearing a tailored dress working the counter for

HAL Properties, an exclusive hotelier in the Southeast, looked a little like...in this light, she sort of resembled...

She could *almost* be mistaken for...

The woman looked up and made eye contact. Then she froze.

Carlotta's eyes bugged. *Hannah?*

CHAPTER ELEVEN

INSTEAD OF WAVING, Hannah did a one-hundred-eighty-degree turn and strode out of the booth in the opposite direction.

Carlotta frowned and walked after her. "Hannah, it's me!"

Ahead of her, Hannah picked up her pace and trotted through the crowd.

Carlotta zigzagged between people to keep up. "Hannah, stop!"

But Hannah was practically running now. Carlotta was ready to give up when she saw her friend trip and go down hard. She hurried to where Hannah had parted the crowd. She was lying on her back, slapping away hands that tried to help her up. Nearby lay a black high-heeled pump, minus the high heel. Carlotta rescued the amputated shoe.

When Hannah saw Carlotta, she squeezed her eyes shut and played dead.

Gone was the Goth makeup and in its place—if Carlotta had to guess from the air-brushed perfection—was Dinair foundation in Golden Tan. Gone were the miscellaneous rings in various face piercings and in their place, diamond stud earrings and a Mikimoto three-strand pearl choker. The fitted colorblock dress covering every inch of tattooed skin was Yves Saint Laurent. And her black and white striped hair had been tamed into a tight bun on the top of her head befitting of a ballerina.

All dolled up, Hannah Kizer was *gorgeous*. And almost unrecognizable.

Carlotta stood over her, hands on hips, taking it all in. "Hannah?"

No response.

"Should I call 9-1-1?" a woman standing next to Carlotta asked.

"No, but thank you," Carlotta said. "I've got this." She smiled and waved off the lookey-loos, then crouched down. "Hannah?"

Hannah cracked open one eye. "Yes?"

"What's going on?"

The other eye opened. "It's a wedding expo."

Carlotta pursed her mouth. "I mean, why were you running from me?"

"I wasn't running from you. I...had to go to the bathroom."

Carlotta arched an eyebrow. "Then you'd better get up." She extended her hand.

Hannah, looking miserable, let Carlotta help her stand. "Damn shoes."

Carlotta held up the leather pump. "You must have put a lot of miles on these. Burberry usually can withstand anything."

Hannah snatched it from her hand. "Good thing I brought flats as a backup. They're back in the booth."

"That would be the HAL Properties booth?"

Hannah squirmed. "That's right."

"Are you moonlighting?"

"Sort of."

"Do you work for HAL Properties, or don't you?"

Hannah's berry-glossed mouth twitched downward. "My family kind of owns it."

Carlotta's jaw loosened. "Your family owns HAL Properties?"

Her friend nodded morosely. "It's named for me and my sisters—Hannah, Anna, Linda."

"And the brother you once mentioned?"

"Sterling. My folks put his name on their flagship hotel."

"The Sterling House?"

Hannah sighed, then nodded.

An exclusive five-star hotel in Midtown that boasted a mere twenty-five rooms of alleged unparalleled luxury—Carlotta had never been through the hallowed doors. But its reputation was the stuff of urban legend.

Disparate pieces of information Hannah had let slip over the years began to fall into place—the disparaging remarks about her family, the implied estrangement. Carlotta had assumed her friend was ashamed of her family, and since she could relate, she hadn't forced the issue. It hadn't occurred to her that Hannah was embarrassed because they were *wealthy.*

A memory bounced into her head—once when the police had questioned Hannah about a theft at the country club where she was waiting tables, an officer had recited the address from her driver's license as West Paces Ferry. At the time, Carlotta had thought it strange that Hannah lived on the same street as the governor's mansion, but the detail had gotten lost in the flurry of the moment. Now it made sense.

"Wow...just...wow. Why didn't you ever tell me?"

Hannah bristled. "What difference does it make?"

"I don't believe it does."

"So why bother?"

"Maybe because you know practically everything about my life?"

Hannah shrugged. "I'm a private person."

Carlotta swept her arm up and down, indicating her friend's drastic change in appearance. "I'm starting to think I don't know you at all."

From the depths of her memory came the voice of Maria Marquez when the profiler had once offered up some unflattering observations about Carlotta's relationship with Hannah. *Is that why she's friends with you—because you don't care enough to ask questions?*

Hannah grimaced. "This isn't me—this is who my parents want me to be."

"And this is so bad?"

"It comes with too many expectations."

Unbidden, resentment rose in her chest. Had she and Wesley been a source of entertainment to Hannah...to see how the other half lived? "So you decided to slum it with the Wrens?"

Hannah's face clouded. "It wasn't like that."

"Then how was it?"

"Don't be mad. Can we go somewhere to talk?"

Carlotta hesitated. The sense of betrayal was keen...but her sense of curiosity won out. "We could go to Moody's. But I rode MARTA, so you'll have to drive."

"Okay," Hannah said eagerly. "I'll change my shoes and meet you by the entrance in ten minutes."

"I can walk with you." She was dying to meet Hannah's family.

"*No*," Hannah snapped, then looked contrite. "One step at a time, okay?"

Carlotta stared after her, reeling inside. How was it possible to spend so much time with someone and know so little about them?

Could she trust anyone except herself?

Feeling numb, she made her way back to the booth to help Patricia tidy up and secure the cash registers. She glanced around, missing Jack and hating herself for it.

"He hasn't been by," Patricia murmured.

"Who?"

The blonde gave her a pointed look. "That cop who doesn't have anything to do with you and Peter breaking up."

She didn't even have the energy to argue…life was sucking the life out of her.

"See you tomorrow," Carlotta said with as much of a smile as she could muster.

When she reached the entrance, Hannah was waiting for her, her startling appearance further enhanced by the addition of a Valentino shoulder bag.

"Nice purse," Carlotta offered.

"Shut up, or I'll choke you with the strap."

"Ah, there's the Hannah I know." She smothered a smile and followed her friend to the parking garage, still marveling over the transformation.

"God, this was the longest day of my life," Hannah said. "What kind of sadist dreamt up the idea of a wedding expo?"

"Oh, come on—no one forced throngs of women to be there."

"Please don't tell me *you* are in the market for a wedding?"

"No, I'm working the show for Neiman's."

"How is Richie Rich?"

"Actually, Peter and I are taking a little break."

Hannah lifted an eyebrow. "Do tell."

"Nothing to tell, I just have too much going on right now."

"Have you talked to your father?"

"No. And at this point I don't know when I will. I have an appointment with the D.A. Monday—I hope I can find out more then."

"How are you holding up?"

Carlotta blinked back sudden tears, and her step faltered. "By a thread," she admitted.

"Hey, hey," Hannah said, her voice surprisingly gentle. "You've made it this long...you can't cave now. I'm sure the paperwork and the jurisdiction bullshit will be sorted out soon."

Carlotta sniffed, then nodded.

"How's your injury?"

"Healing."

"At least that nightmare is over."

So true...but was another one beginning?

Hannah stopped, and Carlotta scanned the rows of parked cars.

"Where's the van?"

The car next to them chirped, then the doors unlocked. "Um, this is my ride."

Carlotta stared at the silver Audi two-seater. "Seriously?"

"Just get in, goddammit."

They didn't talk much on the drive to Moody's—zippy convertibles were convenient that way. The breezy ride allowed Carlotta to study her friend who was, if not wholly comfortable with the designer togs and transportation, at least in command of them.

"Please stop looking at me like that," Hannah said after they'd parked and climbed out.

"Sorry. It's just so—"

"Obnoxious? I know."

"I was going to say disconcerting. It's going to take a while for me to adjust, that's all."

"Oh, no—don't get used to this."

"I can't unsee it."

"Try."

"Hannah, you look terrific!"

"Please—you sound like my sisters." She held open the door to Moody's. "Hurry, let's get a drink."

The inside of Moody's cigar bar was hopping with commuters waiting out rush hour. The bottom floor of the establishment was packed with suited men and women perusing the glass cabinets and counters that held every kind of cigar, loose tobacco, and smoking accessory. The girls headed upstairs to the martini bar, where patrons could lounge in velvet club chairs and deep leather couches around coffee tables studded with interesting ashtrays, lighters, and boxes of wooden matches. Carlotta spotted the proprietor, June Moody, leaning against the bar, chatting with Nathan the bartender.

June greeted her with a concerned smile. "Hello, dear. You made the newspapers again. How are you?"

"Hanging in there," Carlotta said, her heart brimming with fondness for the woman who'd always given her sage advice.

"And who's your friend?"

Carlotta grinned, but Hannah scoffed. "It's me, June—Hannah."

June gaped, then recovered. "I didn't recognize you. You look—"

"Great!" Nathan finished, his eyes bugged.

Hannah made a face. "Can I get a martini—very dirty?"

"Make that two," Carlotta said.

"I'm going to the john," Hannah said, then disappeared into the crowd.

June gave Carlotta a quizzical look, but Carlotta just shrugged.

The older woman laid her hand on Carlotta's arm. "I'm so relieved that awful Dr. Abrams is in jail. He almost got away with driving Coop to total ruin, and hurting you."

"Coop is resilient. And I'm stronger than I look."

"I understand your father is back in town?"

"That's right."

"And you're happy about that?"

"Mostly. I'll feel better when I get to talk to him, and find out where my mother is."

"Of course." June's eyes were moist, probably because she couldn't imagine abandoning her son the way Valerie Wren had abandoned her children. Then she signaled Nathan. "Drinks for Carlotta and Hannah are on the house."

"That's not necessary—"

"Sure it is," June insisted. "You have a lot to celebrate." Then she spotted Hannah returning and lowered her voice. "And I want to encourage Hannah to look normal more often."

Carlotta laughed.

When Hannah was settled on the stool next to her, June left to check on customers.

"People are looking at me," Hannah said.

"It's because you're beautiful," Carlotta said.

"I'm the same person I am in my Goth getup."

"Yes, but you look more approachable. What does Chance think?"

Hannah narrowed her eyes. "He doesn't know...and you're not going to say anything."

"He might like it."

"But I don't. I can't imagine a world where I dress like this all the time."

Carlotta drank deeply of the chilled martini and thought of the Hannah she'd met in the other place she'd visited. "You don't think it's possible that we're all living different lives in other dimensions of the universe?"

Hannah frowned. "Did that Abrams lunatic hit you on the head?"

"That would actually explain a lot," Carlotta admitted.

Between sips of their drinks, they swapped customer stories from the Wedding Expo. "I heard a male model died during a fashion show?" Hannah asked.

"Yeah, I was there. It was sad."

"Figures—the only interesting thing to happen and it's on the day I'm not working the show."

Carlotta gave her a chiding look. "I assume the Expo is the 'catering gig' you texted me you were working?"

"Yep. My sisters want to grow the banquets part of the business, so they set this up, and I couldn't get out of it."

"If your family owns high-end properties, why do you work catering gigs?"

"I want something of my own. I want to be a chef someday."

"At one of your family's hotels?"

"Maybe. But I don't want the job handed to me."

Carlotta nodded. "I admire you for that. If I were in your shoes, I don't know if I could be so independent."

"Sure you could—you're the most independent person I know."

She shook her head. "It's different—I had no choice. You, on the other hand, are choosing the harder way." She lifted her martini glass to Hannah's. "Cheers, my friend."

Hannah smiled and clinked her glass. "Cheers."

They drank the last of their martinis, then Carlotta sighed. "But can I be a little jealous?"

Hannah laughed. "So catch me up. If you and Peter are on the outs, is Jack moving in?"

Carlotta blinked. "Uh—that would be *no*. Jack and I are taking a break, too. Since he arrested Randolph and all."

"Right." Hannah fingered the stem of her empty glass. "So...you and Coop?"

"Also on a break."

"Because of the Abrams thing?"

"Right."

"Cool," Hannah said, looking much relieved.

Carlotta decided not to mention that Rainie Stephens seemed to have set her cap for Coop.

Hannah pulled her ringing phone from her bag, then grinned. "Speak of the devil!" She connected the call. "Hi, Coop!"

Carlotta sat up in surprise. Coop?

Hannah's eyes rounded. "Sure!" Then she glanced at Carlotta. "Actually, Carlotta's with me. Okay...we'll be there in fifteen minutes." She tapped the screen to end the call and squealed. "Coop needs a second on a body-moving job. Let's go!"

Carlotta pushed off the stool and fished in her wallet for a tip. "I wonder why he didn't call Wesley?" Or her, dammit.

"He said he couldn't reach Wes, and he knew you had a bum shoulder."

That hadn't stopped him from calling the time her arm had been broken. Coop was definitely avoiding her...or was trying to. "I'm right behind you."

CHAPTER TWELVE

A SNAPPING NOISE sounded in Wesley's ear. "Wren!"

He jerked his head toward the player on his left.

"Shit or get off the pot, man."

He shifted on the metal folding chair that was killing his bony behind, feigning worry to drag out the hand of Texas hold 'em poker. The community cards had been dealt and he had the nut hand of a straight flush, so he was going home with the pot of about five hundred piled on the table in front of him. But if he slow-bid, he could squeeze another fifty or so out of his three new friends. Chance had told him about the game taking place in the kitchen of a pub in Little Five Points. The kitty hadn't been enough for his buddy to sponsor for a cut, but with a baby on the way, Wes needed every dollar he could get.

Which was why he hadn't taken Coop's phone call. Body-moving money was okay, but the job would have to be a chartered bus wreck on I-285 to match poker money.

Still…he'd missed working with Coop while his boss had taken a self-imposed sabbatical. Now that Coop was back, he was bound to have some good stories to tell.

Wes peeked at his hand again, as if he hadn't memorized it and what everyone else was holding, too. Snappy had a middling pair, probably eights. The greasy aproned guy across from him—the pub's cook—was nursing three of a kind, probably fours or fives. The next guy over wearing a loud plaid shirt had been his only competition all night; Plaid was guarding a full house.

"Call and raise fifty," Wes said, pushing the bills forward. Playing with a clear head for the first time in a long time gave him a renewed appreciation for getting clean. He was firing on all cylinders and the cards had fallen his way all night.

The cook pointed his chin at Wes. "Hey, man, are you related to that fugitive named Wren the police brought down?"

Wes straightened. "He's my dad."

"You're lyin'," Snappy said.

"Nope."

They were all staring at him.

"Are you some kind of crime family?" Plaid asked.

"I've seen the inside of the city lockup," Wes said casually. He didn't add that he'd been scared to death and had taught the other inmates how to play poker to distract them from how beat-upable he was. To add to his street cred, he gave a knowing nod all around. "I work for a loan shark called The Carver."

Snappy and Plaid's heads pivoted to the cook.

"You didn't say he was an ex-con."

"Yeah, I thought it was strange that he was getting great cards all night."

"I want my money back."

"Yeah, I want my money back, too."

The cook leveled a dark gaze on Wes, then retrieved a cleaver from the cutting board behind him. "I think we all want our money back."

Panic blipped through Wes's chest. "Wait a minute, fellas. I don't cheat. And I'm not an ex-con. I was arrested, but I got community service, for God's sake."

Plaid narrowed his eyes. "You don't cheat, huh? Show us your cards."

Wesley swallowed. He'd gotten the straight flush fair and square, but it wasn't going to look that way.

He tossed his cards at them, grabbed two handfuls of wadded bills in the center of the table, and sprinted for the back door. Just as he flung it open, the meat cleaver imbedded in the wood next to his head with a *thwack*. He preferred to believe the cook had missed on purpose, but didn't stop to ask.

He darted across the dark parking lot with the sound of pounding feet closing in behind him. Wes decided Plaid must've played football in high school the way the guy caught up to him and slammed him down on the asphalt. And Snappy must've played soccer because he delivered a pretty decent kick to the ribs. And the cook must've been a volleyball star the way he picked up Wes and spiked him into a dumpster.

He landed face down and spread-eagled in something wet and foul but—thankfully—soft.

Wes lay still, listening. The guys mumbled and cursed as they gathered the scattered bills. Someone kicked the dumpster, sending a gonging vibration through his entire body. Their voices faded as they made their way back to the pub.

Wes gingerly lifted his head and rolled over, wincing at the sharp pain in his side. Once he pulled the rancid remains of salad from his face, the view of the stars in a cobalt blue sky was actually pretty nice. He decided to lie there for a few minutes and think about the gorgeous straight flush he'd been holding—that kind of magic didn't happen often.

In his pocket, his phone vibrated. Thinking it might be Coop again, he dug it out.

It was Meg.

Call him selfish, but he wanted to hear her voice. He connected the call and brought the phone to his ear. "Hi, there."

"Hi, yourself," she said sourly. "I was starting to think you were avoiding me."

"Nah," he lied, then settled back into a day's worth of food sludge. "How's Aruba?"

"Hot…and not as lush as you might think. It's like a big desert."

"A big desert surrounded by turquoise waters and pink skies?"

"Well, there's that."

"Are you having a good time with your folks?"

"Not particularly. I miss you…some."

His heart pinched. "You're just bored."

"That's probably it," she agreed. "What are you into?"

He lifted his free hand and slung off a clump of mashed potatoes. "All kinds of fun."

"Nothing new, huh?"

He opened his mouth to tell her his father was home after years of being on the lam, then he heard her name being called in the background.

"I have to go," she said with a sigh. "My parents are dragging me to some kind of musical and then to dinner."

Dinner and a show with his parents sounded like heaven on earth. "Bummer."

"We get back late Sunday, so I guess I'll see you Monday at work?"

His day of reckoning, when he had to come clean about his impending fatherhood. "Guess so."

"Okay...bye then."

"Bye," he said on an exhale, then ended the call. His nose wrinkled. The special of the day must've been shrimp gumbo. He lifted his sleeve for a sniff—no, crawfish.

Wesley stared up at the stars and imagined he was half a world away, lying on the beach with Meg, with the scent of hibiscus flowers in the air. He missed her, too—present- and future-tense...because even when she got back to Atlanta, she was long gone to him.

CHAPTER THIRTEEN

DUSK WAS STARTING TO descend as Hannah angled the Audi into a spot at a curb in a trendy West End neighborhood. Lights poured from the entrance of a 1960s-era apartment building. A police cruiser and Coop's van were parked on the lawn near the front door.

Hannah was out of the car practically before it stopped moving, but Carlotta understood how she felt—her pulse was elevated, too. She didn't realize how much she'd missed being part of the exclusive club of body movers.

Even though—as Coop had informed Hannah on the phone—the death wasn't suspicious and he only needed a second person on the scene as a formality, it was still more interesting than sitting at home waiting for Randolph to call.

Although she worried where Wesley was and what he was doing that would cause him to miss a call from Coop. She hoped he wasn't in the gutter with Liz—ugh.

"Do you think it's a suicide?" Hannah asked, practically skipping. "Or a dog mauling? Or maybe it was bad hamburger—I heard on the news there was another recall."

"Take the enthusiasm down a notch," Carlotta chided as they approached the door where a uniformed officer stood guard. "This is the worst day ever for this person's family."

"You're right—sorry."

They showed the cop the morgue ID's Coop had given them. "Second floor," he said, then stepped aside to allow them into the foyer.

They took the stairs. A small knot of people stood awkwardly in the tiled hallway, one woman in particular looking distraught and stroking the head of a black terrier. The group stared toward a door where another uniformed officer lounged against the frame, talking on his cell phone. When Carlotta and Hannah walked up, he gave them an appreciative once-over and dropped the phone from his mouth. "Can I help you?"

"We're here for the body," Hannah said, her voice low and dramatic, as if they were auditioning for a TV show.

The cop's eyes went wide. "Excuse me?"

"We work for the morgue," Carlotta corrected, then held up her ID. "Cooper Craft is expecting us."

The officer looked dubious, but let them pass.

When they stepped inside the apartment, Hannah's phone rang. She cursed, but pulled it from her bag. "It's Chance, let me tell him I'm going to be late."

Carlotta nodded, hiding her amusement that Hannah was answering to anyone, much less Fat Boy.

The apartment was a little shabby, Carlotta noticed, but it had good bones—high ceilings and wood floors and tall windows. The decor was trendy and masculine and straight from the pages of a Crate & Barrel catalog, so she gauged the occupant as a thirty-something male. And from the sparse amount of furnishings, she guessed he lived alone.

Had he also died alone?

A framed photograph on a bookshelf caught her eye. In it, a handsome man had his arm around a pretty girl—they were dressed up for some event and were smiling wide. Something about them seemed familiar, but she finally decided it was the kind of happy photo that came in every picture frame.

"Back here," called a voice she recognized as Coop's.

She moved in the direction of the pleasant sound and found him standing in the doorway of a bathroom, holding a clipboard. Cooper Craft was tall and lean and had a ready smile for her. "Hi, there."

"Hello yourself."

The last time she'd seen Coop, she had been at Peter's house, on the verge of leaving for the Vegas trip that had been pre-empted by The Charmed Killer's attack and subsequent arrest.

"For someone who's been through as much as you have, you look..." He reached up and pretended to adjust his glasses. "Good."

She smiled. "Right back at you."

He dipped his chin. "I guess we've both had our trials lately."

They shared an understanding and somewhat wistful glance. There was a time when Carlotta had thought something deeper than friendship might flower between them, but she and Coop suffered from a case of terrible timing.

"Hiya," Hannah said behind them.

Coop looked past Carlotta and pivoted his body to block the doorway. "Um, ma'am, you shouldn't be in here."

Carlotta bit back a smile as Hannah rolled her eyes. "Coop, for fuck's sake, it *me*."

His jaw dropped. "Hannah?"

"I'm in disguise," she said with a dismissive wave. "Long story."

Coop looked at Carlotta, and she gave a tiny shrug.

Hannah clapped her hands together. "What have we got?"

Coop recovered and opened the bathroom door wider to reveal the body of the man from the photo lying on his back, dressed in moto coated Diesel jeans and a crisp Theory button-up shirt. The scent of his cologne—Jarold Jett's fragrance, unless she was mistaken—still hung in the air.

"His name is Greg Pena," Coop said. "Thirty-two years old, looks like he fell and hit the back of his head on the tub. He has a goose egg."

"Fell?" Carlotta asked.

"Slipped on something maybe." Coop gestured to the smooth soles of the man's Cole Haan loafers. "There's a dried sticky substance on the floor over there."

The bathroom sink was littered with grooming products. Carlotta saw something white sticking out from under the shower curtain gathered to one side of the tub. She bent to retrieve it. "Cap from the mouthwash bottle," she said, pointing to the open bottle on the sink. She set the cap on the corner of the aged tub.

"He fell on spilled mouthwash?" Hannah asked. "If I die like that, promise me you'll make up a better story."

"I'll make sure you get a spectacular headline," Carlotta said, then looked up at Coop. "Maybe he didn't slip. He could've passed out for some reason."

Coop nodded. "Maybe he was diabetic, or dehydrated. Regardless, it looks like a fluke accident. If he'd fallen a few inches to the right or left, it might not have been fatal."

"Could someone have hit him on the back of the head?" she asked.

His mouth twitched, then he pointed to a dried brownish smudge on the edge of the tub. "Looks like that's the point of contact." He gave her a wink. "Sorry, Sherlock, this one seems cut-and-dried."

Duly chastised, she bit her lip and nodded.

"Who found him?" Hannah asked.

"A neighbor lady. His dog was barking and she knew something was wrong."

The teary lady holding the terrier. "How did she get in?" Carlotta asked.

He shrugged. "She must've had a key—maybe she dog sat for him. Does it matter?"

"I suppose not." Carlotta nursed a barb of sadness for the handsome man who was only a couple of years older than she. Single, she deduced from the bare ring finger on his left hand, although the woman in the picture seemed special. One minute he was getting ready to go out—perhaps on a date...and the next minute he was mortally wounded by the porcelain-covered cast iron bathtub in his rental. So much for the good bones in this mid-century building—a newer apartment would've had a less lethal acrylic tub insert.

"I'll get the gurney," Coop said.

"We can go ahead and bag the body," Hannah offered, picking up the thick gray plastic bag folded neatly nearby.

Coop hesitated. "Can you manage, Carlotta?"

She rubbed her healing shoulder. "I think so. If not, we'll wait for you to return."

"Okay." He handed her the set of body tags he'd filled out. "Keep an eye out for family. You know what to do."

She nodded, although she was instantly nervous when he left. Dealing with dead bodies on a death scene was one thing—dealing with live bodies on a death scene was something else altogether.

"Let's do this," Hannah said. She tossed Carlotta a pair of latex gloves and snapped on a pair herself, then unfurled the heavy body bag. "I'll lift if you tag the body."

Carlotta swallowed—she'd never handled that little detail before. She scanned the set of three perforated tags Coop had handed her. On each he had printed in neat capital letters the name of the deceased, the address, the date, and the time. The first tag indicated "Attach to Bag." That one she tore away and slipped into a little plastic window on the stiff body bag that smelled like a new shower curtain.

The second tag read "Attach to Toe." She grimaced—that one would be affixed at the morgue.

The last one specified "Attach to Personal Effects," which was more applicable if the deceased had become separated from his clothing, wallet, or jewelry at a hospital or at the scene of an automobile accident. Carlotta left the second and third tags connected to each other and, crouching over the still form of Greg Pena, she gently tied the string of the tags through a tiny buttonhole in his shirt. Beneath her fingers, the smooth skin of his chest was cold, indicating his heart had stopped beating some time ago. Overcome, she blinked back sudden tears. What they did was a necessary and honorable service, but the randomness of death sometimes took her breath away.

However, since Greg Pena deserved her professionalism, she pulled herself together.

Even Hannah, with all her bravado, moved her hands hesitantly before finding a hold on his shoulder and belt loop to angle his body enough to allow Carlotta to maneuver the unzipped bag beneath him. The space in the bathroom was tight, but through a series of tilts and scoots, they were able to get the bag around him. Hannah started to zip it closed, and got all the way to his pale face before she stopped.

"I'll let Coop close it," she said. "He might need to do something...else." She sat back on her heels and surveyed the bathroom covered with white ceramic subway tile. "What do you think about this apartment?"

"It's nice. Why?"

"I'm looking for a place to rent."

Carlotta raised an eyebrow. "Aside from this being an incredibly inappropriate topic of conversation over the body of the current occupant, I thought you were shacking up with Chance."

Hannah made a face. "He's crowding me. And the matrimonial melee at the bride Expo has me a little spooked—that event would be a good setting for a horror flick."

From the direction of the entrance, a commotion sounded. Carlotta heard raised voices—a man's and...two women? One female voice was strident and agitated.

"She has to go in there! Get out of our way!"

They must have succeeded in pushing past the officer because the sound of determined footsteps grew louder. Carlotta and Hannah both scrambled to their feet. But in their haste to get out of the bathroom, they became entangled like Velma and Daphne on a Scooby Doo cartoon and went down on the tiled floor.

When Carlotta looked up from her sprawled position, two red-faced, pony-tailed women in exercise garb were staring down at them.

"Who are you?" the woman in front demanded. Then she looked past them at the bagged body and screamed.

The other woman turned her from the sight and hugged her, shushing and patting. When Carlotta made eye contact with the second woman, she gasped.

"Tracey?" As in, Mrs. Dr. Lowenstein. Although the woman was practically unrecognizable without her fully made up face and perfectly coiffed hair.

The woman's eyes bugged from her blotchy face. "Carlotta? What on earth are you doing here?"

Tracey's voice was accusatory, as if Carlotta somehow were to blame for the incident itself. She picked herself up as elegantly as she could manage and dusted herself off. "I'm, uh...working." She signaled Hannah frantically to close the bathroom door.

Tracey's face went stony. "Oh, right...you mentioned your morbid little part-time job."

Carlotta tried to ignore the disgust that rolled off the woman like a cloud. "Are you a friend of Mr. Pena's?"

"Greg is Iris's fiancé," Tracey said, still patting the other woman.

"Was," Hannah said helpfully as she closed the door.

The sobbing increased in decibels and suddenly Carlotta realized why the woman in the photograph had looked familiar—she was the woman who'd been with Tracey at the Wedding World Expo.

"I'm so sorry," Carlotta murmured as Coop strode up behind the women, his mouth set in a grim line.

Iris lifted her head. "What h-h-happened to Greg?"

"Mouthwash mishap," Hannah supplied.

"Ma'am," Cooper cut in smoothly, giving Hannah a warning glance, "if you'll come into the other room, Officer Merritt will answer your questions." He gently guided Iris away from the scene, letting her lean heavily on his capable arm.

When they were out of earshot, Tracey turned a condemning glare on Carlotta. "So it's true—you actually handle *dead* bodies?"

"Um, I help to move them...yes."

Tracey made a revolted noise. "Can't someone else do that?"

"Yes, but I don't mind."

"Ugh—you are definitely your father's daughter, Carlotta."

She bit down on the inside of her cheek—she couldn't exactly deny that truth.

Tracey sniffed and gestured to Hannah's outfit and grooming with a little wave of begrudged approval. "At least you're not still hanging out with that horrid Goth woman."

Carlotta winced and waited.

Hannah crossed her arms. "It's me." She pulled down the collar of the designer dress for a glimpse of the tattooed skin it covered.

Tracey blinked. "Oh. You look...different."

"Yeah. Hey, I couldn't help but notice your tee shirt. You work out at Turbo City?"

Tracey gave them a little smile. "That's right. Iris and I were doing a hot yoga class when she got the call, poor girl."

"Yeah, well, if you decide you really want to get rid of that huge ass," Hannah said, "you should try Foster's Crossfit."

Tracey's mouth tightened into a knot. "I'm going to check on my friend, who just lost the love of her life."

"Our condolences," Carlotta murmured. When Tracey walked away, Carlotta sent Hannah a withering glance.

Hannah shrugged. "What? You hate her, too."

But Carlotta remembered that in another place, another time, she and Tracey would've been friends. It was disconcerting.

She held up her finger to her lips, then quietly moved to stand at the end of the hallway, her back against the wall, to listen to the conversation in the living room.

From the sound of things, Tracey had supplied Iris with a valium—a strange essential for one's workout bag, Carlotta noted wryly. Iris certainly sounded more calm as she clarified to the officer that she and Greg Pena had been dating for two years, engaged for one, and were in the thick of planning their upcoming nuptials.

"I don't know what I'm going to do now," she said tearfully.

"Be strong," Tracey coached her. "You'll get through this."

But Carlotta knew what Tracey was thinking—that Iris might as well kiss goodbye the deposits she'd paid to the caterer, florist, and band.

Officer Merritt was explaining to Iris a neighbor had found Mr. Pena.

"Which neighbor?" Iris asked, her voice abrupt.

Carlotta frowned—why did that matter?

A rustle of paper sounded—the officer checking his notes?

"That would be Ms. Emma Weatherly," he said, then cleared his throat. "Anyway, like I said, she heard Mr. Pena's dog barking and she thought something was wrong, so she came in—"

"How did she get in?"

Was that suspicion in Iris's voice?

"Er…she said the door was open, ma'am."

"So you think he fell and hit his head, and that's what killed him?"

The cop must've deferred to Coop because he said, "We're not sure how he fell, ma'am. But yes, there's a head injury."

"He probably tripped on that nasty little dog—she was always underfoot."

Carlotta blinked. Iris Kline was obviously not fond on her fiancé's pet.

"Meanwhile," Coop said, "can you help Officer Merritt with the names of the next of kin, and the name of Mr. Pena's employer?"

When Iris started haltingly listing names, Carlotta backtracked to the bathroom and veered into an adjacent room—a bedroom. The door was ajar and a light was on. She stepped inside and scanned the room.

Greg Pena was a neatnik, which she guessed wasn't wholly unusual…but how many men made their bed, then turned down the covers at an angle? Unless he worked for the Marriott, that struck her as strange. She'd thought he was getting dressed to go out, but what if he was expecting someone for a rendezvous? Not Iris, though, since she'd been busy sweating with Tracey.

"Lose something?"

She startled guiltily and looked up to find Coop standing in the doorway wearing a disapproving expression.

She gave him a magnanimous smile. "I was just making sure Mr. Pena didn't have anything on display that might upset his fiancée—you know, pictures of other women, that kind of thing."

He angled his head. "But that's really none of our business, is it?"

"No," she agreed. "His death just seems so random, like there should be an explanation for what happened."

"The M.E. will find an explanation, although it probably will be less exciting than the version running through your pretty head."

She made a face. "Where is the fiancée?"

"I talked her into going with Officer Merritt to assist with notifying the family."

"What about her friend?"

"She left, too, but told me to tell you she'd miss seeing you at the country club. What's that all about?"

Carlotta's cheeks warmed. "Tracey's way of reminding me I don't belong in her social circle."

"I figured Peter's name and money granted you entrance anywhere in the city."

She shifted foot to foot. "Um...Peter and I are taking a little break."

He lifted one eyebrow. "Really? Does this have something to do with your father being back?"

She sighed. "Doesn't everything have something to do with Randolph?"

"Have you and Wes talked to him?"

"Not yet. Soon, I hope."

He nodded, acknowledging it wasn't the place to discuss Randolph. "I see you're back to work?"

"Sort of. I'm working the Wedding World Expo this week."

"Sound frightening."

She laughed. "I don't scare easily."

"No, you don't," he said, then jerked his thumb over his shoulder. "We'd better get this job done before someone else shows up."

"Right."

"But..." He held open the door for her, then lowered his voice. "What's with this new side of Hannah?"

Carlotta gave a little laugh. "Apparently, she's been living a double-life. Her family is wealthy and well-bred. I caught her red-handed today, hobnobbing and conducting herself like a true southern belle, so the jig is up."

He pursed his mouth. "Hm...you think you know people."

"I know, right? Just like maybe Iris Kline didn't really know her fiancé. Maybe there's something else going on here."

He wagged his finger. "Don't, Carlotta. I have new responsibilities at the morgue, and I don't have time to go on wild goose chases...even for you."

She smiled. "What new responsibilities?"

"Just helping out until a new chief M.E. is brought on."

Carlotta's spirits were buoyed by the fact that Coop was being folded back into the M.E. community, even if only temporarily. He didn't talk about it much, but she knew he missed the challenge of heading up the morgue.

But as she followed him back through the hallway, her mind spun with vague frustration. First a young man had died on the runway for no obvious reason. And now another man was dead, his passing equally senseless. There was no obvious connection between the two young men. A wry smile pulled at her mouth—except for the fact they were both about to be married.

Then Patricia's comment came back to her. *Bodies seem to turn up wherever you are.*

Carlotta sighed—Jack was right, and so was Coop. The men's deaths were sad and untimely, but not sinister. In fact, so far the only connection between them was *her*. And that said a lot more about her life than it said about their deaths.

CHAPTER FOURTEEN

WES SLIPPED OUT HIS BEDROOM DOOR and into the hall, his ear piqued for activity. Carlotta's bedroom door was closed, so hopefully she was still sleeping this Saturday morning. He didn't want to have a conversation with her until he could sift through things that were doing figure-eights in his head...like the thing with Liz and the baby...and the thing with Mouse and the headless corpse...and what he was going to do about Meg.

So far, he'd managed to avoid Carlotta by coming in late and feigning sleep when she poked her head inside his room to check on him. Guilt pinged at him. Not being able to see their dad was probably driving her crazy. He knew he should be there for her, but his sister could read him like a road sign, and he didn't want to add to her stress load.

So when he heard sounds coming from the kitchen, he winced and wondered if he could get out the front door without triggering the security alarm sensor.

As he tiptoed across the living room, his gaze automatically went to the forlorn little metallic Christmas tree in the corner. His chest welled in vindication that he'd insisted they leave the tree up until their family reunited. At least when their father came home, he would see proof of how much Wes had believed he would return.

But with the messes he'd created for himself personally and professionally, what would Randolph think of his son otherwise?

"Good morning, stranger."

At the sound of Carlotta's voice, Wes's hand stalled on the doorknob. He turned around to find her standing there fully dressed and holding a vase of cut flowers.

"Good morning," he said sheepishly. "I didn't know you were up."

Her eyes narrowed. "Where are you headed so early?"

"I'm meeting Chance for breakfast."

She frowned. "Do you have a few minutes?"

"Not really—"

"Good, because I'm taking these to Mrs. Winningham, and they're heavier than I expected."

At the flash of pain on her face, he remembered her injured shoulder and reached to take the vase. "Are you okay?"

She nodded, then rubbed her arm. "It's fine. I just overdid it yesterday."

"Is the wedding convention thing still going on?"

"Uh-huh, through Wednesday," she said as she moved to open the front door.

"I don't suppose you've heard from Dad?"

"No," she said, her voice barely above a whisper. "Jack keeps telling me to be patient, but it's hard."

"Liz says the same thing."

Carlotta's mouth tightened as if she had just imagined biting the woman, so Wesley thought it best to change the subject. "What are the flowers for?"

"A peace offering to help make up for the fact that the serial killer who came after me chloroformed Mrs. Winningham first."

Wes scoffed as he walked out on the stoop. "That wasn't your fault."

Carlotta followed him down the steps. "It kind of was since I lured him here."

"That's bullshit."

"Still…she's upset and I feel as if I should make some gesture."

"If my hands weren't full, I could make a gesture," he muttered.

"Shh…there she is."

He looked up to see Mrs. Winningham standing on the other side of the fence she had erected to keep her fugly dog Toofers in her yard…and to keep the Wrens and their crabgrass *out*.

"Good morning, Mrs. Winningham," Carlotta called with a wave.

The woman straightened and pulled at the neck of the blue terrycloth robe she wore. Her hair was a helmet of sponge curlers. She was watching Toofers do his business, standing ready with a plastic bag to remove little turds as soon as they hit her precious zoysia grass.

Mrs. Winningham glared at the intrusion. "What do you two want?"

"We brought you flowers," Carlotta said, then nudged him.

He dutifully lifted the vase of flowers over the fence so she could see them. And so if she said something mean, he could simply dump them on the zoysia.

But to his surprise, the woman blinked and visibly softened. "For me?" She made a beeline for the fence, her pooch's poop forgotten.

Wes marveled over the effect a wad of flowers had on women. He'd taken Carlotta's advice the last time he screwed things up with Meg and bought her a seven-dollar bouquet at a corner stand. She'd acted as if he'd grown and harvested the things himself. He vividly recalled the way she'd removed one bloom and put it in her honey-colored hair, just as sexy as you please.

Remembered images might be all of Meg he would ever have, because an entire hothouse of roses wouldn't help his cause once he told Meg another woman was having his baby.

"Wesley and I feel so bad about what happened to you, Mrs. Winningham," Carlotta said. "We just want you to know we're sorry." She kicked Wesley.

He grunted as the curlered woman took the vase from his hands. "Right. We're sorry a maniac terrorized you before he tried to murder Carlotta."

Carlotta kicked him again. "Anyway, we hope you like them."

"I'm allergic to daisies," their neighbor said primly, and began to pluck the offending flowers from the arrangement. She passed the handful of dripping allergens back to Carlotta. "And I don't care for the vase." After removing the picked-over flowers from the unlikable container, she handed it over the fence. "Thank you."

Carlotta gave her a little smile. "You're welcome."

Mrs. Winningham sniffed. "I read in the newspaper that your renegade father was taken into custody."

Since Carlotta seemed to be struck mute, Wesley piped up. "That's right."

"Will he be coming back here to live with you?"

He lifted his chin. "That's the plan."

The woman surveyed them both with a critical gaze. "I have something to say about that."

Wesley shifted, ready to defend his father, but Carlotta put her hand on his arm.

"I will be glad to have him back," Mrs. Winningham finished.

Wes blinked. "You will?"

"Yes. Your father always kept his yard looking very nice." And with that, she turned around and called for Toofers to follow her inside.

He gave a little laugh. "That was unexpected."

But Carlotta's hand tightened painfully on his arm.

"Ow. Listen, I need to get going—"

"Wes." Her eyes were wide. "I just remembered something Dad told me before he was arrested."

She had his full attention. "What?"

"He said he'd taken care of the fire ants."

He frowned. "The fire ants in our yard?"

"Right…the ones Mrs. Winningham complained about, then later thanked me for taking care of."

"You thought I got rid of them, but I'd forgotten about it."

She nodded. "So then I thought Michael Lane had done it when he—"

"Secretly moved in with us?" Wes cut in dryly.

"Right." She put her hand to her forehead. "But just before Jack took him away, Randolph said he'd been trying to do little things to help us, *like taking care of the fire ants.*"

Wes couldn't stop the grin that spread over his face. "That means he was monitoring the listening device we found in the kitchen from nearby, and not just when you were in trouble, but for a while."

"But from where—a parked vehicle?" She shot a glance toward the busy street at the end of their driveway. "God knows we've had enough strange vehicles stalking us lately that he could've gone unnoticed."

A guilty pang struck Wes—between the loan sharks dogging him and the private investigator Meg's father had put on his tail, he could take credit for the recent traffic jam on their driveway. Then he frowned. "But no one found an abandoned car after Jack took Dad into custody."

"That we know of," she agreed. Although that detail might come up in her Monday morning chat with D.A. Kelvin Lucas.

"But driving around to monitor the townhome seems kind of random, don't you think?"

"I suppose so," she agreed. "So maybe he could've been in a hotel room?"

He mentally mapped the handful of hotels in the vicinity. "Could be. Or maybe he rented an apartment?"

"Or a house," Carlotta added.

Wes's heart rate picked up as this mind leapfrogged ahead. "He and Mom could be living in this neighborhood!"

Their gazes locked and in tandem they turned and looked in the direction of the house on the other side of their townhome.

Quiet, unassuming...convenient.

Wes wet his lips as a preposterous idea bloomed in his brain. "Are you thinking what I'm thinking?"

Carlotta hesitated, then shook her head. "Wes...that's impossible."

But adrenaline began to drip into his bloodstream. "Humor me. When did the gay couple move in?"

"About five years ago."

"And you've never met them?"

"No. I always meant to introduce myself, but...they seemed stand-offish."

"So they're avoiding you?"

Carlotta scoffed. "Maybe they don't want to mix with the next door neighbors who have drive-by shootings and police chaperones."

He ignored her. "They work from home, right?"

"I just assumed so because of all the deliveries they receive."

"Have you ever seen them outside, doing chores or mowing their yard?"

"They have a lawn service."

"As if they don't want to be seen."

"Or as if they don't own a lawn mower."

He ignored her, then gestured toward the sun room the furtive neighbors had added to the back of their small house. "The addition..."

"Infuriated Mrs. Winningham because it blocked her view," Carlotta offered.

"And gave the occupants a great view of *our* house from all angles."

But Carlotta still looked dubious. "That's a stretch, don't you think?"

"How many times have you actually seen someone come and go from that house?" he demanded.

Carlotta shrugged. "Maybe a handful of times."

"And they've never spoken to you?"

"No. It was always a quick glance, maybe a wave." Then she frowned. "Or maybe I waved. But Wes, it's a *gay* couple. Two men."

"Maybe one of them just *looked* like a man."

Her head came up. "You mean one of them could be Mom in disguise?"

"You tell me—you're the one who crashed your own funeral in a getup so good no one recognized you."

"Except Dad," she conceded.

Much later she'd confessed to Wes that a stranger had bumped into her at the fake funeral and placed a note in her pocket identifying him as their father.

"See," he said excitedly. "It could be them!"

But Carlotta was still shaking her head. "Do you hear what you're saying? That Mom and Dad could've been living next to us all this time? That's crazy."

He snorted. "No crazier than anything else that's happened in our lives." He was already moving toward the house. "And there's only one way to find out."

Carlotta caught up to him and grabbed his arm. "Wes, wait!"

He spun around. "Are you kidding? We've waited for ten years to see Mom, and at this very minute, she might be twenty feet away!"

She gave him a tremulous smile. "I meant wait for me."

CHAPTER FIFTEEN

AS THEY CROSSED into the dewy grass of the neighboring yard, Carlotta's heart thudded against her breastbone to the point of pain. Her hairline felt moist. Mixed emotions assailed her. The thought of seeing her mother again was exhilarating—and terrifying. But other emotions crowded her lungs. If, incredulously, Randolph and Valerie had been living next door to them all this time, some part of her might find it comforting that they'd been keeping an eye on her and Wesley. But another, larger part of her would be furious if their parents had been so close and let their children believe they were missing—and worse.

As fantastic as the story sounded, she found herself listing the reasons it made sense that Randolph and Valerie would be hiding in plain sight. Since Valerie had been emotionally dependent on Randolph, she probably wouldn't be content to be parked somewhere alone while Randolph roamed around and made surveillance trips to Atlanta. And if Randolph and Valerie had grown a conscience about abandoning their children, moving in next door would probably assuage their guilt.

Her legs were rubbery when they climbed the steps to the front door. There were no signs of life in or around the little house—no cat in the window, no blaring TV, no aromas of breakfast sausage wafting outside through a vented stove hood.

Which only made Carlotta more anxious because Valerie was allergic to cats, famously hated watching TV, and would ingest sausage only if it had been soaked in vodka.

They stood on the stoop for a few seconds in silence. She knew Wes was waiting for her—the eldest—to make a move, but she was frozen in fear and anticipation. When Wes stepped forward and rang the doorbell, pride welled in her throat. Somewhere along the way he'd gone from being a timid little boy to a gutsy young man. Granted, he didn't always make the best decisions, but she was glad he didn't let life intimidate him.

She wet her lips as the muffled chime of the doorbell echoed throughout the house. As she stared at the door, a strong sense of déjà vu washed over her. There had been another time she'd been standing in front of a door, and when it swung open, Valerie had emerged. Carlotta frowned, her memory churning wildly, and then suddenly, she remembered.

The scene had unfolded in her travel-dream. She had been transported back to the driveway of the lavish home in Buckhead where she and Wesley had grown up. After she had alighted from her Miata and was attempting to orient herself, the door to the mansion had opened, and Valerie had appeared, conversing with Carlotta just as if she hadn't been absent from her daughter's life for a decade. Because in that other-place, she hadn't been. The unexplainable incident was a gift from the universe, Carlotta had come to realize, a glimpse into what her life might've been like if Randolph and Valerie hadn't left.

She still wavered back and forth as to exactly what she had experienced that night, but right here, right now, standing on this stoop, she knew she wasn't dreaming. The thought of being a heartbeat away from being reunited with Valerie made her lightheaded.

Behind the door, they heard a movement. Carlotta straightened and stared at the peephole. Was Valerie squirreled away and afraid, wondering what to do now that Randolph had been taken into custody? Was she looking at them now, panicking? Would she open the door to her children, or would she retreat into hiding?

Open the door, she willed silently, *or I'll break it down.*

The click of a deadbolt sounded, then the knob turned, and the door slowly opened.

A tall man stood there in dark jeans, shrugging into a white dress shirt, which he left unbuttoned. He wore a confused expression on his rugged face. "Yeah?" he asked on a grunt, squinting.

Carlotta exhaled in scathing self-recrimination. What an utterly preposterous notion to think their parents had been living next to them all this time. Beside her, Wesley sagged, his disappointment palpable.

"Can I help you?" the man asked in a sleep-rusty voice.

He was all male, Carlotta registered in a glance, with a platter of muscle for a stomach and shoulders that bowed slightly from the stress of holding up all that bulging protein. A tattoo peeked above the edge of his waistband.

"We're your neighbors," she said brightly, then nodded to their house. "I'm Carlotta and this is my brother Wesley."

"Nice to meet you," he said.

His voice wasn't unfriendly, but neither was his body language welcoming. He spread his arms to span the door frame. His short hair was the color of tarnished brass and stuck up at all angles—it appeared he'd just gotten out of bed.

As further proof, he yawned widely behind his hand. "It's kind of early. Did you need something?"

She glanced at Wes, at a loss. They hadn't discussed what they'd say in the event the person who opened the door wasn't their mother...which now seemed like an obvious oversight.

"We just wanted to welcome you to the neighborhood," Wes offered.

Carlotta looked down and realized she was still holding the vase of allergy-inducing daisies Mrs. Winningham had rejected. She extended it. "Here."

He squinted, then took the vase, which looked ridiculous in his big hands. "Thanks, but I'm just renting this place for a few weeks."

Wes cut her an exasperated look. "We should go."

"Right," she said, nodding. "It was nice to meet you, um...what's your name?"

"John...son. Hey—" The guy scratched his nose—great, the flowers were already inflicting damage. "—what's with the police car parked at the end of your driveway the past few days?"

"Oh, that," Carlotta said. "That's, um..."

"Speed trap," Wes finished, yanking on her arm. "Be careful driving on this street. See you around."

Wes practically dragged her off the stoop and back to their yard. Behind them, the door to the neighboring house closed soundly.

"Easy," she said, rubbing her arm.

"Sorry. I have to get going," he said, his eyes suspiciously moist.

Her heart squeezed for him. "Wes, it was a good theory. I'm sorry it didn't work out, but hopefully we'll get to talk to Randolph soon and get some answers."

He nodded.

"I'm glad you pushed me into going over there," she added with a smile. "Even though we came up empty, it feels good to do something, you know?"

He hesitated, then stabbed at his glasses. "Actually...I'm working another angle to contact Dad."

She frowned. "What other angle is there?"

He squirmed. "A guy I know on my courier job. He has a friend on the inside."

Panic blipped in her stomach. Wes didn't know *she* knew the "courier" job was the lie he'd told to cover for his work as a confidential informant in The Carver's organization, at the behest of D.A. Kelvin Lucas, the toad.

"On the *inside*? Of the prison? Who are you, Baby Face Nelson?"

"I figured if the authorities won't work with us, we'll go around them."

She stared at him with a mixture of pride and dismay. He was so damned resourceful...and how wretched that he had to scheme with thugs to communicate with their long lost father in jail. "And has your *friend* reported back?"

"Not yet. But soon."

Resentment toward her parents for Wes's predicament rose in the back of her throat. But knowing the futility of that path, she swallowed the bad taste. "Okay. Keep me posted?"

"Sure."

Carlotta angled her head. "So, how are things with Meg?"

She caught the darkening of his eyes before he averted his gaze. "She's in Aruba with her folks."

While Wes was here conspiring to make contact with his jailbird dad. The contrast was heartbreaking. "When will she be back?"

He started walking backward toward the garage where he stowed his bike. "I gotta run. Later."

Carlotta hugged herself and watched Wes scramble to retrieve his bike, lower the garage door, and take off. He waved as he pedaled past her. She returned the wave, then pushed her tongue into her cheek.

Since Wes had deflected the subject of Meg, he'd probably done something he shouldn't have...again. Hopefully, it wouldn't be a deal-breaker for Meg because it was clear Wes had lost his heart to her.

Carlotta sighed. Then her head pivoted back to the house next door.

Their fugitive parents hadn't been living there, but something was definitely amiss.

"Johnson," or whoever he was, had gone to great lengths to make it seem as if they'd gotten him out of bed. But while his hair was disheveled, his jaw was fresh-shaven—down to a tiny piece of toilet tissue blotting a cut, and the strong scent of his after-shave was another giveaway that he'd been up for a while.

Also, for someone who'd just rolled out of bed, it was strange he'd had time to put on lace up shoes that were spit-shined.

Plus, the tattoo at the man's waist was a blue and gold emblem—perhaps military, perhaps law enforcement.

And while bracing himself against the doorframe with his shirt hanging open had seemed like a casual pose—and not an objectionable sight—most likely it was an attempt to block them from seeing the big honking camera set up on a tripod facing the Wren house.

The man could be a professional photographer...or a voyeur. But if she were a betting person (like her little brother), she'd wager it was no coincidence they had a new neighbor who was an even bigger snoop than Mrs. Winningham at the precise time that Randolph had returned.

CHAPTER SIXTEEN

WESLEY WALKED INTO the International House of Pancakes, still stinging from the disappointment of the visit to the neighboring house. How epically perfect would it have been for their parents to be living next door all these years?

Chance waved from a booth. "Thanks for coming, man."

Wes swung into a seat. "What's up?" He was wary. It wasn't like Chance to ask to meet for breakfast—or anytime, for that matter. He wanted something—for Wesley to take an exam for him, deliver a package—something. And while Chance always looked a little on the disheveled side, today his chuffy blond buddy looked especially worse for wear.

"I think Hannah is going to break up with me," he blurted.

Wesley sagged. "You dragged me out of bed early to talk about your love life?"

"I'm starting to think she only started seeing me so I would pay to finish the tattoo on her back."

"Well, that was kind of the deal, wasn't it?"

"At first, maybe. Now it's turned into something more for me…but not for her, apparently."

"Is that what Hannah said?"

"No. She doesn't talk much, you know, except to yell at me. But now she doesn't even do that."

"You're upset because she doesn't yell anymore?"

"Yelling means the person cares, man. Like my dad, who screams at me until his face is purple. It's because he cares."

"O...kay."

Chance pulled his hand down his face. "I feel like she's hiding something from me."

"What, like another guy?"

"I don't know, but something."

A harried waitress came by to pour coffee in their cups and take orders for tall stacks.

When she left, to Wesley's horror, Chance teared up. "Hannah didn't come home last night."

"Chill, dude—she probably worked late and went back to her place."

He blinked. "Do you know where that is?"

"No. She's never told you?"

Chance was morose. "No."

"Have you tried calling her?"

"Only about a hundred times."

"Stalker, much? Did you two have an argument?"

"Nah. I thought things were good. I was even thinking about canceling my account with Blackbook."

"Wow, cancel your prostitute service? That's...romantic."

"I know. I've had that account since I was fourteen. But the last time a girl came by, all I could think about was Hannah, couldn't even get it up. Tish and I played Candy Crush all night."

Wes nodded. He'd once shouted Meg's name when he was banging Liz, but Liz had been cool about it. If he ever got the chance to sleep with Meg, though, he doubted he'd be thinking about anyone else.

Not that he was ever going to get the chance to sleep with Meg.

"But when I told Hannah about the service, she got mad."

"Dude, you told her you have a prostitute service? Are you nuts?"

"She already knew about it—that's not what made her mad. She got mad when I said I was going to cancel. Said I was 'crowding' her—what the hell does that mean? Should I buy a bigger bed?"

Wes slurped his hot coffee. "I think she means you're getting too serious."

"Isn't that what chicks want?"

"You're asking the wrong person, man. I got women problems you don't even want to know about."

"You're banging your lawyer, and you got that little piece you work with on the line. What's the problem?"

"Never mind."

"No, tell me, bro. Might make me feel better."

Wes shook his head. "I can't say."

"Fuck, now you have to tell me. It's not as if you got one of 'em knocked up." Chance snorted at his own joke.

Wes felt his face drain of blood, and Chance must have noticed, too.

"Oh, fuck—one of 'em is knocked up?"

"You can't tell a soul, man."

Chance made a solemn X over his chest with his finger. "I'm as silent as the grave. Which one?"

"Liz. I, uh…haven't been with Meg."

"Liz is the attorney?"

"Right."

"Shit. Is she gonna keep it?"

"Yeah, she's old, like almost forty, so she's afraid this is her only chance for a kid."

"What are you gonna do?"

Wes lifted his hands. "Whatever Liz needs me to do. I don't want the kid growing up without a dad like I—" He broke off, then took a quick drink from his cup and burned his mouth.

Chance nodded. "Hannah told me you haven't talked to your old man yet."

"No. Feds got him all tangled up."

"But at least you have good news for him—he's going to be a grandfather."

Wes gave a nervous laugh. "I'm not sure he's going to be happy about it."

"You don't think?"

"Liz used to be his mistress."

Chance did the math in his head—slowly. "Wow, that's…wait—what is that?"

"Messed up," Wes supplied.

"And what about the dish you work with?"

"That's history as soon as I tell her about the baby."

"So why don't you sleep with her first?"

Wes frowned. "That's not an option."

"Hey, it's not like Liz is going to want to have sex with you now that she's pregnant."

That was probably true. This situation just kept getting worse.

"Actually, though, you being a dad is kind of cool."

Wes blinked. "You think so?"

"Yeah, I can see a mini Wes dude running around. You can teach him to ride a bike and shit."

Wes nodded. "I can do that." He smiled. "I'm going to be a dad."

Chance reached over and thumped him on the shoulder. "Yes you are. Just don't fuck it up like our dads did."

Wes's smile wavered. "I'll...try not to."

"Are you going to get a real job, man?"

"Huh?"

"Kids are expensive."

"Liz makes good money."

"What if she decides she wants to be a full-time mom? And what if she has twins?"

"T-twins?"

"Yeah, I heard on TV that older women are more likely to pop them out two and three at a time."

Wes's stomach cramped. "No kidding?"

"Does your sister know?"

"No. And she already hates Liz."

Chance guffawed. "Man, Carlotta's going to stroke out."

Wes swallowed the bile that had backed up in his mouth. "Tell me about it."

Chance's phone rang. He dug it out of his pocket, then grinned. "It's Hannah." He brought the phone up to his mouth. "Hey, baby."

Wes cringed at the moony tone of his buddy's voice...and wondered if he sounded like that when he talked to Meg.

"I'm on my way!" Chance stowed the phone and pushed to this feet. "She has a catering gig today, but she's going to stop by the apartment first to get some of this." He reached down and cupped his balls through his jeans to jostle his manhood.

Wes winced. "What about your food?"

Chance tossed a few bills on the table. "You can have mine. Thanks for cheering me up, bro. Next to your problems, I'm good. See ya."

Wes watched his friend lope away, feeling like he'd been dive-bombed.

His second cell phone rang—the one dedicated to Mouse and all related loan shark activities. He connected the call. "Yeah?"

"Hey, Little Man, I got that information you asked for."

Wes's pulse spiked. "Your buddies talked to my dad?"

"Not exactly. He's in the shoe."

"The shoe?"

"Security Housing Unit. Your dad's in solitary, only comes out to go to the mess hall."

"What did he do to get put in solitary confinement?"

"Don't know. My friends tried to talk to him, but he wasn't interested in being friendly."

Wes wet his lips. "Did they tell him they were asking for me?"

A couple seconds' of silence passed, then Mouse said, "Yeah. He said all the more reason for him not to talk."

Hurt boomeranged through his chest.

"Sorry, Little Man. I know it's not the news you wanted, but at least you know your old man is okay."

"Right," Wes managed, hating the emotion vibrating in his voice. "Thanks anyway, Mouse."

He ended the call before he started crying like a little girl. Randolph had shut him down—apparently he had no intention of communicating with his son.

The waitress arrived and set plate after loaded plate on the table. Wes stared at the piles of fluffy white pancakes and the heaps of bacon, but he couldn't bring himself to pick up his fork. He'd suddenly lost his appetite.

CHAPTER SEVENTEEN

"I'M GOING TO KILL HIM," Edward King said through clenched teeth.

Carlotta rolled her eyes as she booted up the computer kiosk in the *Your Perfect Man* booth. "You're not going to kill Jarold Jett. What happened?"

"He was supposed to judge student designs last night at a televised competition, and he was a no-show. I thought his assistant was going to come unglued."

"She made it in, huh?"

"I guess so…although last night the poor girl seemed ready to board a plane and hightail it back to New York."

"Did the competition take place anyway?"

"I stepped in to cover for Jarold, but those poor kids were devastated, thought they were going to meet a celebrity."

Carlotta gave his arm a pat. "I'm sure they were equally impressed by your expertise."

"It's true I know more about fashion than that lout," Edward said, softening under her praise. "And between us, I've heard his name recognition is slipping. But still, a commitment is a commitment."

"Jarold must've had a good reason for missing the event."

Edward's mouth flattened. "According to Twitter, he was hanging out at the Clermont Lounge."

She cringed. The city's oldest strip club on Ponce de Leon Avenue was known for its kitschy atmosphere and unorthodox dancers—it was more of a tourist attraction for both sexes than a place where men got into trouble, but it wasn't exactly a classy alibi.

"Speak of the devil," Edward said loudly.

Carlotta turned to see Jarold Jett moving their way, with a harried-looking young woman trotting next to him and an irritable-looking Jack Terry bringing up the rear.

Jarold glared at Edward. "I heard that."

Edward glared back. "I meant for you to. I'm sure Nia told you I had to make your excuses last night to a very disappointed group of students."

The slender dark-haired woman—the long-suffering Nia, Carlotta presumed—flushed deep red and glanced at Jarold with something akin to fear. "I didn't—"

"You should be thanking me," Jarold cut in, wagging a finger at Edward. "That competition was good exposure for a patternmaker."

Edward shook his head. "You're going to get your comeuppance someday, Jarold. And I hope I'm there to see it." He stalked off in one direction, and Jarold stalked off in the opposite direction.

Jack stifled a yawn. "This is the longest assignment of my career."

She laughed. "Just four more days. Did the ladies at the Clermont Lounge keep you up late?"

Jack frowned. "I would've rather been home in bed."

"You're losing your edge, Jack."

"Maybe," he conceded, pulling a hand down his weary face. "How's your shoulder?"

"Better, thanks. Guess where I was last night?"

"Do I want to know?"

"Picking up a body, with Coop."

He frowned harder. "Your shoulder must be a lot better."

"Hannah was with me. But get this—the victim died under suspicious circumstances and was also a groom."

He squinted. "So?"

"Like Jeremy Atwater, the young man who collapsed on the runway."

He held up his hand. "Stop. I see where this is going."

"But doesn't that seem curious to you?"

"*No.* I'm leaving now."

"But Jack—"

"Goodbye, Carlotta."

"By the way, I know you put a guy next door to watch me."

He stopped. "What?"

"The guy in the house next to me and Wes—law-enforcement build, has a camera in the window pointed toward the townhouse?"

He threw up his hands as if to deflect responsibility. "Sounds like your run-of-the-mill voyeur. Keep your clothes on." Then he shrugged. "Or don't." He turned and walked after Jarold Jett's entourage.

Carlotta glared after Jack, wishing she could put her finger on what was different about him, something that went beyond a lack of sleep and their pact to stay away from each other...oh, and his general dismissal of any crime theory she had.

He seemed almost...*defeated*. She'd been so consumed with how her father's return had affected her and Wes, she hadn't considered how frustrated Jack must be to have finally collared Randolph Wren—the "get" of a career—only to be banished from the case and sent to stand in the corner.

Or perhaps he was still suffering from the loss of Maria?

Something was eating at him.

Her mind bounced back to the man living next door...something smelled, and it wasn't fragrant.

When an idea popped into her head, she turned to the computer kiosk and looked up a business listing. As she punched the number into her phone, she wondered what kind of reception she might get on the other end.

"Sanders Real Estate Agency," a young woman's voice chirped, "home of Sammy "Sold" Sanders. How can I help you?"

Carlotta rolled her eyes at the cheesy moniker. "Yes, is Sammy available?"

"May I ask who's calling?"

"Carlotta Wren. Please tell her I'm a friend of Jolie Goodman Underwood."

"One moment, please."

Sammy might not be pleased to hear from one of the women who had crashed her upscale pajama party and subsequently been arrested when another unwanted guest—a dead body—had been uncovered during the festivities, but she might be intrigued enough to take Carlotta's phone call.

"Hold on," the woman said. "I'm transferring you to Sammy's cell."

Bingo.

The phone clicked. "Hello, Carlotta. What a surprise. I've been seeing your name in the papers a lot lately." The woman's voice was well modulated, a tad suspicious, but with enough diplomacy to insure she'd get any commissions Carlotta might toss her way.

"Hi, Sammy. How's business?"

"Fabulous. I've been the number one agent in Buckhead for three years running. What can I do for you, Carlotta?"

"Actually, I have a favor to ask."

"A favor?" the woman repeated, with a hint of indignation.

"In return for something I think will be of value to you."

"Which is?"

"A sixty percent off coupon on any item at Neiman Marcus."

"I'm listening. But if it has anything to do with dead bodies, I'm out."

Carlotta smiled into the phone. "I need to know everything you can tell me about the owner of the house next to mine."

"That's simple enough," Sammy said. "I need the street address."

Carlotta gave it to her.

"Are you interested in buying the house?"

"Maybe," Carlotta hedged, knowing Sammy would be motivated to get more information if she sniffed a potential sale.

"Okay. Weekends are my busiest time. Can I get back to you early in the week?"

"Sure. Thanks, Sammy."

Carlotta ended the call and started to minimize the search engine screen, then pursed her mouth.

Just because Jack wouldn't listen to her theory on the suspicious deaths didn't mean she couldn't ask a few questions on her own. While the booth was still quiet, she performed searches for Jeremy Atwater and Greg Pena, just to see if there was any obvious overlap in their lives.

Thank heaven for social media.

There were personal pages, memorial postings, and recycled and forwarded entries filled with shock and sadness for the men, who were separated in age by several years. There were condolences for the family and the respective fiancées—Jenna and Iris—each of whom had posted an endless array of pictures. Funds had been set up for charitable donations to various causes in lieu of flowers. Carlotta didn't find a mention of the men's names in connection with each other, and a cursory review didn't reveal shared friends, hobbies, places of employment, or proximity of address.

Of course, even if they weren't related, it didn't mean that one or both of the men hadn't been murdered.

Then she sighed and rubbed her temples. The awfulness of The Charmed Killer case had left her paranoid. Most likely, Jeremy Atwater had died from some drug and/or alcohol reaction. And Greg Pena had slipped and cracked his head on the tub.

End of stories.

"What did I miss?" Patricia asked, striding into the booth.

"Nothing," Carlotta assured her, zapping the screens she'd been studying. She gave herself a mental shake to get back to the matter at hand—her job. The one that kept a roof over her head and clothes on her back. "Looks like it's going to be a nice crowd today. We should get some good commissions."

"Uh-huh," Patricia said, but she seemed distracted.

"Everything okay?"

She gave Carlotta a watery smile. "Leo and his ex-wife Kaitlin decided to meet here today so she can hand off their daughter Casey to Leo, and Casey can meet me."

"This will be the first time you've met the ex and the daughter?"

Patricia nodded. "Kaitlin thinks it would be best if Casey meets me in a neutral environment. And Leo thinks Casey will be more comfortable with me if she sees me and Kaitlin together."

"That sounds very civil."

Patricia worried her lower lip. "It does, but kids don't usually like me very much."

Carlotta flitted her gaze over the woman's prim suit and hairstyle, and cast about for something to ease her mind. "You're good with people. You'll know the right thing to say."

Patricia brightened. "You think so?"

Carlotta nodded and felt guilty again for all the times she'd had unkind thoughts about Patricia Alexander. Peter hadn't yet gotten her the list of clients her father had allegedly bilked. She wondered how many other familiar names would be on it. "If it makes you feel better, kids don't seem to like me very much, either."

"It's probably your voice," Patricia offered.

Carlotta blinked. "My voice?"

"The pitch is annoying…like a dog whistle." She shrugged. "Maybe it hurts little kids' ears." Patricia turned to straighten items in the display.

Carlotta fumed, then stuck out her tongue at Patricia's back. So much for trying to be nice.

She turned and flinched when she realized a young woman had witnessed her childish behavior.

Minus ten points.

"You're Carlotta, aren't you?"

Great—and the woman knew her. She manufactured a smile as her mind raced to identify the redhead. "That's right."

"I'm Eldora Jones. I meet with Wesley every week."

When recognition dawned, Carlotta wanted to disappear—Wes's probation officer…who now probably believed the entire Wren family had issues.

Which was true, but still.

"Yes, I remember," Carlotta rushed to say. "So good to see you again. What brings you to the Wedding Expo?"

Eldora hesitated, then held up her left hand. "I'm engaged."

Carlotta smiled. "Congratulations."

The woman smiled back, but the enthusiasm didn't quite reach her green eyes. "Thank you."

"I met your boyfriend that night at the Fox Theater…but I'm sorry, I don't remember his name."

"Leonard," she supplied.

"Right. I remember you made an attractive couple."

"Thank you," the woman murmured, barely audible.

Eldora, it seemed, was somewhat less than thrilled to be wearing an engagement ring. Carlotta could relate to that sentiment. Just this morning Peter had texted to remind her she'd promised to take this time to consider wearing his ring. She had deflected his comment by asking if there were any developments regarding Randolph at Mashburn & Tully. He'd replied no, but it had taken him a while. And she hated that the hesitation made her suspicious.

"Can I help you with something?" Carlotta asked Eldora.

"Maybe later. Today, I'm just…taking it all in. This is all new to me, and the show is a little…"

"Overwhelming?"

The woman nodded, looking as if she'd made a big mistake—although whether she was thinking about the engagement, or her decision to come to the show, Carlotta didn't know.

"It was good to see you," Eldora said, and began to turn away.

"Eldora," Carlotta said before the woman could leave. "I'm worried about Wes, and he doesn't talk much. I wouldn't ask you to betray a confidence, but how do you think he's doing?"

Eldora pressed her lips together, clearly torn between her duties and a sister's concern. "Wesley has been through a lot lately, but I think he's turned a corner."

Carlotta released a pent-up sigh. "Are you aware our father has returned?"

"Yes, Wes told me. I'm sure this is a stressful time for you both, but he seems very optimistic."

"Good. I appreciate all you've done for Wes."

"Don't thank me—Wesley is in control of his own destiny."

The woman gave a little wave and continued on to the next booth. Carlotta recalled the Wesley in the "other place" she had visited in her dream—there he'd been a spoiled, petulant jackass. But by the time she'd left, he was on the right path.

A message from the universe that no matter what, Wes would eventually find his way?

It was a cheerful thought to nurse as the day wore on and the Saturday crowd reached a fever pitch. The *Your Perfect Man* display was a bona fide hit. Foot traffic was so heavy, she and Patricia barely had time for bathroom breaks. Carlotta had planned to have lunch with Hannah, but wound up texting her to cancel. Hannah responded she, too, was swamped and would stop by when the exhibits closed.

In the early afternoon Patricia's fiancé Leo Tennyson and an attractive brunette arrived at the booth with a little strawberry-blond girl. Leo was handsome in a raw-boned kind of way, tall and lean and sporting the telltale "lump bump" of snuff that he and many baseball players were known for.

Carlotta covered for Patricia and gave her encouraging smiles when it appeared the little girl was not warming up to the encounter. Kaitlin Tennyson seemed to be doing her best to cajole the little girl forward, but when Patricia knelt to talk to the girl, she retreated to her mother, crying, and causing such a scene that Leo picked her up and carried her away, with a promise to call Patricia later.

The incident left Patricia shaken. "She acted as if she was scared of me."

Carlotta felt compelled to cheer her up. "It'll be okay. Casey is young, and this is a big, noisy crowd. She was probably just feeling bombarded. It'll be better next time, you'll see."

"Thanks," Patricia said. "You're right. You're always right."

The compliment caught her off-guard, but before she could reply, Patricia had retreated for a tissue, then resumed selling like a good little financially strapped sales clerk.

A tiny ripple of pride swelled in Carlotta's chest. She wasn't always right… but she was resilient. And after years of agonizing turmoil, things were finally looking up.

The feds couldn't keep them from their father forever. It was just a matter of time now before they were reunited. And this was a good time for Randolph to reappear: She was relatively happy working for Neiman Marcus…she had good people in her life…she was learning new skills…she wasn't being stalked by a serial killer…and Wes seemed to be on a good path, finally.

Things were looking up for the Wrens.

Hope bubbled in her chest and for the first time in days, she felt as if everything was going to be okay—and maybe sooner rather than later.

She was still smiling when she closed down the booth and Hannah arrived. Her friend's minted designer exterior still triggered a double-take—the silky new Hannah was going to take some getting used to.

"Hiya," Hannah offered. She looked pale...and this time Carlotta couldn't blame the white Goth makeup. "I need to talk to you."

Carlotta gave a little laugh. "Did you lose your black American Express card?"

Hannah scowled. "No. It's about Wes."

Carlotta's pulse spiked. "Is he okay?"

"He's fine," Hannah assured her. "But there's something I think you should know."

"What?"

Hannah leaned in. "His girlfriend is pregnant."

Carlotta's stomach dropped. "How do you know?"

"He told Chance and swore him to secrecy, but Chance let it slip while we were having strap-on sex—"

"Hannah!"

"Anyway, Chance swore *me* to secrecy, but I thought you'd want to know." Hannah winced. "Did I do the right thing by telling you?"

Carlotta nodded, her mind reeling with the potential problems ahead. Her chest welled with anguish. "Wes isn't prepared for this, but at least the mother seems mature."

Hannah gave a little laugh. "I'll say—Liz is pushing forty, isn't she?"

Carlotta squinted. "What does Liz have to do with Meg being pregnant?"

"Who's Meg?"

Carlotta touched her forehead. "Wes's girlfriend."

Hannah's mouth formed an "Oh" but no sound came out. Then she clamped her mouth shut as if she were waiting for Carlotta to figure out the riddle.

The realization hit Carlotta like a kick to the stomach. "Liz Fischer...is pregnant...with Wes's *baby*?"

Hannah took a step back, then nodded.

She couldn't talk...couldn't think. In her mind, Wesley's life unfurled in front of her—tied to a woman with whom he had nothing in common, obligated to a child he wasn't prepared to father.

Father...oh, Jesus, when they saw Randolph, what would he think of this bit of news?

Or had Liz already told him in one of their meetings?

"Carlotta?" Hannah shook her. "Talk to me."

"I...can't." She couldn't breathe either. She leaned over and gripped her knees, gulping air.

"Easy there," Hannah soothed. "It's going to be okay."

"No...it's...not."

"Yes, it is. This is Wesley's life, not yours."

She heard the words, knew it was true...so why did it feel as if her life had just been snatched away? This must be how a parent felt when their child did something irrevocable.

"It could be worse," Hannah offered.

"How?" Carlotta managed to get out.

"Um...*you* could be pregnant?"

She had a point. Carlotta slowly straightened, then groaned. "I thought he was getting his act together. I thought things were...improving."

"They are," Hannah said. "Your dad is back—how amazing is that?"

"Amazingly frustrating."

"For now...but not forever."

Carlotta nodded, then took a deep breath. "You're right."

"You can't tell Wesley you know. You need to let him tell you when he's ready."

She nodded again, although she still felt sick to her stomach. It would take her a while to absorb this new development.

"Let's go out and do something," Hannah urged. "If I have to wear this getup, I might as well get some use out of it."

Hannah's "getup" was a navy belted Akris shirtdress with leather lapels and a price tag that would make even Carlotta cough. Ditto for the Chloe slingback wedges.

"I'm starting to get used to this posh side of you," Carlotta said.

"Don't. This gig was something I got roped into by my sisters. As soon as it's over, I'm back to the Hannah you know and fucking love."

"Are you ever going to introduce me to your family?"

Hannah looked panicked. "Absolutely not. Promise me you won't go near them."

"Okay, relax."

Hannah seemed flustered. "Let's get out of here."

"Do you have something in mind?"

"Something anti-wedding, please dear God."

Carlotta snapped her fingers and dug in her purse until she came up with the brochure for the "After the Dress" art exhibit. "Anti-wedding and free booze."

"Sounds good and bitter to me. Let's go check it out."

CHAPTER EIGHTEEN

"IT'S A WEDDING GOWN GRAVEYARD," Hannah whispered.

Carlotta nodded soberly. In the low light of the warehouse-turned-art-gallery in the industrial Atlanta west side, the row upon row of pale wedding gowns on headless mannequins did have the appearance of tombstones.

The "After the Dress" exhibit featured two hundred gowns from the 1950s and every decade since. Some of the dresses had been pristinely preserved, some were tinged with age and dark spots, some were drooping and dry-rotted. Next to each dress was a small white podium, the kind that might hold a guest book at a wedding, but instead, held a mini computer tablet with a "play" button on the touchscreen.

Carlotta touched the screen of the display nearest her, a tea-length white dress with a Peter Pan collar from the 1960s. On the screen an attractive gray-haired woman appeared, sitting in a chair against a plain background. Marva, age seventy-one, smiled briefly for the camera, then began to tell her story.

"I grew up in a sheltered Catholic home. I was a virgin when I married my husband at eighteen. I was so excited to wear this wedding dress, but I didn't have a clue what to expect." She shifted in her chair and her lips twitched downward. "My husband was an angry man who couldn't keep a job and took all of his disappointment out on me. He was a pathological liar and he cheated on me. After a few years, I finally got the nerve to divorce him, which humiliated my family. I never remarried." The woman shrugged her slight shoulders. "I don't know why I kept the dress…I guess it was the best memory of my marriage. It's such a nice dress." Then the screen went blank.

A pang of sadness barbed through Carlotta at the woman's matter-of-fact abridgment of her unsuccessful marriage.

"And on that note," Hannah said dryly, "I'm hitting the bar. Can I get you something?"

"White wine," Carlotta murmured. "Thanks."

Her interest piqued, she walked among the displays and listened to a few more narratives while studying the corresponding dress. Not all the women told sad stories—some were still happily married, or widowed and mourning their husbands. Some had remarried after a disastrous first (or even second) marriage and had found happiness. But all of them spoke poignantly about how they had bought into the "promise of the dress" and felt duped afterward by their own naiveté.

Yet no matter what their marriage experience had been, all of these women had kept their wedding gowns. It spoke to the immense power of clothing, Carlotta mused, that a single garment—a few yards of pale fabric—could represent so much.

A well-dressed brunette holding a glass of red wine stopped next to Carlotta. "Interesting exhibit, huh?"

Carlotta nodded. "Very compelling."

"That's my dress over there." The woman's bleary eyes and careful gesture made Carlotta think the glass of wine wasn't her first. "The ivory Vera Wang."

"It's lovely," Carlotta said, noting the pristine condition.

"It is," the woman agreed, then took a drink from her glass. "It *was*. I didn't know it at the time, but while I was putting on that dress, my groom was screwing one of my bridesmaids." She gave a shrill laugh.

Carlotta didn't know what to say. "I—"

"It's okay," the woman cut in with an exaggerated shrug. "Men suck. You don't see any men saving their tuxedos, do you?"

"I—"

"Nope. That's kind of an overlooked red flag, don't you think?"

"I—"

"We make ourselves crazy trying to find the perfect wedding gown, pay a king's ransom for it, then starve ourselves to fit in it. Meanwhile, they *rent* the suit they're going to wear on the most important day of their life. I mean, that kind of fucking says it all, don't you think?"

Carlotta hesitated before answering, "I never thought about it, but you're right."

The woman used her pinkie finger to point at Carlotta. "You bet I'm right. Temporary, renting, cheating sons of bitches."

Carlotta gave her a flat smile, then began to inch away. "I'm sorry your marriage didn't work out."

The woman guffawed and held up her left hand that sported a gigantic diamond and a gleaming gold band. "We're celebrating our tenth anniversary next month." She leaned in. "But don't worry, I make him pay—every... single...day." She drained her glass, then tottered off toward the bar, presumably, for a refill.

Carlotta stared after her, marveling over the dysfunctional glue of relationships. Was that how Valerie had felt—trapped in a marriage to an unfaithful man, blurring the sharp edges of her marriage with alcohol? She had asked herself a thousand times why her mother had gone on the run with Randolph. His indictment would've been the perfect excuse to end the marriage. Valerie could've stayed with her children...gotten sober...built a new life for herself. Had she loved Randolph that much...or had she, like the bitter brunette, stayed with him to punish him?

"Who was that?" Hannah asked, walking up to hand her a glass of white wine.

"A sadomasochist. There's a lot of anger in here."

"No kidding. In the bar line women were discussing ways to murder their exes like it was a game show." She clinked her highball glass to Carlotta's. "Cheers."

Carlotta winced. "It's a little depressing, don't you think?"

Hannah scoffed. "Depressing is what we've witnessed at the Wedding Expo this week—women gorging themselves on the idea that a man and a white dress are going to make them happy."

"Some married people are happy."

"Who?" Hannah said pointedly. "Who do we know who's happily married?" She held up her fist, poised to count on her fingers. "There's my mom and dad—oh no, wait—they despise each other. Then there are my two sisters and my brother—no, they have four divorces between them. Oh, but then there's Peter Ashford—no, his wife was a closeted prostitute who ended their marriage by getting herself murdered."

Carlotta gave her a wry look. "What about Tracey Tully Lowenstein?"

"She's a witch and her husband is a creepy twat-doctor."

"That doesn't mean they aren't happy. And hey—there's Jolie Goodman. She and Beck Underwood are still happy and in love."

Hannah harumped. "Okay, that's *one*." She raised her middle finger.

Carlotta laughed. "Did you ever think that happily married people might avoid people like us?"

But Hannah's attention was snagged by something past Carlotta's shoulder. Her finger went from vertical to horizontal. "Holy crap, there's Coop!"

Carlotta turned and sure enough, even from the back and across the room, his tall, lean physique was unmistakable. Pleasure infused her chest. "What's he doing here?"

Hannah was already moving in his direction. "I say we find out."

Carlotta took a drink of her wine, letting Hannah clear a path to Coop, which she did, with flying elbows and violent knees.

"Excuse me...coming through...*move*, already, dammit." When they reached him, he turned at the commotion and Hannah practically fell into him. "Hi, Coop!"

He caught her with a strong arm and a surprised smile. "Hello." After he'd righted Hannah, he gave Carlotta a wink. "Didn't expect to see you ladies here."

"Likewise," Carlotta said with an arched eyebrow. Dressed in dark slacks, a dove grey sport coat and white dress shirt, he looked ridiculously handsome. He was obviously on a date, and she had a good idea who Coop had accompanied.

"He's with me."

Carlotta turned and blinked to see not a certain curvy redheaded reporter, but June Moody standing there looking like a million dollars in a wide-leg black jumpsuit and flat jeweled sandals. "June! What a treat to see you, and how wonderful you look."

"June is one of the guests of honor," Coop supplied.

"One of the dresses is yours?"

June nodded and smiled. "The white crocheted baby doll dress."

"With the yellow daisies around the trim?"

"That's the one."

Intrigued, Carlotta waved in the direction of the dress. "Will you tell me about it?"

June nodded and they left Coop and Hannah to walk back to the exhibit area. The girlish dress was beautifully preserved—the finely knitted cotton circles were snowy white. The full, swingy fabric fell from the neckline and landed mid-thigh. The pale yellow lining that hung a couple inches below the top layer rendered it more modest.

"It's so you!" Carlotta exclaimed. "What year?"

"Nineteen seventy-five. I was a few sizes smaller back then."

"Don't be silly—you could still pull it off." Carlotta gestured to the tablet. "Do you mind if I watch your interview?"

"That's why it's here."

Carlotta pushed the button and June came on the screen, in the same chair as the others, against the same background. June introduced herself with a smile, then said, "My wedding dress was nontraditional for the time—it was short and it wasn't solid white. My mother-in-law didn't know quite what to make of it, but I felt as if my dress represented who I was at the time—a bit of a free spirit." Her eyes shone, as if she were remembering. "The man I married was like-minded. We got married because it seemed like a grand adventure."

On the screen, June gave a little laugh, then her expression sobered a bit. "But after the wedding, we both changed. I got pregnant right away, and he took a sales job he didn't like to cover the extra expenses. He was away much of the time, and I was lonely. We were blessed with a healthy son, but by that time, the writing was on the wall." She shook her head, then lifted her hands.

"The marriage lasted less than two years, but I still have the dress. I guess it represented hope for me...and I couldn't bring myself to get rid of it." She gave the camera a wistful smile, then the screen went black.

Carlotta turned back to her friend, her heart squeezing for the disappointment she'd experienced. "You never remarried?"

"No."

Carlotta had met June's son Mitchell and knew things were tense between them. "Are you and Mitchell's father still on good terms?"

June averted her gaze. "No. Actually, he dropped out of our lives when Mitchell was still a baby. I went back to my maiden name, and changed Mitchell's name to Moody, too."

So he had abandoned them, and June had been a single, self-supporting mother. And Mitchell Moody had daddy problems.

Although that was sort of the pot calling the kettle black.

"He wasn't a bad man," June said. "He seemed crazy about Mitchell—I never thought he'd leave us." Hurt flashed over her face, then she recovered. "But some people just aren't up to the challenge of parenting."

"So true," Carlotta said, feeling ill. She'd managed to go an entire ten minutes without thinking about the fact that Wesley was going to have a baby.

With Liz Fischer.

June suddenly looked stricken. "I'm so sorry, Carlotta. I didn't mean to imply anything about your parents."

"I didn't take it that way," Carlotta assured her.

"I saw how you reacted."

Carlotta sighed. "It's...not that."

"Anything you want to talk about?"

She shook her head.

"Okay. Have you talked to your father yet?"

"No. But soon, hopefully."

June clasped her hands. "You've been through so much."

"So have you," Carlotta returned.

June smiled and nodded. "And we're still kicking."

Carlotta's heart swelled with fondness for the woman who had taken her under her wing. She conjured up a smile that belied her inner turmoil. "Yes, we are."

Coop walked up, with Hannah on his heels. "Hey, sorry to interrupt, but June, I got a work call—I have to leave."

"Go," June said with a wave. "I'll get a taxi home."

"Take us with you!" Hannah pleaded with Coop.

"I don't think this is an appropriate place for you and Carlotta to be."

He might as well have plugged Hannah into a socket. "Where is it?"

"Outside the Clermont Lounge."

"The strip club? Oh, now we *have* to go," Hannah said.

Coop smothered a smile, then glanced at Carlotta. "I couldn't reach Wes. Are you up for it?"

She spent a half second worrying where Wes was, then reminded herself there really wasn't much more trouble he could get himself into. "Sure."

"I need to pick up the van," Coop said. "You and Hannah get some food in you, and I'll meet you there in thirty minutes."

CHAPTER NINETEEN

THE CLERMONT LOUNGE was located in the basement of the Clermont Motor Hotel, which squatted on a seedy stretch of the rapidly gentrifying Ponce de Leon Avenue. Three APD cruisers, a vehicle from the Medical Examiner's office, and an unmarked Crown Victoria in the parking lot sported flashing blue lights. Between patrons, neighbors, bums, and lookey-loos on their way to Home Depot and Whole Foods, there was a bona fide traffic jam of cars and pedestrians.

But Hannah honked and cursed her way through the street—an advantage of having the top down was there was nothing separating a wild-eyed, flailing Hannah from the car next to them. The drivers all caved and let them pass. After she wedged the Audi into a pseudo parking spot, she brought out the elbows and knees and hacked their way through the crowd, holding her morgue ID high and yelling, "Body movers, coming through! If you're alive, get the hell out of the way."

Coop was waiting for them at the back of the transport van. "Nice," he said dryly, handing them scrubs.

"Hey, we got through," Hannah said, pulling on the scrubs on the spot. "What's the deal-e-o?"

"The *situation*," Coop corrected, "is two people were mugged in the parking lot and shot at close range. I'm waiting for the police to give me the go-ahead."

Carlotta stepped between the open rear doors of the van to pull the scrubs over her clothing in as much privacy as one could get at a crime scene. Coop discreetly stepped with his back to her to offer himself as a shield.

"I called Wes again," Coop said over his shoulder. "Has he gone off the grid?"

"I think he's just busy with his two other jobs," she offered.

"You doing okay?"

"Hanging in there," she said with forced cheer.

"Still working at the Wedding Expo?"

"For a few more days." She gave a little laugh. "It's a little overwhelming. Hannah and I decided to take in the art exhibit for the other side of the story, so to speak."

"Ah. I'm glad you did."

She smiled at his back. "So am I. All done here."

As she emerged in her scrubs, a slender female detective Carlotta recognized walked up to them.

"Detective Salyers," Coop greeted her. "This is Carlotta and Hannah—they'll be assisting with the body removal."

All business, she gave them a curt nod. "We're ready for you. This needs to be as quick as possible so we can clear the area."

They sprang into action, she and Hannah rolling a gurney past the crime scene tape, and Coop right behind them with body bags and a transport board. They followed Detective Salyers to the sheet-draped bodies.

The first victim was an Asian male, maybe mid-thirties, Carlotta guessed. Handsome in an exotic way. His casual clothes and shoes were of good quality, and he had a fifty-dollar haircut. He reeked of throw-up, and a bloodstain spread over his chest.

The second victim was a white male, about the same age. Also nice looking and well-dressed in slacks and a polo-style shirt, also reeking of puke, also bloodstained. She particularly noticed the perfect creases in his pants. All the little grooming details that mattered in life seemed incongruous in death.

"Were they at the strip club?" Carlotta asked the detective.

Detective Salyers raised one delicate eyebrow. "I don't believe that's relevant to your job."

Coop threw Carlotta a warning glance, then pulled out the necessary tags to fill in. "Do you have names?"

Salyers shook her head. "We didn't find their wallets or car keys." She glanced at Carlotta, then back to Coop. "They were in the strip club, but they paid cash, so we don't have a credit card receipt. We're checking all the cars parked in the lot, but if they parked somewhere else, it could be a while before we find the right vehicle to run the tags. The M.E. took prints, so we'll run those, too, in case one of them has a record."

"Got it," Coop said. "For now, two John Does."

Carlotta and Hannah worked quickly to bag the first victim. In deference to her shoulder, she allowed Hannah and Coop to move him to the gurney. While they wheeled the body to the van, she knelt to carefully arrange the second victim for bagging, using gloved hands to position his hands close to his body. Something peeking below his sleeve caught her eye—a large flesh-colored adhesive bandage.

Curious, she looked around to make sure Salyers's attention was elsewhere, then lifted the corner of the bandage to find a tattoo so new, it had oozed blood onto the bandage.

At first she thought the design was a set of handcuffs and wondered if the man had a job in law enforcement—perhaps he'd gotten the tattoo to celebrate a new position.

But when she revealed the entire image, she realized it was a ball and chain tattoo.

The kind a guy might get in anticipation of getting married?

It would make sense the men had been at the strip club for some sort of bachelor party.

Under the image was tattooed the name "Kim." Carlotta's pulse spiked. Another groom-to-be, murdered?

Even she recognized the connection as far-fetched. And if it were true, it could simply be a coincidence. Half the people in any given strip club were probably there for a bachelor party, so chances were good that anyone mugged in the parking lot of a strip club would be a member of a wedding party.

"Everything okay here?" Detective Salyers asked.

Carlotta furtively smoothed the bandage back in place. "Yes. I mean…this job never gets any easier."

"I know what you mean."

Carlotta stood. "Detective Salyers, you probably don't remember me, but you and I have met before."

"Yes, I remember you from another body recovery—it was for one of the victims of The Charmed Killer, I believe."

"Yes. But you actually met me—and Hannah—on a previous occasion. Do you recall the Gary Hagan murder?"

Salyers frowned. "Remind me."

"He was reported missing by his girlfriend Jolie Goodman. His car was found in the Chattahoochee River—"

"With a woman's body inside," Salyers finished. "Then later his body was found at a home in Buckhead, during a party."

"That's right." Carlotta cleared her throat. "You arrested Jolie Goodman at the party...along with a couple of her friends."

"You and your helper were the party-crashing friends?"

Carlotta winced and nodded.

"Now I remember," Salyers said. "I seem to recall you were soaking wet when we took you in for questioning."

"There was a pool incident," Carlotta murmured nonsensically.

Salyers squinted. "I'm sorry—what's your name again?"

"Carlotta...Wren."

"Wait—you're the one who was stabbed by The Charmed Killer before he was taken in."

"That's me."

Salyers put her finger to her mouth, and Carlotta could see her mind racing to put details together. "Your father is Randolph Wren, the federal fugitive."

"Yes. Small world, huh?"

Salyers looked as if she wanted to ask more questions, but was interrupted as Coop and Hannah returned for the second body.

The three of them worked in practiced choreography to get the body tagged and bagged, then wheeled to the van where he was deposited next to his buddy. A pang of sympathy barbed through Carlotta's chest as she removed the scrubs and gloves and deposited them in a cloth bag in the van. Not long ago, the two men had been enjoying themselves, feeling invincible. Death could be so random…which accounted for why everyone feared it, she supposed.

Salyers bade them goodbye and strode away to help clear the scene.

When she was out of earshot, Carlotta said, "Coop, the second John Doe has an interesting tattoo."

Coop looked amused. "So do I."

"What is it?" Hannah asked, mesmerized.

Carlotta ignored her. "I think he was about to be married."

"Okay. I'll let Salyers know in case there's a fiancée to contact."

"But this is the third dead groom we've recovered in a matter of days. Don't you think that's strange?"

Coop pursed his mouth. "I'd call it an unfortunate coincidence."

She set her jaw in frustration, then a thought occurred to her and she snapped her fingers. "I might have proof."

Coop looked wary. "What kind of proof?"

She retrieved her purse from the van and rifled through the outside pockets until she came up with a dark, unrecognizable lump which she triumphantly deposited into Coop's hand.

He frowned. "What's this?"

"The gum Jeremy Atwater was chewing when he collapsed on the runway at the Wedding Expo."

"Ew." Hannah wrinkled her nose.

Coop's eyebrows rose. "And why do you have it?"

"I was just tidying up the scene," Carlotta said with a shrug. "I wrapped it in a rose petal, so it's been protected. Maybe you could test it, see if he was poisoned or something."

Hand still outstretched, Coop looked at her as if she'd gone mad.

A shrill whistle sounded, and across the parking lot, Salyers gestured for Coop to move the van.

He secured the van doors then gave Carlotta and Hannah a little wave. "I can take it from here. Thanks, ladies."

"Happy to help anytime someone gets themselves killed," Hannah said cheerfully, staring up at Coop with adoring eyes.

Carlotta stepped up to break Hannah from her trance and propel her toward the car. "Bye, Coop."

The crowd had started to disperse, but it still took a while to wend their way back to the Audi. Hannah shooed a couple of too-interested guys away from the convertible with a promise to "mace their ass" if they didn't relocate. They relocated—proof that Hannah didn't need the Goth garb to incite fear.

"What was all that about back there?" Hannah asked as she started the car.

Carlotta worked her mouth from side to side. "I think someone is murdering grooms."

"Okay, that's insane."

"First there was Jeremy who collapsed at the runway show, then there was Greg Pena, both of whom were engaged to be married. And one of these guys was going to be married."

Hannah gave her a dubious look. "How are things with you and Richie Rich?"

Carlotta frowned. "What does that have to do with anything?"

"I think you're so freaked out over Peter wanting to marry you, you're projecting murder onto these other poor men."

She scoffed. "Peter and I are pretending to be on the outs, so the people in his office don't think there's a conflict of interest now that Randolph is back."

"You mean Peter's pretending, and for you, it's business as usual."

"*Nooooo*. In fact, I told Peter I'd take this time that we're apart to consider wearing his engagement ring."

"And are you?"

"Am I what?"

"Exactly," Hannah said, putting the car in gear. "Detective, detect thyself."

Carlotta frowned and sat back in the seat, happy for the summer air whipping around them that made conversation difficult.

Because she didn't want to waste her breath trying to convince Hannah how wrong she was...about the mysterious deaths *and* about her and Peter.

Dead wrong.

Probably.

CHAPTER TWENTY

WHEN CARLOTTA OPENED her eyes the next morning, she heard a drum-beat. A few seconds later, she realized the pounding was in her head, keeping time to the throb of her shoulder. Bits of troubled dreams lingered in the corners of her brain. Snatches of the current state of her life assaulted her—Randolph's stoic silence…her tedious stint at the Wedding Expo…Wes's pregnancy predicament.

From the nightstand, her cell phone vibrated. She reached for it in time to see Peter's text scroll across the screen. *I woke up thinking about you.*

Carlotta squeezed her eyes closed, willing herself to go back to sleep for a few days. Maybe she'd get transported to the alternate universe she'd visited before, where she was happily married to Peter, and her parents were walking around living relatively normal lives.

She toyed with her phone, weighing a response to Peter. The man had demonstrated his love for her—he'd passed up a nice promotion to go to New York to stay in Atlanta to be with her. He'd showered her with gifts, including this phone. He'd let her live in his extravagant home while The Charmed Killer was on the loose. He'd once paid a hefty sum to get Wesley out of a scrape. He'd even risked his job by not revealing that Randolph had once called him. And now he'd agreed to be her lookout in case someone in Mashburn & Tully did or said something that might help Randolph.

And all he'd asked in return was for her to think about wearing his ring… to think about becoming his wife…to think about realizing the dream she'd fostered most of her adult life.

She was being a brat, as Hannah had implied. Making Peter jump through hoops to make up for his actions as a scared young man faced with an impossible choice.

Why couldn't she let him off the hook? Because the power felt good...or because deep down she was afraid her and Peter's window had closed, and their relationship was best left to play out in the other place, where their lives had taken the expected path.

Carlotta pursed her mouth, then texted *I am thinking about you, too. Any news?*

Yes. I miss you...but I guess that's not news.

At a loss, she texted back a smiley face.

Have you or Wesley talked to Randolph?

Suspicion stirred in her chest. It occurred to her that texting left a paper trail. And on the heels of that revelation came the realization that Peter owned her phone—he could have her account records pulled any time he wanted to.

When the scent of bacon wafted under her door, her stomach growled and she grasped at the diversion. *Talk later...Wes made breakfast.*

She set down the phone, then climbed out of bed and grabbed her fuzzy chenille robe on her way out of the room. Wes sat at the table behind a section of the Sunday *Atlanta Journal-Constitution*. His plate was piled high with bacon and eggs.

"Did you make enough for me?" she asked.

The paper didn't move. "Nope."

Carlotta bit her lower lip, then tried again. "You were out late last night."

"Yep."

She walked to the coffee pot to pour herself a cup. "Hannah and I helped Coop on a body pickup. He said he called you first."

"Uh-huh."

She took a sip, then leaned against the counter, knowing Wesley must be tied in knots over his impending fatherhood, maybe wondering how to tell her. "Is something wrong?"

She realized the absurdity of the question as soon as the words left her mouth. What *wasn't* wrong?

Wes snorted, then tossed down the paper and gestured to a story. "Your gal pal Rainie Stephens wrote a fabricated story about Dad."

Carlotta frowned and glanced at the headline. *Infamous Fugitive Faces Fraud Charges.* She skimmed the story, which focused on how many investors' lives Randolph had destroyed—dozens—and hinted he'd lived a life of luxury on the lam with the stolen money while his own children had been left behind to fend for themselves.

The last half of the report was certainly accurate. "At least they didn't mention our names."

"It's total bullshit. I wonder who her source is?" His voice was accusatory.

"It's not me, if that's what you're implying."

He studied her, his face sullen. "Promise?"

"*Yes.* Rainie came to the Expo and asked for an interview, but when I declined, she didn't press."

He didn't say anything, but his gaze strayed to the pile of mail on the counter.

"Dad hasn't sent the visitation forms," she murmured. "Yet."

His mouth tightened. "He will."

She pulled a smile out of thin air, then nodded. "Of course he will. Have you heard any news from your friend inside the facility?"

He hesitated, then nodded.

She lunged forward. "And?"

"And he's in solitary confinement, only comes out for meals."

"Why is he in solitary confinement?"

He shrugged. "I don't know. The guy said he tried to talk to him, told him he was asking for me, but Dad wouldn't respond."

His expression of angst made her heart pinch. No son should have to do what Wesley had done...only to be rejected again. Emotion welled in her throat over the fact that Wes's life hadn't turned out the way it should have. And now a baby on the way...

He looked concerned. "Are you okay, Sis?"

She blinked back moisture, then rubbed her aching arm. "I must have slept on my shoulder wrong." She turned her back to rifle a cabinet for ibuprofen, then downed a couple of tablets with her coffee. It gave her time to gather herself. When she turned back, Wes had divided the heaped up food onto two plates.

He pushed one toward her, then licked his thumb. "You need protein to heal."

She smiled, then joined him at the table. He handed her a fork, and she dug in. After a few bites, she was already feeling better. "Guess who was at the Wedding Expo yesterday?"

He shrugged. "Who?"

"Eldora Jones."

He took his time swallowing. "Yeah, she's engaged to a lughead."

"I remember meeting him at the Fox. Do you know him?"

Another hesitation. "I think I met him through Chance once."

"So he's into something shady."

"Not everything Chance does is illegal."

But he didn't correct her where the fiancé was concerned. So maybe the uncertainty she'd detected in Eldora Jones was warranted.

"Hey, are things okay with Hannah?"

She looked up from the eggs. "Why do you ask?"

"Chance said he thinks she's…I don't know—keeping something from him."

Her identity, like she'd been keeping from all of them. Carlotta conceded she felt deceived, but it was Hannah's secret to tell. "Maybe he should ask her."

He frowned. "I don't think they talk much."

"Ew."

"I know."

She took a few more bites, noticing Wes's ragged fingernails. He had started biting them when he was a little boy, after their parents had left, chewing them obsessively until they bled. At the time, she had resorted to all kinds of preventive remedies, from coating them with nasty-tasting solutions to putting Band-Aids around them, but nothing worked. Finally she realized the nail-biting was simply a way to keep his hands busy while his mind raced with problems no child should have to deal with. She'd given him a wad of Silly Putty to keep with him at all times, and the nail-biting had stopped. Eventually the putty had been set aside, too.

But under the stress of their dad returning and now the situation with Liz, apparently the old habit had resurfaced.

"You've been scarce," she said lightly.

He took his time responding. "Just busy."

"How is your community service job?"

Wes shifted in his seat. "Fine."

"How are things with Meg?"

"She's still on vacation with her folks."

"Ah. When does she get back?"

He looked despondent. "Tomorrow."

And he would have to tell her he'd gotten another woman pregnant. Carlotta felt like crying herself—or giving him a good shake for being so careless. "You're not looking forward to seeing her?"

He dropped his fork with a clatter, then stood abruptly. "I gotta go."

"What? Where?"

He gestured vaguely. "I have a...thing."

Carlotta closed her eyes and opened her mouth to let the painful words spill out. "Wes...I know Liz is pregnant." When she opened her eyes, Wes looked like a trapped animal.

"How do you know?"

"It doesn't matter—"

"Chance told Hannah and Hannah told you, didn't she?"

"Wes, the point is I know. What's going to happen?"

His arms flailed as if he were fighting the universe, his eyes wide. "It's none of your business. It's no one's business but mine and Liz!"

"That's not true," she said as calmly as she could. "It's going to affect my life, and Meg's...and Dad's. Does he know—has Liz told him?"

"No!" He pulled his hand down his face. "I don't know. I don't think so." Then he made a chopping motion in the air. "Look, this is my problem and I'll handle it."

Carlotta wanted to throttle him. "Like you handled your gambling problem? Or your drug problem?"

When angry tears filled his eyes, she wanted the words back. Wes had developed all his bad habits under her watch—didn't she share some of the blame?

"I shouldn't have said that—"

"Shut up!" Wesley yelled. "And stay out of my life!"

He turned and strode through the living room and out the front door with a bang. Carlotta fought back tears. When would her world right itself? She leaned her head back and let out the pent up frustration in a therapeutic scream.

Which made her feel marginally better...good enough to drag herself to her feet and think about getting dressed to head to the Wedding Expo.

The sound of the doorbell startled her. She padded through the living room and checked the side window.

The man from next door—Johnson—stood on the stoop holding the glass vase she'd forced on him yesterday. He saw her and waved.

Carlotta jerked back. She didn't trust the guy, and she was alone. Had he seen Wesley leave? Did he mean her harm?

She ran to the bedroom, grabbed her cell phone, and called Jack with one button. He answered on the second ring. "What's up, Carlotta?" From the background noise, she could tell he was in his car.

"Jack...the guy next door with the camera I told you about? He's ringing my bell."

"Trying to make me jealous?"

She frowned. "I'm serious, he's ringing my doorbell. And Wes isn't here."

"If you're afraid, don't answer the door."

"But he knows I'm here."

"So?"

"So...that's rude."

He sighed. "So what exactly do you want *me* to do?"

"Stay on the phone...I'll put you on speaker so you can hear our conversation. That way, if anything happens, you can—"

"Come running? I get the picture."

She walked back to the door, set the phone on a nearby table, then hit the speaker button. She glanced down at her robe and realized the yoga pants and tee shirt underneath were more presentable, so she peeled it off, wadded it into a ball and tossed it toward the hallway. Then she finger-combed her hair and pinched her cheeks.

"Are you primping?" Jack asked dryly.

"Shhh!" she hissed, then opened the door.

Her neighbor gave her a smile. "I thought you weren't going to answer."

"Why would I not answer the door?" Carlotta asked loudly to make sure Jack heard her.

The man shrugged. He was wearing jeans, a fitted tee shirt, and black athletic shoes. "It's Carlotta, right?"

"Yes." He was even more attractive than she'd first noticed, but she wasn't going to let his Abercrombie good looks distract her. The man could be an assassin. "And you're Johnson?"

"That's right."

"Is that your first name or your last name?" Jack would need some details to be able to check him out.

"It's just a nickname," he said with a laugh. "My dad's name was John, and everyone called me John's son, so..." He shrugged again, displacing lots of muscle.

"So what *is* your name?" she pressed, then realized she sounded like an interrogator. She gave a little laugh. "I mean, I like to know who's living next door."

"That's funny," he said with an amused expression. "The guy I rented the place from said he'd never met the people who live here."

She felt herself blanch. "I...that is, we...are kind of private, I suppose. But we're...trying to...be better. Better neighbors, I mean."

He squinted, then extended the vase. "I just came to return this. Er, thanks for the flowers."

Her face flamed as she took the glass vase. "You're welcome." But she steeled herself because now both his hands were free.

"Okay, well, I guess I'll see you around," he said, backing down the steps.

"Wait!" Carlotta practically shouted. "What do you do for a living?" Then she tried to appear casual. "I'm interested in why you're only renting the house for a few weeks."

He stopped. "I'm a freelance photographer, and I'm in town on assignment."

She deflated a little. "What kind of assignment?"

"Nothing too exciting—I'm here to shoot pictures for Google Maps."

She narrowed her eyes. "I thought Google Maps used cameras on robots." Wes had told her that once.

"They do. I'm shooting pictures of things the robots can't get to, just to fill in the blanks." He lifted his hands. "Like I said—nothing exciting."

"Oh," she said, mildly disappointed.

"Say, since I'm going to be in town for a while, would you like to get a drink sometime, maybe have dinner?"

She blinked in surprise. "Oh…thank you, but…I'm seeing someone."

"Ah." He inclined his head. "Okay, then, I'll be going. Bye."

"Goodbye," she murmured, then watched him walk his really nice body from her unkempt mortgaged yard back to his neatly groomed rented one. She stepped back and closed the door.

"Gee," Jack said from the speaker, "you've never given me flowers."

"Shut up, Jack." She turned the phone off speaker mode, then put it to her ear. "It was an excuse to see who lived there. Wes got it in his head that since Randolph was apparently monitoring us…"

"That he and your mother might be living next door?"

She sighed. "It sounded plausible at the time."

He made a thoughtful noise. "I guess you haven't heard from Randolph?"

"No…and it's wearing on us."

"I know, but hang in there a little longer. Are you still meeting with Lucas tomorrow?"

"Yes. And I took your advice—Liz will be there, too. I'm hoping she'll have some news." She thought about the other news Liz was sitting on, then added, "From Dad."

The chime of the doorbell filled the room.

"Is your neighbor back?" Jack asked.

Carlotta peeked out the side window and swallowed a groan. "No...it's Peter."

"Put me on speaker again, would you? This might be more interesting."

"Goodbye, Jack." She stabbed a button to end the call, then opened the door.

Peter, dressed in business casual clothes, had a ready smile for her. "Hi."

"Hi," she said, and met his lips in a quick kiss. "But I'm so sorry I don't have time to talk—I need to get ready for work."

He nodded. "But I have some news and I thought I'd tell you in person. I don't know if it's related at all to Randolph, but I thought you'd want to know."

She frowned. "What happened?"

"Walt Tully was rushed to the hospital this morning."

Randolph's former partner wasn't her favorite person, but she didn't wish him ill. "Is he okay?"

"I'm afraid not. He's in a medically induced coma after an accidental drug overdose."

CHAPTER TWENTY-ONE

"DON'T JUMP TO CONCLUSIONS," Jack said.

Carlotta glanced over his shoulder to make sure Patricia was out of earshot in the booth. "You don't think it's a pretty big coincidence that Walt Tully takes an overdose of prescription pills a few days after my father returns?"

"Accidental overdose," he corrected. "I had a friend pull the medical report."

"So you *are* interested."

"It's an interesting development. But even if there's a connection, it doesn't have to be menacing. You said yourself that Walt Tully and your dad were more than coworkers."

"Yes, they were best friends. Walt is our godfather."

"He didn't exactly fulfill his duties after your parents left you."

"No," she admitted. "But it speaks to how much my father trusted him."

"So...maybe now that Randolph is back, Walt Tully feels bad about not doing right by you and Wesley. A couple of sleeping pills...a couple more...an alcohol chaser, and suddenly he's in the hospital."

"There's another possibility," she said.

He sighed. "There are about a hundred possibilities, but because I need to go powder Jarold Jett's ass, I'm going to let you tell me the one you have in mind."

She smirked. "Thank you. What if Walt is so guilt-ridden about the firm railroading my dad, he couldn't take it anymore?"

Jack nodded. "That is definitely one possibility."

"Are you going to look into it?"

"You forget I'm technically on vacation for a few more days. Besides, there's no criminal investigation here. The man had a legitimate prescription for the pills. He took too many, and now he's suffering for it."

Carlotta bit into her lip. "Did the medical report mention the prognosis?"

His mouth twitched downward. "Fair to good."

"Peter is going by the hospital. He's going to call me later with an update."

"I thought you and Peter had split."

She squirmed. "That's right."

"You told your neighbor you were seeing someone."

"Maybe I just didn't want to go out with my neighbor."

"Ugly, huh?"

She laughed. "Sure, Jack, whatever you want to think." Then she sobered. "So Jack...why would Randolph be in solitary confinement?"

He frowned. "There could be lots of reasons. But how do you know that?"

"I...heard."

"From Liz?"

"Not exactly."

He pinched the bridge of his nose. "Who, exactly?"

"From a friend of a friend of Wesley's who's on the inside."

His eyebrows flew up like two angry birds. "You two are trying to communicate with your father through another criminal?"

"It didn't work—Randolph wouldn't talk."

If she thought the pronouncement that the scheme had failed would take the wind out of Jack's sails, it didn't. He leaned in, his face almost purple. "Godammit, Carlotta, stop playing detective before someone gets hurt."

She frowned. "I think you're angry because I found out information about Randolph that you can't."

Her words found their mark. He drew back, as if to reaffirm their pact to maintain a safe distance from each other. "I'm late." Then he spun on his heel and stalked away, disappearing into the crowd that had swelled since church services had ended.

Carlotta sighed. She and Jack seemed to be designed to rub each other the wrong way.

And the right way.

But Jack was right about the development with Walt Tully—it might have nothing to do with Randolph's return.

But what if it did?

Carlotta thought about calling Tracey to say she was thinking of the family, but wasn't sure her call would be welcome, and she didn't want to add stress to an already upsetting situation. After all, Tracey didn't know that if Randolph and Valerie hadn't left, she and Carlotta would've been best friends.

Patricia walked across the booth, her expression bright and shiny. "Leo and Casey are coming by in an hour or so to take me to a late lunch—will you cover for me?"

"Sure." Carlotta smiled. "It'll be better this time, you'll see."

Patricia nodded, then turned back to a customer. The *Your Perfect Man* booth was hopping, and Carlotta was swept into sales mode as she explained the warrior, the king, the lover, and the magician archetypes over and over, and helped women decide which best matched the man they were shopping for. The sales spiel, she realized, was helping her to understand more about the men in her life. The confusion over her feelings for the men came from the fact that at different times in her life, she needed a warrior…and other times she needed a king, or a lover, or a magician.

It was much the same for men, she suspected, who consciously and unconsciously categorized women as the kind of woman to befriend or date or sleep with or take home to mother. With all the moving parts and bad timing, it was a miracle men and women got together in the first place…and as evidenced by the women featured in the "After the Dress" art exhibit, staying together seemed more like an endurance challenge rather than a labor of love.

Carlotta glanced over the throngs of brides-to-be, some arm in arm with their betrothed who seemed to be along for the ride. She admired how fearless they were in the face of the odds against them. And was it so wrong if a beautiful white dress was part of a bride's emotional arsenal, to equip her with a strong dose of dopamine and oxytocin to carry her through some of the lows in a marriage?

Her phone vibrated and she glanced down to see Peter was calling. Eager for an update on Walt's condition, she connected the call. "Hi."

"Hi, there," Peter said, his voice low. "Can you talk?"

"Briefly. How's Walt?"

"He's improving, thank goodness. If things go well for the next twelve hours, the doctors are going to bring him out of the coma tomorrow."

Carlotta exhaled. "That's good news."

"Yes, it is. But he's still not out of the woods."

"Has anyone said why this might have happened?"

"His wife said he's been really stressed lately and hasn't been sleeping. She thinks he just didn't realize how big of a dose he'd taken."

Carlotta bit into her lip...just a few nights ago, an extra dose of the pain meds for her shoulder had triggered the fantastic trip across time. "I've heard that's fairly common," she murmured.

"I know. But..." The background became muffled, as if he'd covered the microphone with his hand. "But I heard his son say something about a note."

"A suicide note?"

"I don't know that for sure, but I did see his sister pull him aside and it looked to me as if they had some harsh words."

"Tracey?"

"Right. Anyway, I'm going to stick around the hospital for a while. The partners are here."

"Okay. Thanks for the update."

"I miss you," he said, his voice earnest.

"I miss you, too. Bye." She ended the call and stowed her phone.

It wasn't a lie—she missed the way she and Peter used to be. Carlotta glanced down at her bare left ring finger. Would it be so bad to be married to Peter now? She wasn't getting any younger. And while she'd had passing fantasies about Jack...and some missed opportunities with Coop, neither of them was offering her a ring.

"You look deep in thought."

Carlotta lifted her gaze to see Rainie Stephens standing there. She dropped her left hand, then crossed her arms. "I could be thinking about the interesting story regarding my father in this morning's paper."

Rainie nodded. "That's why I'm here. I wanted to let you know it wasn't my idea to run the piece."

"Your byline was on it."

"Yes. But I didn't initiate the story. And I had your and Wesley's names removed."

"Thanks for that anyway. And I guess this isn't the first time the information has been printed."

"I know. But I like you, Carlotta, and I don't want to see you hurt by this situation with your father any more than you probably already have been."

Carlotta pressed her lips together. "I appreciate that."

"That said, I'd really like to keep my job. So what I'm about to say is for your ears only."

Her interest was piqued. "I'm listening."

"I got the impression that there was some pressure to run the piece on your father."

"Pressure from whom?"

Rainie's shoulders lifted in a slow shrug. "Who would benefit from making your father look bad?"

"Mashburn & Tully, of course...or any of the clients who lost money. Did you know one of the partners of the firm, Walt Tully, is in the hospital for a prescription drug overdose?"

Rainie blinked. "No. When did that happen?"

"This morning." A thought burst into Carlotta's head and she could tell Rainie was thinking the same thing—had something in the article triggered a self-destructive reaction from Walt Tully?

Carlotta hesitated, then said, "There might have been a note."

"A suicide note?"

"I don't know...and I'm not even sure there was a note. It's...a rumor."

"Who told you?"

"I'd rather not say."

Rainie angled her head. "Doesn't your boyfriend work for Mashburn & Tully?"

Carlotta's cheeks warmed. "Peter Ashford works there, yes…but I wouldn't call him my boyfriend."

Rainie smiled. "What would you call him?"

"A good friend. Now that my father is back, I don't want anyone at the firm questioning Peter's loyalty."

"Ah," Rainie said, although she looked…concerned? "Okay, well, I have some digging to do. I'll let you know if I find out anything interesting."

Carlotta nodded. "Same here."

Before she dove back into sales, she checked her phone in case Wes had called. He hadn't. She hated the way they'd left things this morning. She punched in his number and when it went straight to voicemail, she said, "Wes, it's me. I'm really sorry about this morning. I know you have a lot on your mind right now with…everything. Just know I will support you any way I can. Just…don't shut me out, okay?"

She ended the call and sighed. Wesley usually came around when she gave him time, but she was afraid this time he'd reached some sort of breaking-away point…that she'd gone too far, maybe pushed him out of their family duo and toward Liz—*ugh*—and his new family.

Brides shopping for their grooms kept her busy all afternoon—the women loved the certainty of matching a gift to their man's archetype. The gift of choice for warriors appeared to be boots. For kings, golf bags ruled. For lovers, electronic gadgets held the most power. And for magicians, designer sunglasses were the perfect fit.

Carlotta looked over and saw Patricia on her phone, obviously distraught. She walked over and touched her arm, then whispered, "Is everything okay?"

Patricia shook her head, then covered the mouthpiece. "Leo can't bring Casey to eat with me—a friend of his died suddenly. He's so upset."

"Oh, I'm sorry," Carlotta said. "If you need to leave early, I'll cover the booth…and we'll split the commissions."

"But—"

"No buts."

Patricia nodded gratefully, then uncovered the mouth piece to resume her conversation.

Carlotta tended to customers, thinking about what Patricia had said once about bodies turning up around her. The truth was, death had always been nearby—she'd just never noticed how indiscriminate it was until she'd started body-moving.

When Patricia ended the call, she walked over, dabbing at her eyes. "How awful. His name was Jeffrey Oxblood. He was so young—only thirty-eight."

"How did he die?"

"He was out for a run and collapsed. They think it was a heart attack."

"Very sad," Carlotta agreed.

"He had just started a new job, and he was engaged. Leo said he was really stressed out."

Carlotta pressed her lips together. "Engaged?"

Patricia nodded. "His fiancée is devastated. They were planning their wedding."

"That can certainly be stressful."

"If you don't mind, I think I will take you up on your offer and go be with Leo. Would you like to take a bathroom break before I leave?"

"Yes," Carlotta said. "I'll be back in a flash."

She walked in the direction of the restrooms, but detoured over to the HAL Properties booth, where she spotted an impeccably groomed Hannah talking to a young couple, handing them vacation brochures. Carlotta smiled to herself to see Hannah behaving almost—genteel. At the same time, she couldn't help feeling she'd been deceived by this woman whom she'd allowed into her life.

"Can I help you?"

Carlotta turned to see a tall woman with honey-colored hair and Hannah's eyes standing behind a counter. One of Hannah's sisters, she presumed, and model pretty. "I'm waiting to talk to Hannah," she said, then waved when Hannah looked in her direction.

"You know my sister?" the woman asked.

"Yes."

She put out a beautifully manicured hand. "I'm Anna Kizer."

Carlotta shook her hand. "Carlotta Wren."

The woman's brow furrowed. "Wren?"

Apparently the woman read the newspapers.

Hannah appeared suddenly and grabbed Carlotta's elbow to shepherd her away from the booth.

"Hello to you, too," Carlotta said, trotting to keep up with Hannah's long stride.

"I asked you to stay away from my family," Hannah said, her tone irritated.

"They seem normal to me. Besides, I needed to talk to you."

"About what?"

"Were you serious about renting Greg Pena's apartment?"

"The guy who slipped in the mouthwash? Yeah. I even called, but the manager said he wanted to wait to show it until the guy's stuff is out of there."

"Perfect. Can you call him back and get him to show it to you anyway, like this evening?"

"Let's see."

Hannah pulled out her phone and searched her call log until she found the number, then connected the call. She reminded the manager who she was, then said she needed to see the apartment that night because she was getting ready to go out of town...and no, she didn't mind that the previous renter's stuff was still there...and did she mention she was willing to pay the deposit and six months' rent in advance—in cash? "Great," she said, giving Carlotta a nod. "I'll be there." She ended the call. "We're in."

"Great. Meet you at the entrance when the show closes?"

"I'm counting the minutes."

CHAPTER TWENTY-TWO

"THANK YOU," Hannah said as the manager pushed open the apartment door.

"We'll lock up when we leave," Carlotta added.

The man looked back and forth between her and Hannah. "Since I'm not supposed to let you in, I probably should stay."

Hannah leaned in and gave him a flirtatious smile. "But that's the very reason you shouldn't stay. We don't want to see you get into trouble."

"Right," Carlotta added with her own smile.

"Besides," Hannah said, "do we look like the kind of women who would talk our way into a place just to do something underhanded?"

The guy looked them up and down. Hannah preened in her Kate Spade colorblock dress that emphasized her knockout figure. Carlotta felt less dazzling in a red pleated mini-skirt and white silk tank, but it seemed to suffice.

"Er...no," he murmured, a flush tinging his ears.

"We won't be long," Carlotta said.

"Meanwhile," Hannah said, angling herself between him and the door, "why don't you go ahead and draw up the lease agreement? I'd really like to get this wrapped up tonight."

He hesitated, then shrugged. "Okay. I'll be in the office."

As they walked inside, Hannah shook her head. "I mean, it's scary how easy this is sometimes. We could loot this entire place."

Carlotta flipped on light switches. "Well, he does have your phone number."

"Hello? If I were going to commit a burglary, I obviously would use a burner cell phone. After I move in, I'm going to complain about the lax security."

Hands on hips, she glanced around to take in the high ceilings, large windows, and aged wood floors. "Yeah, I think I'm going to like this place."

"I didn't mean to force you into making a decision today," Carlotta said.

"No, it's better that I do this while I'm working at the Wedding Expo—if I came dressed as myself, the manager probably wouldn't have shown it to me."

"You think?"

She shrugged. "Hey, it comes with the territory. People see tats and leather and they think I'm a criminal. Like your buds at the country club."

"What country club does your family belong to?" Carlotta asked lightly.

Hannah ignored her and walked into the tiny kitchen to the right. "Nice appliances…gas stove—that's a plus."

"Have you told Chance you're moving out?"

"I never really moved in. But no, I haven't told him…yet."

Carlotta walked through the living room, set down her purse, then began opening drawers and peeking under magazines. "It doesn't bother you that a man died here?"

Her friend scoffed. "Something tragic has happened or will happen in just about every apartment, condo, and house that's ever existed—a terrible accident, a fire, flood, or tornado, or yes—a silly, senseless, needless death."

"Or a murder," Carlotta said, moving through the hall and into the bedroom. She glanced over the neat room, which was much the same as when they'd been here, the covers folded down at an inviting angle.

"Ooh, nice fixtures," Hannah called from the bathroom, her voice echoing. "I didn't notice before because the body was taking up so much room in here." The shower came on, then went off. "Good water pressure!"

"Be careful—we don't want to disturb any potential evidence."

"What exactly should I be looking for?"

She opened the closet door and poked around. "I'm not sure…something suspicious that proves he didn't slip on mouthwash."

"Like a homicidal banana peel?"

"Very funny. Or something that would point to motivation. It looks to me as if he was expecting company—maybe he was having a last-minute fling before he walked down the aisle."

"And you think his girlfriend did him in?"

She lifted the lid on a wooden box that was a catchall for jewelry, odd keys, paperclips and ticket stubs. "You felt his body—rigor hadn't set in, he hadn't been dead very long. Iris had been working out with Tracey, remember?"

"Maybe they're in on it together."

Carlotta pursed her mouth at the unlikely scenario.

"Or maybe," Hannah said in a sing-song voice, "like Coop said, he slipped on mouthwash and whacked his head on the tub and that was that."

Carlotta sighed—Coop was probably right. She lifted the pillows from the bed and felt along the sheet. When she came across a small lump, she looked underneath to find a red acrylic fingernail.

"Someone's back was getting scratched," Hannah observed from the doorway.

"Not by Iris," Carlotta said, holding it up between finger and thumb. "This is a press-on nail. I think that's a little beneath her manicure grade."

Hannah clapped. "This is getting good."

A sound of the door opening and closing reached them. Her first thought was the manager had returned...until she heard female voices.

"Why are the lights on?"

"Whose purse is that?"

She met Hannah's wide-eyed gaze. They were trapped.

"Who's there?" a woman called.

"I have a weapon!" another female voice cried.

With nowhere to hide, Carlotta led the way out. "It's okay, it's just—" She stopped at the sight of Iris Kline and Tracey Lowenstein. "—us."

Tracey gasped. "You two!" She wielded a large wooden spoon.

"Were you going to spank us?" Hannah asked.

Tracey lowered her weapon, her face a mottled red. "What are you doing here?"

"How did you get in?" Iris demanded.

Carlotta opened her mouth. "We...we're...that is—"

"I'm taking over the lease," Hannah blurted.

Jaws dropped, faces contorted, Iris covered her mouth with her hand.

"That's just—" The woman broke off in a sob.

"Sick," Tracey chirped.

Carlotta felt Hannah bristle, so she spoke up before any more damage was done. "The manager was kind enough to let Hannah take another look while he finished the paperwork. If we had any idea you would be coming by, Iris, we wouldn't have dreamed of imposing. We're very sorry." She bumped Hannah.

"Right. Sorry."

Iris seemed to believe them, sniffed mightily and nodded. "I wanted to get some personal items."

"We didn't bother anything," Carlotta assured her.

From the bathroom came a crash, a clatter of glass on porcelain.

Hannah grunted. "I might have glanced inside the medicine cabinet."

Tracey glared and pointed to the door. "Get out!"

"We're going," Carlotta said, stopping to pick up her purse. Then she turned back. "Tracey...I was very sorry to hear about Walt."

Tracey's eyes watered. "You should be. It's your father's fault."

"Hey," Hannah said, hands on hips. "That's not fair."

"It's true," Tracey said, sending lasers at Carlotta. "My father's been cleaning up your father's mess ever since he ran like the thief he is."

Anger sparked in her stomach, but she recognized that Tracey was lashing out from worry over her father's condition. "We're all hoping for a speedy recovery." Carlotta tugged Hannah toward the entrance.

Once they were out in the hallway, Carlotta exhaled.

"Don't let her get to you," Hannah said.

"It's okay," Carlotta said. "Tracey's entitled to vent. And there's probably a lot of truth in what she said." Still, the encounter had left her shaken. As they descended to the first floor she held onto the handrail a little more tightly than she had going up.

When they reached the bottom of the stairs, she heard the sound of a faint bark and followed it.

"What is it?" Hannah asked.

"I was going to ask the manager for the apartment number of a woman I saw when we were here before, but I think I can find it on my own."

"What woman?"

"The officer said a neighbor who dog sat for Greg found his body. I want to talk to her."

The closer they walked to the apartment at the end of the hall, the louder the barking. Carlotta knocked on the door, and the barking escalated.

"What are you going to ask her?"

"Just if she noticed anything."

In a few seconds, the door opened, revealing the woman Carlotta had seen before. She was pretty and curvy, and snuggled the black terrier that was in some of Greg Pena's photographs. "Yes?"

"Hi," Carlotta said with a smile. She searched her memory banks for the name the officer had given to Iris, who'd been curious about which neighbor had found her boyfriend—and curiously irritated when she heard it was the dog sitter. "It's Emma, right?"

The woman nodded. "I recognize you. You two were here Friday...when Greg died."

"That's right," Carlotta said. "We know you're a friend of Greg's."

She tightened her grip on the little dog until it yelped. "Yes."

"That's his dog, isn't it?"

"I don't mind keeping Peppy. I was going to take him anyway, when Greg got married. His girlfriend doesn't like dogs."

"That's very nice of you. I recall that you were the one who found Greg."

Emma teared up and nodded.

"What do you think happened to him?"

"I don't know. When I came in, he was lying in the bathroom floor." She sniffed. "He must've had a heart attack or something."

"How did you get in?"

She hesitated. "The door was open."

"Did he always leave the door open?"

She pressed her lips together, then shook her head.

"But he was expecting you?"

"I...I...yes, he was...because I...was going to walk Peppy."

"Were Greg and his girlfriend getting along?"

Emma bit into her lip.

"It's okay," Carlotta urged with a conspiratorial smile. "You can tell me what you think."

"Greg was having second thoughts about getting married. He said he was going to break up with Iris." She teared up. "But he didn't get a chance."

Carlotta made a sympathetic noise. "Thank you for answering our questions." She started to turn away, then gestured to the woman's hands. "I like your nail polish."

She held up her red-tipped fingers and smiled. "Oh, these are just press-on nails."

"I see you lost one," Hannah piped up.

Emma frowned at the naked nail on her pinkie finger. "Yeah...that happens sometimes."

"Have a nice day," Carlotta said, then smiled and turned away.

When they walked out of earshot, Hannah said, "So she was sleeping with Greg."

"Looks that way."

"Just because the guy was fooling around on the side doesn't mean he was murdered."

"I know. I'm just asking a few questions." She pulled out her phone and dialed Rainie Stephens's number. After a couple of rings, Rainie answered.

"Hi, Carlotta. What can I do for you?"

"A favor, I hope."

"If I can."

"A list of the obituaries of single men in the metro area who died in the last thirty days."

"Should I ask why?"

"If it turns out to be something, the scoop is yours."

"Okay. Might take me a couple of days. Since I have you on the phone, any more news about Walt Tully's condition?"

"Not since we talked earlier. How about on your end?"

"Still digging."

"Okay. Let me know when you get those obits."

When she ended the call, Hannah was staring at her. "Don't you have enough going on right now?"

Carlotta bit into her lip, then sighed. "Apparently not."

CHAPTER TWENTY-THREE

UNDER THE TABLE IN THE APD INTERVIEW ROOM, Wesley's leg jumped as if he were high, but this time there was no Oxy coursing through his system—just pure, white-hot fear. He noticed a ragged edge on his thumbnail and bit it off. Too late, he realized he'd bitten it down to the quick. His thumb began to throb. Between this interview and having to face Meg afterward, he'd be down to the knuckle soon.

"Relax," Liz said, pushing his hand away from his mouth. "Even if they can prove you mailed in the note with the victim's name, they can't prove you knew anything about his death."

Wes nodded, then couldn't seem to stop bobbing his head. The repetitive movement was calming somehow. Along with the knowledge that Liz was probably going to do everything she could to keep her baby-daddy out of the clink.

The door opened and Jack Terry walked in, all attitude. He was flanked by a suited slender black woman who also wore a badge.

"Hello," Jack said in a brusque tone. "Wes, Liz, this is Detective Salyers. Detective, this is Wesley Wren and his attorney Liz Fischer."

"Wren?" Salyers asked. "Any relation to Carlotta Wren?"

They all turned to look at Salyers.

"I know her from another case," Salyers murmured.

No one seemed surprised.

"She's my sister," Wes supplied.

"Enough of the family tree," Jack said with a frown. "I have to be somewhere, so let's make this quick."

Liz crossed her long legs that looked great encased in sheer hose. "I'm surprised you're here at all, Jack. I heard you were suspended."

A muscle worked in Jack's jaw. "You heard wrong. I'm just taking a few days of vacation. But I thought this was worth coming in on my day off." From an accordion folder, he removed an evidence bag and slid it onto the table. "Look familiar, Wes?"

At the sight of the scrap of paper he'd mailed from Piedmont Hospital along with the envelope he'd sent it in, Wes decided his fingernails could use another trim...the bonus of having his fingers in his mouth was he didn't have to talk.

Liz leaned forward. "It's not familiar to me, Jack. What are we looking at?"

"The APD received this anonymous note a few days ago. On one side it reads 'Decapitated man in county morgue,' and on the other side it reads 'Crosby Newell or maybe Croswell Newton.' And then 'Newt Crossen' with a question mark."

"And what do you make of it?" Liz asked mildly.

"That the person who sent the note was offering up the identity of the headless John Doe in the morgue."

Liz pursed her lips. "Looks like two different handwritings to me."

Jack nodded. "But only one set of prints—Wes's."

"That doesn't mean he sent the note."

"It's a self-sealing envelope, but we can have the stamp checked for DNA." Jack looked at Wes. "Why don't you save the taxpayers some money and just tell us what we already know—that you sent the note."

Wes glanced at Liz and she gave a little nod.

"Okay, I sent the note," he said on an exhale. "But I didn't kill the guy."

"Who did?" Jack asked.

Liz put her hand on Wes's arm. "My client doesn't know."

"He clearly has some knowledge of the crime," Salyers said.

Liz smiled. "Wes occasionally works for the county morgue as a body mover, so he knew about the John Doe. He also knew the body had a tattoo that had been lasered off. He decided to play detective and found someone who thought they recognized the tattoo. Those were the names his source gave him." She glanced back to Jack. "Have you been able to identify the body?"

Jack nodded. "His name is Croswell Newton."

"Ah, so the tip actually helped. The way I see it, instead of treating Wesley like a criminal, you should be giving him some sort of medal."

Jack gave her a flat little smile. "Maybe we will. Especially if he's the anonymous phone tipster."

Wes frowned. "Huh?"

"The anonymous phone tipster who told us he knew who had committed the murder."

Wes's heartbeat began to pound in his head. "I didn't make the call."

"Are you sure? Think about it...because if it *was* you, then I would assume you weren't involved. But if it *wasn't* you, then I might be forced to put you on the suspect list."

Wes's mind raced as he chewed on his nails. If this phone tipster knew who did it, maybe the guy would give the police what they needed, and he'd be off the hook. Because while he'd hate to see Mouse get locked up, at least it wouldn't be because Wes had snitched on him.

"Give me and my client a chance to confer," Liz said.

"I'm not the phone tipster," he blurted. "But I didn't have anything to do with the murder—I swear."

"Okay," Jack said. "Then maybe you can corroborate some of the details the caller gave us."

Wes shrugged. "I'll try."

"He said he has the jacket the perp was wearing when he committed the murder. He said the victim's blood is all over it. Do you know anything about that?

Wes felt faint...it was his jacket, complete with his monogram inside. He could explain that he'd left it in the trunk of Mouse's car and when he'd later tried to retrieve it, had found a severed finger wrapped inside and had thought better. But who would believe that? He gave Liz a panicked look.

"This interview is over," Liz said, pushing to her feet. "My client has told you everything he knows. Come on, Wes, let's get out of here."

"This isn't over," Jack said.

Liz smirked. "Enjoy the rest of your *vacation*, Jack."

Wes followed her out of the interview room, feeling numb. How had things gotten so screwed up?

"Liz, I—"

"I have to find a bathroom."

He knew that look—she was about to hurl. He trotted along behind her and when she rushed into the ladies' room, he stood by the door awkwardly.

"Everything okay here?"

Wes turned his head to see Jack standing there. What an asshole. He jerked his thumb toward the door. "Liz had to go…you know women."

From inside the bathroom came the distinct sound of retching.

"I think she mentioned she's coming down with the flu," Wes said to cover. "You really need some of those hand sanitation stations around here."

Jack frowned. "I'll get right on that. Listen, Wes, if you know who offed the Newton guy and it's one of The Carver's soldiers, you need to tell me. The D.A. didn't put you undercover to be an accessory to murder."

Wes shook his head. "I don't know what you're talking about."

The door opened and Liz emerged, white-faced and sucking on a breath mint.

"You okay?" Jack asked.

She managed a smile. "Too much wine with dinner last night, I guess. Walk me out, Wes? I know you have to get to your community service job."

"Right," he said glumly. He fell in step next to her. "Liz, I—"

"Not a word about anything until we get outside."

He obeyed, miserably keeping up as she *click-clacked* her way through the Midtown precinct on high, pointy heels. Scenarios regarding the headless man raced through his head, and none of them were reassuring. Mouse had once reminded him his blood-stained jacket had been retained as incentive to keep his mouth shut…was Mouse planning to throw him under the bus?

They exited the building under dark, cloudy skies that reflected his mood.

"Now," Liz said. "What do you have to say for yourself?"

"I'm totally innocent."

She gave him a dubious look.

"Okay, I'm mostly innocent."

She closed her eyes briefly. "Oh, Wes, what have you gotten yourself into now?"

"I didn't kill that guy. But I kind of helped to cover up his identity."

She frowned. "How?"

"Um...by pulling the teeth out of his decapitated head."

She brought her hand up to her mouth and swallowed hard.

"But I swear, when I got the head it was already separated from the body."

Her throat convulsed. "I can't deal with this right now. I have back to back appointments all day." She headed toward the entrance, briefcase swinging. "By the way, one of the meetings is with the D.A. and Carlotta."

He frowned. "Carlotta? Why?"

"Allegedly, it's to wrap up The Charmed Killer case. But she asked me to sit in because she's afraid the D.A. will ask about Randolph."

He pulled a hand over his face. "She knows about the baby."

Liz's eyes widened. "You told her?"

"No...it's a long story, but she knows, okay?"

Liz looked as if she were going to be sick—again. "Okay, well, it was bound to come out sooner or later. But the timing seems especially bad with your father being back."

"Did you tell him about the baby?"

"Of course not. Not that I've talked to him lately."

"I thought inmates were allowed to see their lawyers whenever they want to."

"Generally, yes, although there are limits. But..."

"What?"

She wet her lips. "Your father refuses to see me."

Wes frowned. "Has he hired another attorney?"

"No, he says he still wants me to represent him, but he just doesn't want to talk."

He was stunned—and confused. "But where does that leave me...and Carlotta?"

"Frustrated, I know. Be patient. He'll come around, you'll see." She glanced at her watch. "I have to go."

"By the way, you're not drinking, are you?"

"What?"

"You told Jack you might've had too much wine with dinner."

She frowned. "No, Wesley, I'm not drinking. It was the first excuse I could think of." Then she smiled. "But it's nice that you're concerned."

Something warm unfolded in his chest. "Of course I'm concerned. I'm in this, too." He pulled his hand over his mouth. "I'm going to get my life together, I promise. You won't be alone."

Liz looked almost…teary? "Why don't you come over tonight for dinner?"

He'd been planning to cook dinner for Carlotta and try to make up for being a general pain in her ass, but he had new priorities now. He was going to be there for the baby, which meant being there for Liz, too. "Okay…as long as you let me cook."

She smiled and nodded. "Deal."

Wes walked to his bike feeling marginally better about things…but the feeling didn't last long. In fact, by the time he rode up in front of the building that housed Atlanta Security Systems, mockingly referred to as ASS, he was nauseous. Meg would be there and bouncing around as if everything was right with the world, thinking they were a couple and expecting them to go to movies and to the zoo and shit.

He walked into the building and endured the security line and metal detector.

The depressing thing was he *wanted* to go with Meg to the movies and to the zoo and shit.

He stepped onto the elevator with a morose crowd and punched the number for his floor.

But what was done was done.

When the doors opened to his floor, he almost lost his nerve. He could leave and call in sick, and handle this situation with Meg tomorrow. Or tonight, on the phone.

No, a text would do. Yeah…

"This your floor?" a bored, heavyset guy asked.

"Changed my mind," Wes said, then pushed a button to close the doors.

"*There* you are."

A flowered sleeve reached in and the doors bounced back open to reveal Meg Vincent in all her girly, bohemian glory. Her hair was bright and sun-streaked, her skin was tan and glowing, and her smile was like the Aruban sun.

"If you don't go," the guy next to him muttered, "I will."

Wes stumbled out and managed to smile. "Hey."

"I was getting worried about you. I tried to call a couple of times."

"I...had an appointment I couldn't get out of." He walked past her and headed down a hallway toward their work station. "Is McCormick pissed?"

She followed him. "No."

"Are Ravi and Jeff working on the human resources firewall?"

Suddenly he came up short, his head snapping back from the abrupt yank from behind. "Ow!" He contorted to see Meg had a handful of his backpack. "What the hell?"

Her expression was thunderous. "Yes...what the hell? In case you haven't noticed, I've been gone for a while. I missed you...and I kind thought you were missing me."

He'd missed everything about her—the way she wouldn't use a pencil unless it was perfectly sharp, and the way she twirled her hair when she was deep in thought, and the way she sighed into his mouth when he kissed her.

"Things have changed since you left."

She frowned. "What things?"

He glanced around to make sure no one could overhear them. "My father is back."

Her eyes flew wide, then a grin split her face. "But that's great news!"

He nodded, then said, "Except he was taken into custody."

"But you've talked to him, right? And is your mother back too?"

"No...and no." Then he sighed. "Look, I can't really talk about it here."

"Okay...let's have dinner."

His throat ached from wanting to scream *yes*. Instead he said, "I already have plans."

"Okay, how about lunch? Ravi and Jeff will be upset if we ditch them, but—"

"I can't." He hated the little furrow of hurt between her eyes, so he kept talking. "This thing with my dad is taking up all my time because...he asked for my help to prove his innocence."

"Really? That's—wait, I thought you said you hadn't talked to him."

He nodded. "That's...right. But he's been sending me messages...in code."

"How?"

"Uh...through another guy who's in lockup with him...by way of a buddy of mine."

"Wow, that's...wow."

He nodded solemnly. "So you see, I'm too busy for movies and the zoo and shit."

She squinted. "Hm?"

"I don't have time for...you know, dating and stuff. I have more important things to do."

She bobbed her head. "Of course you do. Have you found anything in the database dump that might give you some idea of what the state has against your dad?"

"I'm still going through the files. It's a lot to wade through."

"But I'll help you. We'll do it together."

He shook his head. "I have to do this alone."

"No, you don't." She reached forward to squeeze his arm. "Wes, don't you know?"

"Know what?"

"I love you, silly."

His jaw loosened, allowing his mouth to fall open. Meg was everything in the world he wanted. With her by his side, he could accomplish anything... and he would move heaven and earth to make her happy.

She laughed. "Well? Say something."

He had to stop this train now, tell her another woman was having his baby. Meg would be dismayed and likely would never speak to him again, and it would reinforce everything her father already thought about him. But no matter the consequence, it had to be said. And since his mouth was conveniently open, he pushed out the words.

"I love you, too."

CHAPTER TWENTY-FOUR

CARLOTTA ARRIVED EARLY for the lunchtime meeting with Kelvin Lucas, so she decided to sneak a cigarette to calm her nerves. Since the government building was a nonsmoking facility, she stood under a tree in the parking lot and sucked on the cancer stick until her cheeks went concave.

She really needed to quit smoking.

Later…after her life settled down.

Of course, she might be dead by then from old age.

"I thought that was you," Liz Fischer said, walking up in her Albert Nipon skirt suit and Gucci shoes.

The woman had such a great sense of style, Carlotta almost hated to hate her. "It's me," she said with forced cheer. "Thanks for coming."

Liz nodded, but when the smoke from Carlotta's cigarette drifted in front of her, she waved it away and looked a little green.

Carlotta shifted to shield the smoke, then smirked. "A little afternoon morning sickness?"

Liz pressed her lips together. "Wesley told me you know about the baby."

"Yep."

"I'm sure you're not happy about it."

"Nope."

"I didn't expect this to happen."

"And yet, it did." She turned her head to exhale in the opposite direction— her niece or nephew was going to have enough problems without her second-hand smoke in utero. "How is this supposed to play out, Liz? You must know that Wes can't even take care of himself, much less a child."

"It's not ideal," Liz agreed. "But we'll figure it out. And if you don't mind, I'd like to keep this as quiet as possible, for all our sakes."

"Isn't it against some ethical code to sleep with your client? Oh, but wait—you did that with Randolph already, didn't you? Same song, different instrument."

Liz didn't respond.

"By the way, how is dear old Dad? He must be busy since he hasn't gotten around to sending out that invitation for his children to visit him."

"All I know is he's well. Your father refuses to see even me now."

"Does he know you're pregnant?"

"Of course not."

"Do you know why he's in solitary confinement?'

Liz blinked. "Who told you that?"

"That doesn't matter. Did he do something wrong?"

Liz sighed. "I'm going to tell you, but you can't tell anyone—not Wes, and not Jack."

Carlotta frowned. "I won't tell Wes. And Jack and I don't…share things… anymore."

Liz registered that tidbit with an arched brow, then said, "Apparently, a relative of one of Randolph's clients is housed in USP."

Understanding dawned. "Randolph is in danger."

"The warden thought there was enough of a threat to move your father into solitary confinement for his own protection."

"But he takes meals with this man who might hurt him?"

"There's some kind of disruption in the food service at the prison. I'm told it will be resolved soon and Randolph will take his meals in solitary. Meanwhile, he says he's not ready to talk…to anyone."

Carlotta stooped to snub out her cigarette on a rock. "Randolph is still in control."

"Yes," Liz murmured. "When you care about someone, they have the power to control you."

"Did you hear about Walt Tully?"

"Yes."

"Do you think it has anything to do with Randolph's return?"

"I couldn't say."

A finger of suspicion trailed up Carlotta's neck. Liz couldn't say...or wouldn't say? She studied Liz's cool, detached demeanor. She could see why men were attracted to her—she was gorgeous and as aloof as a cat. It was impossible to pinpoint where her loyalties lay.

Carlotta had the feeling that Liz could play all sides.

She glanced at her watch. "Let's get this interview over with. I need to get back to work."

"How are things at Neiman's?"

"Actually, I'm working the Wedding World Expo this week."

"And how's that?"

"Surrounded by thousands of women planning their happily ever after? Just peachy."

Liz smiled. "You don't ever think of marriage?"

Carlotta squirmed over the personal turn of the conversation. "I guess I haven't ruled it out."

"I gathered you and Peter Ashford had become an item."

"Peter and I have history. But we've decided to take a break until this situation with Randolph is resolved."

"Oh, that's right—he works for Randolph's old firm."

"Yes."

Liz sighed. "The past and the present have a tendency to fold back on each other, don't they?"

So the woman *was* nursing her own demons. When Carlotta had visited the other place where everyone's lives had taken a different path, Valerie suspected Randolph of an affair with Liz there, too. Was the beautiful barracuda of a lawyer destined to have bits and pieces of different men whose hearts belonged to other women?

At the District Attorney's office, they were led to a meeting room to wait for Kelvin Lucas. An administrative assistant offered them bottled water and said Mr. Lucas would be in shortly.

"Lucas likes to make an entrance," Liz offered. "I'll stop the interview if he goes too far, but you don't have to answer anything that makes you feel uncomfortable. This should be routine."

But that didn't keep her pulse from accelerating when Kelvin Lucas, a reptilian man, strode into the room with a young man at his heels. To make matters worse, GBI agents Green and Wick brought up the rear. They smirked at Carlotta, no doubt remembering their last encounter at the city detention center.

Lucas grunted a greeting and made introductions. "This is ADA Finke, Agents Wick and Green of the GBI. Liz, I didn't know you'd be here."

Liz smiled. "I guess that makes us even since we didn't know the GBI would be here."

"The Charmed Killer case is theirs," Lucas said, gesturing for everyone to sit. "Are you representing the entire Wren family now?"

"I'm here in the event Carlotta needs an advisor, that's all."

Lucas's attention shifted to Carlotta. "Ms. Wren's always been able to take care of herself. But I guess she's had to, since her daddy ran out on her when she was still in knee socks."

Anger ignited in her stomach, but she didn't want to rise to his bait. "I don't mean to be rude, but I'm on my lunch break."

"Then let's get to it," Lucas said. "Finke here is going to take notes. Ms. Wren, this interview is to get your version of the events that took place during and around the incident where Dr. Bruce Abrams was taken into custody at your residence. Agents, she's all yours."

She gritted her teeth over the misogynistic tone, but endured Wick and Green's questions about how well she knew Dr. Abrams and what had happened the day he'd attacked her at the townhouse.

"How did he get in to your home?"

"I don't know. I had stopped there to get some clothes. I was on my way out of town, so I was in a hurry. I might've left the door unlocked."

"Where were you attacked?"

"In the kitchen. I was taking aspirin for a headache, and I was struck from behind. As I fell, I hit my head again on the edge of the countertop. I nearly blacked out. I saw it was Abrams and that he had a knife."

"What kind of knife?" Finke asked, scribbling away.

"I…don't remember exactly. It was serrated, I think, maybe eight inches long."

"Then what happened?" Agent Wick prodded.

"I talked to him, tried to stall. He seemed happy to tell me about his plan to frame Cooper Craft by killing all those women."

"Did he say why he wanted to frame Craft?"

"He said he didn't like the way his employees deferred to Cooper. I've heard that when Coop was the chief medical examiner, he was well liked. I guess Abrams felt as if they respected Coop's opinion more than his."

"Did Abrams mention why he used charms as his signature?" Green asked.

"He said he got the idea when he saw Shawna Whitt's charm bracelet."

"Shawna Whitt was one of the victims."

"Yes."

"And did he indicate why he wanted to kill you?"

She swallowed hard. "He said I had caused too much trouble, and I got the feeling he thought my death would hurt Coop."

"Because you and Craft have a relationship?"

"I work with Coop sometimes as a body hauler."

"And that's all?"

"We're good friends, but Coop and I have never had a romantic relationship, if that's what you're getting at."

"Back to the attack," Wick said. "What happened next?"

"Abrams was holding a knife to my throat. I was screaming for help, and suddenly someone came through the front door. It distracted Abrams and I pulled away, but he sliced my shoulder." She touched her arm and smoothed a hand over the bandaged area. "Then I heard a shot, and when I turned around, Abrams was lying on the floor bleeding."

"And who fired the shot?"

Carlotta shifted in her chair. "My father, Randolph Wren."

"And when was the last time you saw your father?" Lucas asked mildly, as if he were trying to slip the question into the flow of the conversation.

She glanced at Liz, who sat forward.

"I don't see how that's relevant to this case."

"It's relevant if Ms. Wren had an expectation that her father would come and save her life."

"I didn't," Carlotta said with a frown. "No one was more surprised to see Randolph than I was."

Lucas scoffed. "So did your fugitive father explain how he just happened to be strolling by when you were being attacked by a serial killer?"

"No."

"What *did* he say?"

"We didn't exactly have time to chat. Detective Terry arrived and placed him under arrest."

Lucas crossed his arms in slow motion and settled a heavy-browed scowl on her. "So how do you think your father knew you were in danger?"

Liz made a noise of protest. "Carlotta can't be expected to know what her father was thinking or doing. Why aren't you asking Randolph yourself?" When he didn't respond, Liz angled her head. "The feds aren't letting you near him, are they?"

Lucas's face flushed to burgundy, but he kept his cool. After a slow blink, he said, "I'm merely asking Ms. Wren to speculate. Her father was never there for her before—he didn't even show up for her funeral."

"My fake funeral," Carlotta said through gritted teeth. And Randolph had been there, in disguise. She longed to throw that info in Lucas's toady face, but exercised restraint.

"He didn't know that," Lucas said. "Unless you and your brother have been lying and you've been communicating with your father all along."

"We haven't," Carlotta said evenly. Not knowingly. She wasn't about to mention the listening device they'd found in the kitchen, or that her father had said he was keeping tabs on them.

"Because if you *have* been communicating with your father," Lucas said, as if she hadn't spoken, "now's the time to come clean in order to avoid aiding and abetting charges."

Sheer loathing pumped through her veins. "We. Haven't."

"Then help me out, Ms. Wren. What would explain your father's uncanny sense of timing to show up at precisely the right moment to save your life?"

Carlotta lifted her shoulders in an exaggerated shrug. "The Charmed Killer was national news, and if you recall, Agents Wick and Green—" She smirked in their direction. "—even named Randolph as a suspect. Maybe he decided to come back and keep an eye on things."

"Lucky for you," Lucas said.

"Yes, wasn't it?" Carlotta pushed back from the table and stood. "Gentlemen, I've told you everything I know. I need to get back to work. The taxpayers aren't paying *my* salary."

She walked out of the room, and Liz followed.

"I think Lucas was right," the blonde said as she stabbed the elevator call button. "You didn't need me in there."

"It helped," Carlotta said grudgingly.

"It helped me, too. No wonder Lucas is chomping at the bit—the feds are keeping him out of the loop. He's trying to get his information sideways."

"Why wouldn't law enforcement be working together?"

Liz gave a harsh laugh. "It's all territorial. The big cases draw a lot of media attention. A lot of media attention means bigger budgets and promotions. You can bet the feds are going to get their meat and toss the scraps to Lucas, if there are any left."

"But why is it taking so long?"

Liz hesitated until the elevator doors opened. "My guess? They're making Randolph sweat, letting him see what life is like in a federal pen."

Carlotta chewed on the inside of her cheek as they rode down with a small knot of people. What did it say about her that she was okay with Randolph suffering a little for all he'd put them through? She wouldn't wish anything terrible on him, of course, but bland food, a narrow cot, and a stainless steel toilet seat might shrink his ego down to size.

She and Liz exited the building together. "Thanks again for coming, Liz."

Liz inclined her head. "Glad to help."

Carlotta pressed her lips together, conscious of the fact that this woman was going to be part of their family—whatever that might look like when the dust settled. She opened her mouth to extend an olive branch, but Liz's phone rang and she waved goodbye, connecting the call as she strode across the parking lot.

Whew, saved by the bell.

In profile, the whip-slim Liz was definitely sporting a little tummy pooch. As Carlotta watched her, Liz set her briefcase inside her car, then, still talking into her phone, her free hand moved to caress her stomach.

The gesture was so offhand and gentle, Carlotta was struck with a sense of wonder. She knew in that moment Liz was going to handle motherhood like she handled everything else—in stride, and with no apologies.

And then another sensation, this one more alien, curled deep in her own abdomen, an ages-old primitive pull that caught Carlotta by surprise.

Envy?

The conversation she'd had with Jack about children came back to her. She loved Wes dearly, but she well remembered the difficult times of raising him alone—the times when he'd cried and she'd cried along with him because she couldn't fix whatever ailed him. She'd nursed him through skinned knees and near-sightedness, chicken pox and puberty, all while trying to banish the sadness and feelings of neglect that lingered after their parents had left.

She'd always told herself that her mothering was done…but she realized now that her view of parenting had been skewed—both because her parents had been lousy at it and because it had been forced upon her.

But having a child of her own…

She gave herself a mental shake at the wildly premature thought—before she did the baby thing, she really needed to get the man thing right.

Which reminded her: The *Your Perfect Man* booth beckoned.

CHAPTER TWENTY-FIVE

MONDAY AFTERNOON, THE FIFTH DAY of the Wedding World Expo, was decidedly slow, Carlotta observed.

Security was soft—she was able to walk in the "employees only" show entrance without even flashing her lanyard. After the frantic foot traffic of the weekend, the booths and decorations were looking a little tired and picked over—balloons drooped and bunting sagged. And the workers themselves were looking a bit done in—smiles had faded and eye contact was dodgy. For the most part, everyone seemed to be using the time to clean, straighten, and resupply their stock for the show finale on Wednesday. To draw customers in on the last day, most booths would be giving away prizes and the runway area would be busy with back to back entertainment.

Melissa Friedman, the director of the show, seemed to sense the lull in enthusiasm because she was walking around in her pink pantsuit like a one-woman cheerleading squad trying to rally the team for the last quarter of the game.

"Great show!" She clapped her hands and pumped her fist in the air. "Great show, everyone! Keep it up!"

Carlotta appreciated the effort, but she, too, was suffering from vendor fatigue.

"There you are," Patricia said when Carlotta walked up the booth. "I was getting worried."

"Sorry," Carlotta said. "My meeting took a little longer than I thought."

"You didn't miss anything, it's dead around here."

"Still, thanks for holding down the fort. How's Leo dealing with the loss of his friend?"

"He's devastated. And he feels so guilty."

Carlotta frowned. "Why?"

Patricia glanced around as if she were afraid someone would overhear her. "He thinks his buddy might have been taking a little, um, sex booster to keep up with his fiancé...and his girlfriend."

"Oh. And Leo thinks his friend might have overtaxed his heart?"

"Right. And Leo feels awkward around Jeffrey's fiancé. I told him not to tell her."

"You don't think she knows?"

"That's the point—I do think she knows. I mean, don't you think most women know when their man is stepping out?"

The way she asked the question gave Carlotta the sense there was something driving it. "I believe a woman's intuition is generally strong—and accurate. Is everything okay between you and Leo?"

Patricia rubbed her thumb over her engagement ring. "Just a rough patch, I guess, first the blip with his daughter, and now this."

"Relationships are complicated. But it speaks well of Leo that he and his ex are on good terms."

"Actually, I give Kaitlin most of the credit for that. Leo says she has obsessive-compulsive issues, but I admire the way she tries to do everything just right."

Rather unconsciously, Carlotta was sure, Patricia smoothed a hand over her perfect bob. She wondered if Patricia saw a little of herself in Leo's ex... and perhaps feared the woman's present situation as Leo's ex-wife would be her future situation?

"They were probably opposites in a lot of ways," Carlotta offered.

"She hated that he dipped snuff." Patricia made a face. "I kind of hate it, too."

Carlotta understood, but since she sneaked cigarettes, it didn't seem fair to pile on. "I'll give you some advice a wise older man once gave me. He said an engagement ring is just something nice to wear while you make up your mind."

Patricia curled her hand over her engagement ring as if she were protecting it. "But I made up my mind when I told Leo yes."

"I think what he meant is an engagement is a time when you try each other on for size before you make a legal commitment. I'm sorry you and Leo are going through all of this," she added gently, "but isn't it better to go through it now to see how you interact rather than after you're married?"

Patricia pulled back in a defensive posture. "What do *you* know about being engaged or being married?"

She balked. "I…not much, I suppose."

"Well, don't give up hope, Carlotta. Maybe Peter will change his mind."

Carlotta's mouth twitched to say she could marry Peter anytime she wanted to…but in hindsight, Peter hadn't put up much resistance when she'd suggested they not see each other for a while. And what would happen if Randolph was tried and convicted?

"By the way," Patricia added, "Jarold Jett was here a few minutes ago asking for you or that detective."

"Did he say what he wanted?"

"No. But he seemed kind of upset."

"Do you know where I can find him?"

"He said something about the mattress booth. Everything's fine here if you want to check in with him." She turned her back as if Carlotta had already left.

Carlotta decided to let the woman stew—she had a feeling she'd touched a nerve earlier.

After consulting the Expo app on her phone to find the mattress booth location, she headed in the general direction. On the way, she spotted Hannah getting a cup of coffee. She was hard to miss, standing over six feet tall in heels and topknot. Carlotta took a moment to marvel over her statuesque beauty… and her dual personality. Carlotta held back to make sure Hannah was alone since her friend had made it clear she didn't want Carlotta talking to her family members—apparently she didn't intend for her two worlds to overlap. Carlotta pushed down the resentment and waved to get Hannah's attention.

"Oh, thank God," Hannah said. "Someone sane. I feel like I'm in *Groundhog Day* and this show will never end."

"We're in the home stretch," Carlotta said with a laugh.

"Want a coffee?"

"I'm good, thanks."

Hannah sipped from her cup. "Where are you headed?"

"I have a wedding gown designer in crisis. Want to come with?"

"Will you need some muscle?"

"Maybe."

"I don't have anything better to do."

Carlotta led the way. "When do you move into your new apartment?"

"Not soon enough."

"Trouble at home?" Carlotta asked sweetly.

"Chance is being a big baby, don't get me started. So, what did you do with the info we got from Greg Pena's neighbor?"

"Nothing yet. Everyone thinks I'm being an alarmist. And maybe I am."

"How are things with Wes?"

"Evolving. We're both...stressed."

"No word from your father?"

"No. And honestly, I don't know what to do."

"Isn't the next move up to him?"

"I guess so. I just feel so...powerless." She blinked back sudden moisture. "I'm just tired of waiting for my father to acknowledge me."

Hannah looked pained.

Carlotta inhaled to gather herself, then tried to smile. "Sorry—didn't mean to get all emotional on you."

"It's fine," Hannah murmured, although she looked unnerved, as if she were out of her depth. "So *this* is where the crowd is."

Carlotta looked ahead to see the sign for a well-known local mattress company. Peachy Mattresses had one of the largest booths in the exhibit, hoping to sell lots of marital beds. "No wonder Jarold is a little freaked out."

"Hm?"

"The designer—he has a problem with crowds."

She didn't see Jarold, but assumed he was inside the booth. As she threaded her way through the throng of people, she noticed a camera crew. When she reached the front, she saw lenses and lights focused on the set of an elaborate bedroom, complete with sparking chandelier overhead. But the feature was a bare white mattress and pillow. Dressed in a black tuxedo, Jarold Jett was evidently filming a commercial.

She saw Edward standing nearby and worked her way over to him. "What's this?"

He rolled his eyes. "Diva time."

Indeed, from the body language of the crew, things weren't going well.

"Quiet please!" a guy yelled in a bored voice. "Commercial for Peachy Mattresses, take seventeen." He turned back to the set and held up cue cards.

Jarold looked into the camera and gave a watery smile as he walked toward the bed. "When it comes to the mattress I sleep on, I won't settle for anything less than a ten."

It was a takeoff of the way he scored aspiring designers on his popular television show—on a scale of one to ten. And the notoriously cranky designer was famous for never awarding a ten.

"He looks tense," Hannah whispered, and Carlotta agreed. The man's forehead was shiny with sweat, his movements were stiff, and his voice sounded unnatural.

He sat on the bed awkwardly, then reclined on the pillow and pulled a large placard from his jacket with the number ten written on it. "Peachtree Mattresses gets a perfect score."

"Cut!" the man in the crew yelled, obviously the director. He looked heavenward as if he were summoning patience from a higher source. "Mr. Jett, it's *Peachy* Mattresses. Peachy as in peachy keen, got it?"

Jarold set up, glowering. "How am I supposed to work with all these people around?"

"I can't watch this," Edward said. "See you later."

Jarold spotted Carlotta and waved frantically. "Carlotta, come here, please."

"Take five, everyone," the director yelled.

Nia, Jarold's personal assistant, her brown ponytail sagging, was standing guard at the booth entrance. She pivoted to allow Carlotta inside.

Jarold pushed himself up from the bed, and strode over to meet her. "Where is that detective?"

"You mean Jack Terry?"

"I suppose," the man said with a dismissive wave. "I've called him numerous times."

"It's not like Jack to be late."

He mopped a handkerchief across his brow. "My idiot assistant forgot to put this commercial shoot on my schedule." He shot lasers at Nia, who shrunk from his gaze. "I didn't know about it myself until an hour ago."

"Oh. Well, Jack must've had another commitment. Can I help with something?"

"Can you get rid of some of these people? I'm feeling quite anxious today."

"I'll see what I can do."

"You can leave, too," he barked in Nia's direction.

Carlotta gave the girl a sympathetic look when she reached her. "He must be a handful."

She gave a curt nod. "I'll help you try to disperse the crowd."

"Maybe if we just ask everyone to move back a few feet, he won't feel so claustrophobic." She recruited Hannah's help and soon they established a wider boundary around the booth.

The director resumed his place by the camera. "Quiet, please! Commercial for Peachy Mattresses, take eighteen."

Jarold smiled into the camera and walked toward the bed. "When it comes to the mattress I sleep on, I won't settle for anything less than a ten."

He sat on the bed, then reclined on the pillow and pulled the card from his jacket. "Peachy Keen Mattresses gets a perfect score."

"Cut!" the director yelled. "It's not Peachy Keen Mattresses—it's Peachy, by itself. Peachy Mattresses!"

Jarold sprang up from the bed. "This is absurd!"

A whooshing noise sounded, then a terrific crash of glass. The crowd gasped, including Carlotta, who wasn't sure what had happened.

Jarold Jett had scrambled from the set, away from the noise. Carlotta rushed forward to see the chandelier hanging over the bed had plummeted straight down. And from the splintered glass and how deeply it had imbedded in the mattress where Jarold had been lying only seconds earlier, it was clear he had escaped serious physical harm.

"Jesus," Hannah muttered to Carlotta. "He was almost human hamburger."

The director took control of the situation, clearing the set area. "Watch the glass, everyone, watch the glass."

Jarold Jett was reduced to wide-eyed silence as he stared at the impaled mattress. Carlotta touched his arm and guided him away from the scene. "Are you okay, sir?"

He nodded, shaking shards from his clothing. He searched the crowd. "Nia?"

"I'm here," the woman said, emerging to take over. "Let's get you to a chair."

Carlotta and Hannah helped to wave back the growing swarm of people trying to get a look. When security officers and Melissa Friedman arrived, they slipped away, but instead of heading back to their booths, Carlotta jerked her thumb toward the back of the booth. "Let's go this way."

"Why?"

"Humor me."

They walked around the outside perimeter of the booth built from sturdy walls that were ten feet tall. Because it was so large, the structure was free-standing, with no other booths adjacent to it. Situated in the area behind the booth was a series of wedge-shaped supports to shore up the walls, and multiple outlet boxes to supply electricity to lights and displays. Carlotta picked her way over the hardware until she estimated they were standing behind the commercial set. A large square weight sat on the floor, and from the closed metal loop on top dangled the end of a thick rope that had been secured with a complicated series of knots.

"This must be where the chandelier was attached," Carlotta said, then pointed up. "The rope was looped over those two bars to allow it to hang down into the set."

Hannah picked up the end of the rope. "A lot of good these knots did. Looks like the rope frayed here, past the knots."

Carlotta brought the rope closer for a better look.

"And what do you think you're doing?"

At the sound of a man's voice, Carlotta turned, half-pleased, half-irritated to see Jack making his way toward them. Their last conversation was still stuck in her mind, like a thorn.

"Exploring," she said innocently. "When did you get here?"

"Just now. Jett told me what happened. Were you there?"

"Yes. He was almost killed."

"I kind of got that from seeing the mutilated bed." He stopped next to them, then looked at Hannah. "Sorry—do I know you?"

Carlotta bit back a smile.

"It's me, Detective Dickhead."

His eyebrows spiked. "Hannah?"

"You seriously need to brush up on your observation skills."

He frowned, then indicated the bulky weight at their feet. "I *observe* this is where the chandelier was tied off."

"Looks like it," Carlotta said, handing the end of the rope to Jack. "But that's a pretty clean break for wear and tear, don't you think?"

He studied the broken strands. "Did you see anyone back here?"

"No. But we weren't exactly paying attention."

"That girl," Hannah said. "The one who works for Mr. Fancy Pants—she disappeared for a while."

"Nia," Carlotta confirmed to Jack. "Jarold yelled at her to leave."

"She was with Jett when I got here," Jack said.

"She came back after the incident." Carlotta snapped her fingers. "And Jarold said she forgot to put the commercial shoot on his schedule. Is that why you weren't here?"

He nodded.

"Maybe she left it off the schedule on purpose so you wouldn't be here."

"So she could drop a chandelier on Jett?" Jack scoffed. "I can see why she'd want to, but that's reaching, even for you."

"There's another possibility."

Jack sighed the sigh of a long-suffering man. "I'm going to hate myself for asking, but what is it?"

"Jarold Jett is engaged…maybe he's being targeted by the Groom Slayer."

"Did you just make that up?" Hannah asked.

"I did."

"Not bad. Kind of catchy."

Jack pinched the bridge of his nose. "I was right…I hate myself."

"Jack—"

"Carlotta, stop this nonsense! This was just what it looks like—a freak accident." He put his hands on his hips. "Now, don't you ladies have somewhere to be?"

Carlotta frowned. "Come on, Hannah."

Hannah grumbled as they stepped over and around obstacles to get out. "I think you were brilliant. He's such an asshole, I don't know what you see in him. He must be hung like an elephant."

Carlotta let her friend rant, nursing her own bruises over Jack's dismissive behavior. After all they'd been through, he continued to regard her as a nuisance.

But when she reached the end of the wall and looked back, the vexing man was using his phone to take a picture of the end of the rope. Carlotta smiled to herself.

Plus ten points, Jack.

CHAPTER TWENTY-SIX

TRAFFIC WAS MORE BRISK at the Wedding World Expo on Tuesday thanks to charter busloads of brides streaming in from Birmingham, Charlotte, and Nashville. Savvy trip guides had packaged a two-day experience called Wedding & Whales. For one price, women received admission to the Expo and the Georgia Aquarium.

It appeared most of the bride tourists were saving the belugas for tomorrow.

Carlotta was glad for the increased business because it kept her and Patricia from stepping on each other's toes. She didn't see Jack all day, and resisted the urge to call him and ask about yesterday's chandelier incident. Likewise, he obviously didn't feel the need to call and give her an update.

Peter had called a couple of times with news about Walt Tully, whose condition continued to slowly improve. And to suggest they sneak away Friday night to have dinner outside of town where they would be less likely to run into anyone who knew them. She had agreed, and conceded to herself that she was looking forward to seeing him.

She was lonely.

Wes didn't seem to be angry with her anymore, but he had become so withdrawn, she was seriously worried about him. When she'd asked if he'd talked to Meg since her return, he had looked as if he were going to cry and retreated to his room. Her heart ached for him—in love with one woman, and having a baby with another. But she also wanted to shake him for being so careless. One dumb decision would affect a lot of people's lives.

At the end of the day she walked out with Hannah, who was also growing wedding-weary. "One more day of this crapfest and I get my life back."

"If that's what you want."

Hannah stopped. "Don't tell me you like me better like this."

"Of course not. I like you whichever way you want to be. I just don't understand the extremes...and the secrecy."

"It's hard to explain," Hannah said, suddenly flustered. "Do you want to grab a drink?"

"I'm sorry—I have to be somewhere."

"Oh, okay. Need a ride?"

"No, I drove the rental. But thanks."

"See you tomorrow."

Carlotta nursed a pang of remorse as she watched her friend stride away. It seemed as if Hannah had been on the verge of confiding something...or maybe not. Maybe there was no explanation for her behavior beyond the fact that Hannah felt different from the rest of her family and dressing Goth-style gave her an outlet for her quirky personality.

Still, Carlotta felt guilty as she climbed into her car because if Hannah knew where she was going, no way could she shake her.

The Fulton County morgue looked more like an elementary school than a repository for dead bodies. Most people who drove by it didn't even know how close they'd come to death.

She parked in the visitor's lot and entered through the front door, remembering the first time she'd come to this place, under duress. She'd accompanied her friend Jolie Goodman to identify the body of her boyfriend, Gary Hagan. It had been as horrific as Carlotta had imagined it would be, offending every girly sensibility she had. Which made it all the more incredulous that she'd become a body mover.

The desk clerk greeted her by name. "Don't see you coming in the front door much."

"True enough. Is Coop around?"

The woman smiled. "For you? I'm sure he is. Let me see what floor he's on." She picked up the phone and pressed a couple of buttons, talked briefly into the mouthpiece, then set it down. "Second floor lab. He's expecting you."

Carlotta thanked her and took the stairs, chiding herself for being nervous about seeing Coop. Sure they hadn't spent much time together lately—Coop had been away from the morgue and from body-moving for a while during The Charmed Killer murders—but he'd been a good friend to her and to Wes, and she missed seeing him. More than that, though, she didn't like the wall he'd put up between them.

She pushed open the door to the laboratory and saw Coop standing next to a sink, washing his hands. He looked just as much at ease in a white lab coat as he had in the elegant jacket at the art gallery—tall and lean and handsome.

He smiled. "This is a nice surprise." He shrugged out of the lab coat and hung it on a peg.

"Are you on your way out?"

"I have a few minutes. To what do I owe the honor?"

She handed him a gift bag. "Happy birthday."

He seemed genuinely pleased. "You shouldn't have. Can I open it?"

"Sure."

He reached inside and pulled out a blue folded item about the size of an umbrella.

"It's a kite," she supplied.

"And a nice one, I see. Five foot wing span, counterweighted." He grinned. "I can't wait to take it to Piedmont Park. Thank you."

He stepped forward to hug her, and his embrace was like a moor in a storm. Coop was warm and solid and comforting because he didn't expect anything from her. The contact lingered longer than it should have, but it seemed as if both of them had left things unsaid, and wanted to make the most of this opportunity. Coop broke their contact first.

He stepped back. "Sorry—I shouldn't have done that. Did I hurt your shoulder?"

"No." She smoothed her hand over the area. "It's healing well."

"Good," he said, but his expression was still guilt-ridden. "I can't tell you how sorry I am about what Abrams put you through."

"It wasn't your fault, Coop. Besides, he put you through a lot, too. He's an evil man, and he'll be locked up for the rest of his life. I sat down with the D.A. yesterday to give my statement."

"Since Abrams signed a confession, hopefully everyone will be spared a trial."

"That's what Jack said."

"Speaking of, I just talked to Jack."

"Oh?"

Coop walked over to a printer and removed a report of some kind. "I have a present for you, too. That wad of gum you gave me from the young man who collapsed at the Expo tested positive for anticoagulant rodenticide."

She frowned. "What's that?"

"Rat poison."

Her pulse bumped higher. "You're saying Jeremy Atwater was murdered?"

"I'm saying he was poisoned. Rat poison is common, so it pops up in a lot of strange places, like in people's homes and schools and restaurants and public toilets." He spread his hands. "For all we know, Jeremy dropped his gum in it and put the gum back in his mouth."

"*Ew.*"

"But it's suspicious, so I called Jack, to tell him the case needs to be reopened."

"And what was his reaction?"

Coop gave a little laugh. "He was pretty upset that you and I, as he put it, had gone behind his back. But he also admitted you were suspicious from the beginning, and he'd written it off."

"So you're going to take another look at Jeremy's body?"

"Yes."

"And Greg Pena's?"

Coop frowned. "What does he have to do with it?"

"What if he was poisoned, too? He was having an affair with the neighbor, by the way, the lady who found his body."

"The dog sitter?"

"Right. I found one of her fingernails in his bed." She rummaged in her purse and came up with a tiny plastic bag that held the wayward fingernail.

Coop pursed his mouth and reached for the bag. "And when was this little fact-finding mission?"

Carlotta lifted her chin. "Sunday evening. Hannah's interested in renting the apartment, so she and I went back to look around."

"Uh-huh. I take it Jack doesn't know about this?"

"Can it be our secret until you take another look at Greg Pena's body?"

"Unfortunately not…because I identified another possible victim who died prior to Jeremy Atwater."

"You did?"

He nodded, then reached for a clipboard and thumbed back a few pages. "Simon Markhall, African-American male age twenty-eight died suddenly in his home." He pointed to a wall calendar and counted back. "Six days before Jeremy Atwater."

"Was he poisoned, too?"

"Looks that way. The guy was overweight and had a big last meal, so I'm still going through the stomach contents."

She made a face. "What made you suspicious?"

"Unexplained death in the young always bothers me, but there was something else on his profile that jumped out at me."

"What was that?"

"He was engaged to be married."

Carlotta's jaw dropped. "Really?"

"But wait, there's more," he said in the voice of an infomercial spokesman. "Remember our shooting victims in front of the Clermont?"

"Of course."

"We identified them as Grant Monk, and Timothy Chin, and you were right—one of the men, Grant Monk, was about to be married."

"But they were shot, not poisoned."

"Yes, they were shot, but maybe as a backup. Both men had vomited."

"I remember the smell."

"So I tested the throw-up."

"And?"

"Grant Monk had been poisoned. Throwing up probably saved his life until he was shot."

"But not the other victim?"

"Right, no poison. But I found defensive wounds on his hands, so he might have been shot simply because he put up a fight."

She gasped. "So someone really is targeting grooms?"

"I didn't say that. But it's a strange coincidence shared by five victims that we know of that I'm willing to pursue further. So I'll be reexamining Greg Pena's body, too."

"And Jack knows all of this?"

He nodded. "He mumbled something about "Groom Slayer" and now he'd never hear the end of it?"

The smile she swallowed went down like a happy little bubble. "Can you add another name to the list?"

He looked surprised. "Sure."

"Jeffrey Oxblood. He died Sunday, collapsed while he was running."

"That name sounds familiar. The body might be here. Another groom?"

"About to be."

"Wow. Okay, I'll look into it."

"Thank you, Coop." Impulsively, she reached up to kiss him on the mouth. He seemed surprised, but kissed her back.

It was a good kiss.

At the sound of someone clearing their throat, they parted to see Rainie Stephens standing there, giving them both an amused look.

"Rainie, hi," Coop said. "Carlotta was just…"

"Wishing Coop happy birthday," Carlotta supplied.

"Right," Coop said, nodding.

Rainie looked dubious, but kept smiling. "I didn't know you'd be here, Carlotta, but I have something for you." She reached into her bag and pulled out a thick report. "Obituaries of all the single men in the metro area who died in the past thirty days."

Coop gave Carlotta an exasperated look, then turned back to Rainie. "I'll take that."

Rainie didn't ask questions, just handed him the report. "Ready to go?"

"Yes." He walked to the coat rack, removed the fedora Carlotta had helped Rainie pick out and set it on his head. He wore it well. "Carlotta, we're going out to get a bite to eat, want to join us?"

"Yes, join us," Rainie added.

Carlotta could tell the pretty redhead didn't mind if she tagged along, but Carlotta she didn't want to intrude, didn't want to impede anything that might be developing between the couple. "Thanks, but I need to get home."

Her phone rang. Carlotta retrieved it to see Sammy Sanders was calling. "I need to get this. Do you mind if I stay and take it in here?"

"Close the door when you leave," Coop said.

She gave them a little wave, and connected the call. "Hi, Sammy."

"Hi, Carlotta. I have some information for you on the house next door, but I don't know that it's going to be helpful."

She'd forgotten she'd asked Sammy for info on the owner. After talking to the photographer renting the house, her suspicions now seemed silly. But she felt obligated to feign interest since Sammy had gone to the trouble. "What did you find out?"

"The deed is recorded to a business called Property Group Holdings. The mailing address is Virginia, but that's where the trail goes cold. I can't locate a phone number or email address, and it's not a registered corporation. But if you're interested in making an offer, I can send a letter of inquiry to the address of record."

"That's okay, Sammy. Thanks anyway."

"If you're interested in looking at other properties, I'd be happy to show you some nice homes. Interest rates are terrific right now."

Not for people with her credit rating. "I'll keep that in mind. Meanwhile, where shall I send the Neiman's coupon I mentioned?"

"You can send it to my house...I think you know the address."

Carlotta smirked—a reminder of the time she'd crashed a pajama party at Sammy's home which had ended with Carlotta being arrested for murder. "Um...yes, I remember."

"Good. Sorry about the house next door, but if it's any consolation, it's probably not worth your trouble anyway."

"What do you mean?"

"In my experience, those generic property holding companies in Virginia are almost always government related and a real hassle to deal with. Bye, now."

"Bye, Sammy." Carlotta ended the call, her mind racing. Government related?

Minus ten points.

CHAPTER TWENTY-SEVEN

"HOW'S IT GOING at your community service job?" E. Jones asked.

Wes lifted his hand to his mouth and chewed on a straggly piece of skin. It was torture. For the past two days he'd had to endure Meg's sunny optimism, snug jeans, and spontaneous declarations of affection. And now that she'd confessed her feelings for him, she didn't care who knew. Ravi and Jeff sent daggers of loathing at him when Meg wasn't looking.

He knew how they felt—he loathed himself, too. After receiving a full-body kiss goodbye from Meg Monday, he'd gone to Liz's and cooked dinner for the two of them. He'd tried to put Meg out of his mind, but the dreamy look on Liz's face when she talked about the baby made his stomach hurt and the goodbye kiss had been the place he'd escaped to in his mind. Yesterday he'd made vague excuses not to spend the evening with Meg, but in a weak moment today, he'd agreed to come by her dorm later, with the implied understanding he'd sneak into her room and they'd make out. Just the thought of it made his balls tingle.

He was in such deep shit.

"It's going great," he said.

"Good," E. said, although she was staring at his hands.

He cracked his knuckles casually, then tucked his hands under his legs so he wouldn't be tempted to bite his nails.

"Have you talked to your father?"

"Not yet, but soon."

"I'm sure you'll have a lot to talk about."

Including the fact that he'd gotten his father's mistress pregnant. He pulled his hand out from under his leg and found another jagged piece of nail to bite off.

"Have you been staying out of trouble? No drugs, no gambling?"

"Right. You can take my blood if you want."

She studied him for a few seconds, then shook her head. "Not today. That's all."

He jumped to his feet and headed for the door.

"Wesley?"

He turned back. "Yeah?"

"Your father will be proud of you for taking responsibility for your actions."

Wes swallowed hard and walked out the door. He had so many problems, his problems had problems.

And when he walked out of the building and unlocked his bike, one of his problems pulled up next to him in a black Town Car.

"Hey, Little Man."

He bit back a groan. "I thought we weren't going to collect today."

"Change of plans," Mouse said, then popped the trunk. "Get in. I got a surprise for you."

Wes felt the sweat pop out of his pores as he walked his bike to the back of the car. Did Mouse know he was working undercover for the D.A.? Was he going to work him over, beat a confession out of him? Or worse?

"And grab the driver," Mouse added.

Wes stared at the golf club, wondering if it was intended for *his* head today. He stowed his bike, then pulled out the club and trudged to the passenger side.

When he swung inside, he was afraid to make eye contact with Mouse, so he just stared straight ahead. "Where are we going?"

"You'll see."

Wes slumped in his seat and watched the passing scenery. Mouse steered the car onto Peachtree Street and drove north.

"Have you heard from your old man?"

Wes shook his head.

"You got a mother?"

"Yeah. She left with my dad." He brought his hand to his mouth to trim the uneven bits of nail he had left.

"Where is she now?"

He shrugged. "Dunno."

"Your sister raised you?"

It occurred to him that if Mouse felt sorry for him, he might not kill him. "Yeah. It was rough."

"Yeah, lots of people have it rough."

He sagged. So much for sympathy.

The traffic of downtown gave way to Midtown, then Buckhead, then the perimeter, and still they headed north.

"Going a little out of our jurisdiction, aren't we?"

"I thought we'd take a little drive."

He was a dead man. Anyone who watched television knew that taking a drive was code for going to an isolated location to be executed. He examined the head of the club, checking the grooves for blood or bits of flesh. "Mouse, I really appreciate all you've done for me."

"Yeah?"

"Yeah. Teaching me the ropes, putting in a good word for me with The Carver, and helping me to get clean."

"You're welcome."

The man seemed unmoved. Wes gave up on his nonexistent nails and picked at his raw cuticles.

"You nervous about something?" Mouse asked.

Wes's stomach cramped. "No."

Mouse seemed unconvinced. "You sure you don't have something you want to tell me?"

"I'm sure." That, at least, was no lie.

They were on Peachtree Industrial now, well north of the city, driving through fits and spurts of old commercial property and residential housing. Mouse chewed on a toothpick, and Wesley chewed on his fingernails.

215

When they reached Norcross, Mouse veered the car left onto Peachtree Parkway into an increasingly residential—and rural—area. Wes couldn't recall ever being this far north.

After a few more miles, he couldn't stand it anymore. "Are you going to tell me the surprise?"

Mouse made a sudden right turn onto a smaller road. "Then it wouldn't be much of a surprise, would it?"

Wes stared at the passing trees and fields and wondered if the look of surprise would be frozen on his face when his body was found. *If* his body was found. There were a few stacked-stone entrances for subdivisions he couldn't see with names that had words like "Estate" and "Colony" in them. He supposed people paid big money to live in big houses with big yards and good schools…and lots of undeveloped countryside in between.

He had to hand it to Mouse—no one would think to look for him way out here in—

"What county are we in?"

"Forsyth, I think."

No one would think to look for him way out here in Forsyth County. He wondered if Meg would raise the alarm when he didn't show up tonight…or if she'd think he'd flaked out, like before.

When Mouse started craning his neck and tapping the brake as if he were looking for a place to pull over, Wes began to panic. At this point, he figured he had nothing to lose. "Mouse…actually, there is something I want to tell you."

"Thought so. Well, might as well get it off your chest."

Wes was going to be sick. "I, um…that is…" He coughed and a bitter taste filled his mouth.

"Spit it out." Mouse slowed the car and flipped on the turn signal.

Wes squeezed the armrest, then noticed where they were turning. "St. Marlo Country Club?"

"Yeah," Mouse said with a big grin. "I thought we'd play a round of golf, just you and me."

"That's the surprise?"

Mouse's grin dissolved. "You don't want to play with me?"

Relief flooded his limbs. "Are you kidding?" He whooped. "Yes, I want to play. This is…this is *great*, Mouse."

Mouse grinned again. "Yeah?"

"Yeah." Then Wes stopped. "But what about clubs?"

"Relax, we'll get everything we need at the golf shop."

"I don't have much cash on me."

"It's all on me, Little Man."

It was perhaps the worst, ugliest game of golf ever played, Wesley decided as they slogged, chopped, and hacked their way through eighteen holes. His swing was awful, and Mouse's was even worse. They trash-talked each other relentlessly. He drove the golf cart while Mouse sucked down a couple of beers. In the essence of time, they set a maximum number of shots per hole. By the time they'd reached the eighteenth green, they'd lost nine balls and both of them were knocking on a score of 140.

Wes couldn't remember ever having so much fun.

"You were actually getting pretty good there toward the end," Mouse said as they left the clubhouse.

"Better maybe, but not good."

"You just need practice. Me, I doubt I'll ever get the hang of it."

"I doubt it, too," Wes said, then ducked a playful punch. It was a far cry from the kind of punishment he thought he was going to get today. When he climbed into the car, he was pleasantly tired, and…happy.

Mouse started the engine. "Say, what was it you wanted to tell me earlier?"

"Huh?"

"You said you wanted to get something off your chest."

He shifted in his seat, his mind racing for a plausible answer. "I…got a woman pregnant."

Mouse winced. "Jeez, no wonder you've been so jumpy. Is this your Meg?"

"No," he said morosely.

"Aw, shit. What's the situation?"

"The woman is older."

"Not married, I hope?"

217

"She's single, and she wants to keep the baby."

"And how do you feel about that?"

"It's her decision. I told her I would help anyway I can."

"Is this someone you care about?"

Wes wet his lips. "It's complicated. She's my attorney."

"Aw, hell."

"And my dad's former mistress."

"Aw, fuck."

Wes sighed. "I know—it's a mess."

"Does Meg know?"

He shook his head. "I haven't had the nerve to tell her yet."

"You gonna call her from the hospital waiting room?"

"No." Although that wasn't a bad idea.

"All I'm saying is you gotta tell her sooner, rather than later."

"She's going to hate me."

Mouse nodded. "Probably so. Women are funny about their guys having kids with other women."

Wes puffed out his cheeks in an exhale. "I don't know what to do."

"Sure, you do. If you want to be a man, you do the hard thing."

"The hard thing?"

"Yeah—the hard thing is usually the right thing. Especially where your kids are concerned."

That gave Wes something to chew on other than his nails. Mouse was right. Carlotta had done the hard thing by sacrificing her twenties to raise him.

So did that mean Randolph had taken the easy way out?

No. His dad had a good reason for leaving...*leaving* had been the hard thing. Somehow.

"But how do you know what the hard thing is?"

Mouse gave him a little smile. "Easy—it's the thing you don't want to do most."

"That's what I was afraid you'd say."

"Welcome to adulthood, Little Man. It sucks for a while...and then it doesn't. You'll see."

"If you say so." He saw the sign for a MARTA station and sat up. "Why don't you drop me at the train? That'll save you time and I won't have to sit in traffic and smell you."

"Okay, smartass."

When Mouse pulled up to the MARTA dropoff, Wes rolled out, then turned back and leaned in. "Mouse...thanks, man. For everything."

"You're welcome. Collections Saturday. I'll call you."

Wes shoved the door closed, then retrieved his bike from the trunk. His mind whirled on the long train ride back into Midtown. He rehearsed what he was going to say to Meg over and over. On the short bike ride from the station to her dorm, he worked up a little irritation—it wasn't as if Meg had been putting out...and they weren't even dating. She couldn't really blame him for being with someone else when she would barely give him the time of day. He was a red-blooded man, after all. And virile, according to Liz.

What did Meg expect him to do—wait for her to decide if and when she might bestow upon him the gift of her uptight self? Did she think she held his balls in her hand?

She had no right to be angry with him for doing what men do...and he'd tell her so.

He called from her dorm lobby while the lady watchdog at the desk eyeballed him warily. "Meg, I'm here."

"Oh, good, you're early. Have you thought of a way to sneak in?"

"Um, maybe you'd better come down first."

"Okay."

As much as he'd psyched himself up, every defense he had constructed evaporated when she bounced off the elevator and into his heart. Her hair was loose around her shoulders, and she wore a yellow onesie-romper thingy that exposed her tanned arms and legs. She'd gotten a henna tattoo on her wrist while on vacation and the colors were still vibrant. Meg smiled wide and opened her arms to invite him into her personal space.

He went. He deserved this, one last hug to inhale the scent of her shampoo and feel her lithe body snug against his. He ran his hands down her back and when the woman at the desk glared at him, he went a few inches lower for a blissful handful. Meg kissed him with her pink berry mouth, then pulled back and frowned.

"Is something wrong?"

"Uh...I need to tell you something."

She smiled. "Okay. What?"

He should ease into it, he decided...tell her how much she meant to him, and he wished he had waited for her because after all, he'd pretty much made a career out of thinking about having sex with her...

She gave a little laugh. "Wes, whatever it is, just tell me. I mean, how bad can it be—"

"I got someone pregnant."

She stopped midsentence, mouth open. He was ready for anything—a slap to the face, a knee to the nuts. Crying, shouting, name-calling. He braced himself.

Instead, her eyes got quiet and faraway. "You'll be a great father," she said softly, then turned and walked back the way she'd come.

He was too stunned to follow her, couldn't even get his breath until the elevator doors had closed. He ran after her, but was stopped by one beefy arm across his chest.

"I don't think so," the dorm monitor said, pointing to a sign that read 'No male visitors past lobby.' "Why don't you just go?"

He nodded and left, still reeling from Meg's response and how it only made him love her more.

And it made him more determined to do the right thing—the hard thing. Now it was clear what he had to do: Ask Liz to marry him.

But if he was going to propose to the mother of his child, he needed a ring, and for that he needed money.

He pulled out his phone and connected a number. "Chance, man, it's Wes. I need a poker game."

CHAPTER TWENTY-EIGHT

JACK SURVEYED THE bedazzled runway and snorted. "Whose idea was it to set up another fashion show after last week's disaster?"

Carlotta gave a little laugh. "It was already on the schedule. But lucky for us it's set up like last week's show so we can recreate the scene of the crime."

"Yes, lucky for us."

"Are you still mad that I was right about someone killing grooms?"

"You seem to have overlooked one very real possibility."

"And that is?"

"The men might have done themselves in rather than walk down the aisle."

"Very funny, Jack. Just because you're allergic to commitment, doesn't mean every man is."

"Says the girl playing Spin the Bottle with three boys in her sandbox."

Her mouth tightened with annoyance, but for the life of her, she couldn't think of a comeback.

"Speaking of your sandbox," he said with a sardonic grin, "what's going on with the photographer next door?"

"I haven't seen him around, but I had a real estate friend look into who owns the house."

"And?"

"And the information was a little vague, but she seemed to think it's owned by the government."

He shrugged. "That's pretty common, with all the foreclosures through federal financing programs and grants for affordable housing."

"I suppose you're right." Leave it to Jack to squash anything remotely intriguing about the situation.

He glanced at his watch. "How was your interview with Lucas Monday?"

"About what I expected. He's irritated because he hasn't gotten to talk to Randolph yet."

Jack pursed his mouth. "Interesting."

"And Liz was…surprisingly helpful."

"See? Liz has some good qualities."

Carlotta burned to tell him that managing birth control wasn't one of them, but bit her tongue. Liz had asked her to keep quiet about the baby and she would, for Wes's sake. Besides, if word got out and Randolph got wind of the situation, it could complicate Liz's ability to represent him.

At least Wesley had seemed to be in a better frame of mind when he'd come home last night. He still didn't want to talk, but he'd given her an unsolicited hug, and that was like gold.

"Wonder what's keeping Salyers?" Jack said, checking the time again.

"I'm here," the woman called from the curtained rear entrance. She walked up and nodded a greeting to Carlotta. "Sorry I'm late. It took me a while to wade through that crowd. Has it been like this all week?"

"Mostly," Carlotta said. "But today is the last day of the show, so it's a little crazy."

"Do you still work at Neiman's, Ms. Wren?"

So Salyers had reviewed her notes from the old case…which did not paint Carlotta in the most favorable light. Her cheeks warmed. "Yes. The Expo is a temporary assignment."

"So trouble follows you around?"

Jack guffawed. "You have no idea."

Carlotta shot him an exasperated look—he was more cranky than usual today.

Salyers glanced at Jack. "I thought you were baby-sitting some hotshot celebrity."

"Jarold Jett. He's lying low for the time being."

"He's a possible target of the Groom Slayer," Carlotta supplied.

Salyers frowned. "Is that what we're calling the UNSUB?"

"No, we are not," Jack said, frowning at Carlotta. "Jarold Jett had a near-miss yesterday, which might not even be related, but we're taking extra precaution."

"The near-miss—that was the chandelier incident?"

Jack nodded. "Jett will be here for the runway show—he's going to emcee. That's why you're here, on the remote chance that something would happen."

"Where is he now?"

"At his hotel. Apparently, something called Twister blew up?"

"He means Twitter," Carlotta said. "The footage of the chandelier falling went viral."

"Yeah, that," Jack said to Salyers, clearly uncaring that he was out of the social media loop.

"His fiancé Sabrina Bauers flew in this morning," Carlotta said, then added, "According to Twitter."

Jack gave a curt nod of confirmation. "She's with him at the hotel. Salyers, I'll show you the scene of the accident later. For now, this is the basic setup of the show where the first victim collapsed."

"Second victim," Carlotta reminded him. "Simon Markhall was probably the first victim."

He scowled. "Coop talks too much."

This probably wasn't the time to mention Coop had confirmed in a text that Jeffrey Oxblood and Greg Pena had both been poisoned. "Coop *communicates*."

Salyers glanced back and forth between them. "Is it going to be like this all day?"

"No," they said in unison.

Salyers raised an eyebrow. "Okay. We have at least six victims, five of whom were poisoned. Since Jeremy Atwater is the only victim who died with an audience, let's start at the top. Where do you think he was most likely poisoned?"

Carlotta opened her mouth, but Jack gave her a warning look. She dipped her chin to defer to him.

"In the tents behind the stage," he said and led the way to the row of temporary structures.

Carlotta held back, sensing Jack was near some sort of breaking point with her. And now that he was on the scent, she knew he wouldn't let up until the case was solved. Plus she had no interest in undermining him in front of his colleague.

"This is where they were getting dressed, the brides in here, the grooms over there. Carlotta was in the tent with the grooms."

"Did you talk to Atwater?" Salyers asked her.

"Yes." She repeated as much of the conversation as she could remember while Salyers scribbled in a notebook. "He was slurring his words, seemed agitated. He also mentioned he was getting married next month."

"Did you see him eat or drink anything?"

"Bottled water. And there was a food cart of donuts and things. Edward had it removed so the guys wouldn't spill something on the suits, but some of them had already eaten from it."

"But no one else got sick."

"Right," Jack said. "That's why we think the poison might have originated in the gum."

Salyers referenced her notes. "Who's Edward?"

"Edward King," Carlotta said. "He's a coworker at Neiman's."

"How many people were back here?"

"A dozen male models, a dozen female models, a few helpers. Edward can get you those names. Plus Jarold Jett was back here, and his assistant."

"No," Jack corrected. "His assistant didn't arrive until the next day."

Carlotta smiled. "Oh, that's right—you had to carry the giant buzzer the first day."

"Don't remind me."

Salyers studied the distance to the stage. "Did the men go straight from the tent to the runway?"

"Yes," Carlotta said. "Around the back. And Jeremy was the first groom in the group to walk out onto the stage."

"Alone?"

"No, he was escorting a female model."

"Did you interview her?" she asked Jack.

He shifted from foot to foot. "No. But Carlotta talked to her."

Salyers looked back to her. "Did she say he'd taken any drugs or mentioned he was feeling ill?"

"No. She said he was flirting before they walked out, then he just fell to the ground."

"Is that when the gum fell out of his mouth?"

"Either then or when the paramedics arrived," Jack said.

Salyers swung her head back to him. "But that's when you collected it?"

He pursed his mouth. "Actually, Carlotta collected the gum."

Salyers looked back to her with a frown. "When?"

"The next morning. I came back in to look around."

"To snoop," Jack corrected.

"It's a good thing for us she did," Salyers said lightly.

Carlotta wanted to enjoy the moment, but a memory chord stirred, trying to push something to the forefront of her mind. Then it clicked. "I just remembered something else I found that morning—a red wig. I didn't think much of it because the models all wore red wigs. But maybe someone wore it to blend in...or as a disguise."

"I don't suppose you kept it, too?" Jack asked dryly.

She shook her head. "But I remember there were a couple of dark hairs mixed in that looked real."

"Anything else, *Hart to Hart*?" Salyers asked.

They both frowned and chorused, "Who?"

Salyers waved her hand. "Never mind. Jack, you said you wanted to show me the scene of the other incident?"

"Right. Carlotta probably needs to get back to work." He gave her a pointed look.

"Yes," she agreed. "Good to see you again, Detective Salyers."

"You, too. Will I see you at the runway show?"

"I'm afraid not. My coworker's boyfriend is one of the celebrities in the show, and I promised her I'd cover the booth so she could attend."

"I understand it's going to be quite the lineup."

Carlotta nodded. "The mayor, some local TV anchors, a couple of radio personalities, some reality show stars—I'm sure it'll be packed. Enjoy."

She gave Jack a little wave and grudgingly left the runway area to return to the main exhibition hall. The decibel level was terrific. As she made her way to the *Your Perfect Man* booth, she tried to catch hold of the happy enthusiasm in the air, but her mind was still cranking the details of the disconnected cases, including the chandelier incident.

"Oh, good, you're back," Patricia said when she stepped into the booth. "I was getting worried. I know there's plenty of time before the runway show starts, but I wanted to freshen up, and help Leo with his tux."

"Of course," Carlotta said. "Leave whenever you need to. Listen, Patricia… if I said something the other day that offended you, I'm sorry. I'm sure you and Leo will be very happy together."

Patricia inclined her head. "That's very nice of you, Carlotta. I'm sure you'll find someone, too. Someday."

"Er, thanks."

With that cheery thought to keep her company, she worked the *Your Perfect Man* booth like the veteran sales associate she was, giving the warrior, king, lover, and magician spiel over and over, and moving a lot of merchandise. When the crowd ebbed and she realized people were heading to the runway show early to get a good seat, she felt a twinge of envy—she hated not to be there in case something interesting happened. Although she was sure Jack and Detective Salyers could handle it.

"Hello."

She looked up and exclaimed in surprise to see Coop and Rainie…until the implication of the two of them attending a wedding show hit her. "Interesting destination for a date," she teased.

They both laughed. "Rainie is in the fashion show," Coop said.

"And Coop decided to tag along," she finished. "In fact, I'm running a little late, so I'm going to head over there."

"Look for me in the audience," Coop said. "See you afterward."

The look of fondness they exchanged made Carlotta's chest tighten. Coop watched Rainie until she disappeared into the crowd.

Was she jealous of the sentiments? Or jealous of Coop?

"Interesting booth theme," Coop offered, surveying the display. "I'm not sure I want to know which archetype I am."

Which was silly—it wasn't as if he was cheating on her.

"Rainie and I decided you're a lover," Carlotta offered.

"That's a conversation I'm sorry I missed," he said with a wink.

*Cheating on her...*Bells rang in Carlotta's head as unrelated bits of info fell into place. Jeremy Atwood was a player...Greg Pena had been having an affair...so had Jeffrey Oxblood...and two of the victims were outside a strip club.

"Coop, do you know if the first victim had a girlfriend on the side?"

He frowned. "Strange that you would ask...the M.E. who was at the scene said it was awkward because two women showed up at the guy's house—his fiancé, and his girlfriend."

"Maybe that's it," she said excitedly. "The victims weren't just getting married—they were cheating on their fiancées."

"Are you saying it was a pact of some kind to off their grooms?"

"Could be. Maybe they met somehow through planning their weddings, maybe even at a show like this."

"Or online?"

"Or through their gift registries?"

"And bonded over their cheating boyfriends?"

Carlotta put a finger to her mouth. "Although if I decided to murder my cheating fiancé, why wouldn't I wait a few more weeks until we're married to make sure I get the life insurance?"

Coop shrugged. "To save on the wedding expenses?"

"That's the way a man thinks. A woman would simply take the expenses out of her insurance proceeds."

"I'm not sure I wanted to know that."

"But you met Iris Kline, Greg Pena's fiancé. She had an alibi. And she did seem devastated about Greg's death."

"So...no pact among the brides?"

"Wait a minute...where do women go to complain about a cheating fiancé?"

He lifted his hands. "I don't know. To their mother, their girlfriends…"

"Their gynecologist…"

Coop winced, but nodded.

She snapped her fingers. "Their therapist. Maybe he or she is the culprit."

"But what are the chances the fiancées of all the victims see the same therapist? Plus we're talking about a professional who would have some serious mental problems of his or her own." He pushed up his glasses. "It might take some time to find and interview all the fiancées."

"Iris Kline and I have a mutual, um, friend. I can contact her, although I'm not sure how well I'll be received."

"I remember the confrontation at Pena's apartment," Coop said. "But it's worth a try. We're grasping at straws here."

Carlotta retrieved her phone. Luckily, the booth was almost empty of customers. From the applause sounding in the direction of the runway, the celebrity fashion show had started.

She texted Peter. *Important…do you have Tracey Lowenstein's mobile #?*

After what seemed like an interminable pause, he texted back the number, along with *I miss you.*

Carlotta tamped down a ping of guilt and dialed the number, willing Tracey to answer. She did.

"This is Mrs. Frederick Lowenstein."

From the public announcement noises in the background, it occurred to Carlotta that Tracey was probably at the hospital, keeping vigil at her father's bedside. "Tracey, this is Carlotta."

"How dare you call me? My father is still lying in a coma because of your father."

Carlotta closed her eyes. "Tracey, not now. Do you know if Iris was seeing a psychiatrist…or maybe a marriage counselor? I know she and Greg were having problems."

"How do you know that? And even if it were true, it's Iris's business."

"Please, Tracey, it's very important. I'll explain later."

Tracey sighed. "Yes, she was seeing someone, alone. Greg had been known to stray, and she was trying to work through it. But she doesn't want anyone to know."

"Do you know the name of her doctor?"

Another exasperated sigh sounded. "I can't remember."

"Try, Tracey, please. This could help a lot of people."

"Jenson, maybe? Or Denison?"

Carlotta froze. "Could it be Tennyson?"

"That's it. Dr. Tennyson. It's a woman."

Patricia's statements about Leo's ex came back to her. *Kaitlin thinks it would be best if Casey meets me in a neutral environment...Leo says she has obsessive-compulsive issues, but I kind of admire the way she tries to do everything just right.*

Like purge the world of lying, cheating husbands? Rat poison for ratty men.

"Thanks, Tracey. I'll explain everything later." She ended the call, her mind racing.

"What?" Coop asked.

"I think the person behind all of this is Leo Tennyson's ex-wife, Dr. Kaitlin Tennyson."

His head jutted forward. "Leo Tennyson the baseball player? Are you sure?"

"It all adds up...Leo recently proposed to my friend Patricia. Wait—when was the first victim killed?"

"Last week—"

"The night of the full moon," Carlotta finished.

He squinted. "How did you know?"

"That's the night Leo proposed to Patricia...that must be what set off Kaitlin. She's killing grooms who cheat before they're even married."

Coop grimaced. "Sounds personal."

Applause roared from the direction of the runway show. Then Carlotta remembered. "Leo's in the show!"

CHAPTER TWENTY-NINE

ON A FULL RUN to the runway area, Carlotta dialed Jack's number, but he didn't answer.

"Either his phone is turned off, or he doesn't hear it," she told Coop. "I'll try Patricia."

She pulled up the woman's number and connected the call.

Patricia answered, but there was a lot of background noise. "Hello?"

"Patricia, are you with Leo?"

"Carlotta, if this is you, I can't hear you. It's too noisy."

"Are you with Leo?" she shouted.

"Leo? He's about to go on stage and I'm missing it! I have to go."

Carlotta turned to Coop as another burst of applause sounded from the runway area. "Leo's going onstage. If I'm right, his ex-wife might've already planted the poison on him."

"How?"

Her mind sprinted over the cases she was familiar with. Jeremy Atwater chewed gum obnoxiously...for Greg Pena, swishing mouthwash had been his last act of vanity...runner Jeffrey Oxblood got dosed in his water bottle... and overweight Simon Markhall ate tainted food. The answer hit her like a thunderbolt.

"Leo dips snuff, and Patricia mentioned how much his ex-wife hates it. I'll bet she put the poison in the can."

"That'll do it," Coop said. "I'm calling 9-1-1 to get an ambulance on standby in case we need it."

Carlotta sent a text to Jack. *Leo Tennyson in danger; think ex-wife Kaitlin is Groom Slayer, might be in crowd, 30s, dark hair.*

Although if the woman was there to watch her handiwork and see Leo die onstage, she was probably in disguise.

Carlotta rushed the door of the area sectioned off for the runway show. The room was packed with several hundred people, many of them standing behind and around the seated audience. Her heart sank with the realization that finding the woman would be next to impossible. But she took consolation in the fact that medical help was on the way if Leo collapsed, and even if Kaitlin Tennyson escaped, the police would eventually catch up with her.

Applause sounded. She glanced to the stage to see Jarold Jett was once again emceeing the show. He stood behind a slim podium and entertained the audience with an ease and good humor that belied his underlying anxiety. After he was told yesterday's accident might not have been an accident, she suspected he was on edge.

Indeed, he kept dabbing at his shiny brow, and glanced often toward his beautiful fiancé, redheaded Sabrina Bauers, who sat in the VIP area near the stage.

Jarold introduced Leo Tennyson to great applause. Leo emerged with an athletic swagger, wearing a black tuxedo and a Gwinnett Braves ballcap. She could see he held a dip of snuff under his lower lip, but he looked fit and tan. She spotted Coop standing near the front of the stage, also studying Leo, poised to spring into action if the man fell ill.

To her great relief, Jack and Salyers appeared next to her. "I got your text," Jack said. "What's going on?"

In as few words as possible, she told them what she and Coop had learned. "Coop is keeping an eye on Leo, and an ambulance is on the way."

"What does this Kaitlin Tennyson look like?" Salyers asked.

"I met her only once—she's maybe five eight and slender, dark shoulder-length hair."

Jack frowned. "That's not much to go on." He settled his serious gaze on her. "How sure are you about this?"

Doubts crowded her mind. Jack had accused her more than once of making a mountain out of a molehill. What if she wrong?

But what if she was right?

She lifted her chin. "I don't know if I have all the details correct, but the big pieces fit."

He nodded. "Okay, let's find this woman."

"Wait," Carlotta said. "Coop mentioned one of the shooting victims had put up a fight—what if Kaitlin has bruises she's trying to hide?"

"Okay, so maybe look for someone wearing a scarf, or sunglasses?" Salyers asked.

Then the last piece fell into place in Carlotta's head, and she nearly thumped herself on the forehead. "Or a wedding veil."

They turned and scanned the room. Between models and hostesses, there must have been over a hundred brides milling around.

"Great," Jack muttered.

"I have an idea," Carlotta said, then pulled up Patricia's phone number again and pushed send. "Answer," she murmured.

She did. "Carlotta, for goodness sake, I'm trying to watch the show!"

"Patricia, do you know what kind of wedding gown Leo's ex-wife wore in her wedding?"

"What? I can't hear you."

She cupped her hand over the mouthpiece. "This is important, Patricia. What kind of dress did Kaitlin wear in her wedding with Leo?"

"Um...old fashioned...Gibson Girl-style, I think. Leo hated it." A gasp sounded over the phone. "Leo!"

On the stage, Leo Tennyson was down. The crowd gasped, frozen for a few seconds as Coop leapt onto the stage. The sound of an ambulance siren grew louder.

"I'll get the paramedics," Salyers said, and ran toward an exit.

"What kind of wedding dress are we looking for?" Jack asked.

"Gibson Girl."

He gave her a clueless look.

She motioned with her hands. "High neck, puff sleeve at the shoulder, then tight on the arms. And look for a hat with a veil."

They split up. By now, most of the crowd had pressed toward the stage to get a better look. She kept an eye out for anyone peeling off to the exits, especially brides.

And spotted one.

Wearing a Gibson Girl-style dress. High neck, puff cap sleeve at the shoulder, fitted sleeve on the arm, and jaunty hat, with a veil pulled down over the bride's face. She was moving at a fast, steady pace in front of a wall of red roses which were trending now because of a recent Kardashian wedding. Carlotta moved to cut her off before she reached the exit.

The bride turned her head and made eye contact with Carlotta. It was Kaitlin. When she recognized Carlotta, she picked up her long skirt and made a run for it.

"Kaitlin, stop!" Carlotta shouted, sprinting after her.

The woman didn't stand a chance in her little side-button boots with the kitten heel. Carlotta tackled her, sending them both rolling into the wall of roses like a couple of bowling balls.

Carlotta came to a stop on her back. She lay still for a few seconds, praying she hadn't broken anything vital, like her nose. Then she opened her eyes and spit rose petals out of her mouth.

Jack's face appeared over her. "You okay?"

"Never better. Kaitlin?"

"She's not going anywhere, snapped an ankle."

"Leo?"

"Having his stomach pumped as we speak. Coop just gave me the thumbs up." He extended his arm and helped her stand. "Anything broken?"

"I don't think so, but I'm going to be sore tomorrow."

He guided her to a chair. "Sit tight while we clear everyone out."

"Are you coming back?"

He gave her a defeated smile. "Don't I always?"

Within a few minutes, the room was vacated except for the group close to the incident. Sabrina Bauers comforted Jarold. His assistant Nia stood nearby, looking pensive. Edward sat a few chairs away. From the looks of the frazzled show director Melissa Friedman, this might her last Wedding World Expo.

Coop and Rainie had left so, she suspected, Rainie could submit a story on what had happened to run in tomorrow's paper. Patricia had ridden to the hospital with Leo and texted Carlotta he was feeling fine, considering he'd almost been murdered.

Carlotta studied the group, trying to put the final pieces together. Something still didn't seem right.

And then suddenly, it did.

"Are we free to leave?" Sabrina asked. "We have a plane to catch, and I'm afraid Jarold is quite upset. This entire week has been one disaster after another."

"Lucky for Jarold," Carlotta said.

They all turned to look at her.

"What's that supposed to mean?" Sabrina asked.

"Why don't we ask Nia?"

Heads swung toward Nia, who looked panicked. "I d-don't know what you're talking about."

"I believe you do," Carlotta said.

The woman pressed her lips together. But her gaze darted all around.

"Nia?" Jarold said.

The girl's face crumbled. "No one was hurt."

"When?" Jarold asked. "What are you saying?"

"It was Sabrina's idea."

"That's a lie," Sabrina said.

"What's a lie?" Jarold asked.

Sabrina blanched. "Whatever she was about to imply."

All eyes went back to Nia. "Sabrina wanted me to do something to get your social media stats up. She had me fly ahead to scout out the show so I could look for a good opportunity to set up something that could go viral."

"Shut up, you idiot!" Sabrina hissed. "She's lying, Jarold."

"Sabrina said the commercial shoot was the perfect chance to set up an accident while the cameras were rolling."

"I could've been killed!" Jarold roared.

"But you weren't," Sabrina said, splaying her hands. "It all worked out—you didn't have to finish that hideous commercial, no one was hurt, and your social media exploded." She smiled. "Win...win...win."

In the stunned silence, Salyers stepped in front of Nia. "Why don't you and I go down to the precinct and talk about this some more? You, too, Ms. Bauers."

Sabrina Bauers protested until Salyers threatened to handcuff her. Sabrina looked at Jarold.

"You have to come with me, to help them understand this is all just part of the business."

Jarold looked at her as if he were seeing a stranger. "You're on your own."

Sabrina sputtered and shouted until they were out of earshot.

Carlotta touched Jarold's arm. "Are you okay?"

He looked dazed. "Just trying to process it all." He emitted a sad, little laugh. "All this time I've been worried about what strangers might do to me, and it was the people closest to me who almost got me killed."

Jack walked up and nodded to Jarold. "A car is outside to take you to the airport. I'll help you with your bag."

"Thank you, Detective." Jarold patted Carlotta's hand. "If I ever decide to open a wedding boutique in Atlanta, I'm going to hire you to run it."

Carlotta smiled. The idea of someday leaving Neiman's was a little exhilarating, actually.

Jarold looked at Jack. "Don't you think Carlotta would make a beautiful bride someday?"

Jack surveyed her with his glittery gold eyes in a way that made her toes curl. "Yes, she would."

"Well, when that day comes," Jarold said, "call me and I'll design you a gown fit for a queen."

She laughed. "I will, thank you."

"I'll walk out with you," Edward said to Jarold. "If that's okay."

Jarold looked surprised, then he nodded. "I'd like that." The men headed toward the exit.

Jack gave her a little smile as he backed away. "You did good today."

She angled her head. "Thanks, Jack. See you around?"

"Probably." He winked, then turned and followed the two men out the exit.

Carlotta walked toward the exhibition hall, rubbing a bruise on her arm. Most of the booths were either empty or closing down. The area resembled a wedding reception hall the day after the ceremony—littered with bits of trash and stray balloons, with confetti in strange places.

It was a little sad.

She was pulling up Hannah's phone number when she spotted her friend walking toward her. "I was just about to call you."

"When I heard the sirens, I figured you were involved," Hannah said dryly. "But they wouldn't let me back there. What happened?"

"One groom slayer, subdued."

"Wow. So you were right?"

"Looks that way. What a week, huh?"

"A week of my life I will never get back."

Carlotta laughed. "Do you want to grab some dinner?"

"I...can't," Hannah said, then gestured vaguely in the direction of the HAL Properties booth. "I have a family...thing I can't get out of."

And obviously, Carlotta wasn't invited to attend. "I understand," she said. Even though she didn't.

"How about dinner tomorrow night?" Hannah asked.

"Sure, call me."

She watched Hannah walk away and wrestled with the old familiar feeling of rejection. It cut deeper when it came from an unexpected source.

She rode the train home and walked the remaining few blocks from the station in the dusk, happy to breathe fresh air after being cooped up in the exhibition hall most of the week.

As she walked up her driveway, she discreetly surveyed the house next door, looking for any signs of shifty activity. There were none. Johnson what's-his-name was probably sitting in front of his computer, stitching together photos of sidewalks and street signs and wishing he'd gone into porn like the rest of his photography friends.

When she walked into the townhouse, she was comforted by the beep of the security system that let her know it hadn't been breached since she'd set it that morning. On the other hand, she'd been hoping Wes would be there because she really didn't want to eat dinner alone.

She pulled out her phone and texted him. *Coming home soon?*

A few minutes later he responded. *Staying with Chance tonight, pasta salad in the fridge.*

She sighed, hoping he and Chance weren't doing something criminal. She wondered, too, how the next few months were going to play out with Wes and Liz. But it was too much to think about tonight.

She put on a comfy sleep shirt and padded to the fridge to find a covered bowl of her favorite pesto pasta salad, topped with olives and pine nuts. Food was Wes's way of apologizing. She scooped a bite of the creamy, zesty pasta into her mouth and murmured, "You're forgiven."

She grabbed a beer and carried the bowl to the living room, then settled in to watch bad weeknight television on their bad TV. When she was full, she stowed the leftovers, and walked around the kitchen and living room surveying the damage to the walls from Wes's less-than-expert installation of the security system. She finished her beer staring up at the round disc of a listening device that might have saved her life the night Abrams had attacked her.

She wondered if anyone was still monitoring it—her mother?

"Where are you, mother?" she said aloud. "Don't you miss us at all?"

The doorbell rang, spooking her. She wondered if Hannah had changed her mind about hanging out. And there was the neighbor next door.

And what if Valerie *was* monitoring the device, and simply waiting for the right time to stop by and catch up over a cup of coffee?

Despite the absurdity of the notion, her pulse ticked higher as she walked to the side window and pulled aside the curtain.

Jack waved at her.

Carlotta swung open the door. "Hello, there."

His tie was loose and his jaw was shadowed. He leaned on the door frame. "Hi."

"What brings you to this part of town?"

"Your sandbox," he said, then pulled her into his arms and nuzzled her ear. "Can I sleep in your bed tonight?"

"Not if you plan to sleep," she murmured.

He closed the door behind him and practically carried her to her bed. He knew the way.

They shed their clothes and he kissed a path to the place that made her cry out. He knew the way.

Then he covered her body with his and stroked into her so deeply and so fully, it was as if he were claiming every inch of her for himself. He slanted his mouth over hers and took her breath, then gave it back, slowly jackknifing his body into hers over and over to carry them to a frightening height before they crashed over the edge together.

Afterward, Carlotta lay still, recovering...shaken. With Jack, the sex was always intense and satisfying, but something was different this time. Something had shifted.

"I can't stay away from you," he breathed into her ear. "I love...this."

She closed her eyes, and listened to the sound of his heart beating against hers. "I love this, too."

CHAPTER THIRTY

"THREE GRAND FOR YOU," Chance said, counting out the bills. "And three grand for me." He grinned. "Man, that was one marathon game."

"Yeah," Wes agreed, leaning over to the stuff the wad of bills into his sock. He hadn't slept since getting out of bed the previous morning, was running on the fumes of energy drinks and Snickers bars. And the high of winning a decent pot.

"You played like your life was on the line."

Which it was, kind of. "Thanks."

"What are you taking, man?"

"Taking?"

"Ritalin, Adderall?"

"No, nothing."

"Something made you uber focused, you didn't make a single mistake."

"Just motivated, I guess."

"What are you going to do with the money?"

"I'm going to buy a ring."

"What kind of ring?"

"An engagement ring."

Chance's eyes bulged. "You're getting married?"

"If she says yes."

"Wait—which chick are you asking?"

Wes scoffed. "Liz. She's having my baby, and I'm going to do the hard thing."

"The hard thing?"

"Yeah, you know…the thing you don't want to do, but you know you should. The hard thing."

Chance looked at him as if he were insane. "Whatever, man. When are you going to pop the question?"

"Today, I guess. As soon as I buy the ring. I mean, she's going to start showing soon, and I don't want people thinking badly of her, you know?"

"That's cool."

"How are things with Hannah?"

Chance shrugged. "Okay, I guess. I don't know—I still think she's hiding something, but I can't put my finger on it."

"You don't think it's another dude?"

"Naw…once a girl gets a ride on my Johnson, no other guy's gonna measure up."

"Uh-huh. So where's the best place to buy a ring?"

"Pawn shop."

"Really? Do girls like that?"

"That's the great thing about diamonds, man—she's not gonna know. Put it in a fancy box and throw a bow on top, and she'll think you went to the mall."

"I guess you're right."

"And you'll get a lot more for your money."

"Okay. Wanna go with me?"

"Sure, I'll take you to my regular spot."

He stowed his bike in the trunk of Chance's BMW, and they rode to the west side of town to a pawn shop that looked a little seedy, even for a pawn shop.

"Are you sure about this?"

"Yeah, it's righteous. When the tennis types in the burbs have to sell their jewels, they don't want to go to a pawn shop in their backyard because they're afraid their neighbors will see them. And they don't want to drive through a bad part of town. But this place is convenient because it's right off the interstate. They can get in, and out."

They pulled around to park and Wes counted three Mercedes, two Cadillacs, and a Volvo, so apparently Chance knew his shit.

They sauntered in through a metal detector into one large room lined with shelves and cabinets that appeared to house anything of value—musical instruments, leather coats, even a motorcycle. The cycle made Wes's mouth water. He'd be getting his driver's license back soon and needed to upgrade on horsepower.

In the back, women wearing tight pants and dark sunglasses were conducting business across a counter with a couple of beefy looking guys. A stocky older woman with hair piled on top of her head approached them, chin down to peer at them over reading glasses.

"What can I do for you fellas?" Her nose wrinkled and Wes conceded that after a night in a smoky illegal card hall, they probably were not the most fragrant of customers.

"We're buying," Chance said.

As opposed to selling, Wes presumed. The woman's nose wrinkle disappeared.

"You got something in mind?" she asked, giving them another once-over, as if trying to assess their net worth.

Chance jerked his thumb toward Wes. "He's getting married, needs a ring."

The woman's jowly face heaved upward in a smile. "Right this way."

They followed her to a glass cabinet that held an array of rings so vast, Wes wondered about the rate of divorce in the metro area. How on earth would he pick one?

"How much are you looking to spend?" she asked.

"Three grand," he said.

"Two grand," Chance said at the same time.

"Twenty-five hundred," he corrected.

She looked back and forth between them. "Okay, let's start over here." She unlocked the cabinet and withdrew a tray of rings, then slid it on top of the glass counter.

Wes's heart beat faster in his chest. He was really going to do this. Really. He wiped a hand across his forehead and it came away sticky.

"What's your girl like?" the lady asked with a grandmotherly smile.

Meg's face popped into his head and his first thought was he could never describe her in a way to make someone else understand the way he saw her.

"She's pregnant," Chance supplied in his silence.

With a start, Liz's face replaced Meg's. Right.

"I see," the woman said.

"She's classy," Wes said. "She's an attorney and she likes nice things."

"She's older," Chance said helpfully.

"Ah," the lady said, as if she'd grasped the situation. "How about this one?" She removed a ring from the tray and held it up. "It's one carat, beautiful setting, 14K gold."

Wes took the ring and swallowed hard. "Do you think she'll like it? It's really important that she likes it."

The woman hesitated, then reached for a different ring and held it up. "One and a half carats, emerald cut, white gold." She handed it to him. "She'll like it."

He turned the ring in the light and the diamond sparkled like a thousand fires...that would consume him forever and ever and ever.

"It's pretty. How much?"

"Cash?" she asked.

He nodded.

"The tag says twenty-eight hundred, but I'll take twenty-five, tax and all."

He glanced at Chance and his buddy nodded.

"Okay."

The woman smiled. "Let me get this to Sam. He'll clean it and put it in a nice box." She returned the tray to the cabinet, then headed toward the back.

"I'm gonna look at the stereo stuff," Chance said.

Wes nodded, too tired now to work up an interest in speakers. He rubbed his eyes, then leaned on the counter...and spotted a bracelet inside that made him look closer. It was dainty. Some kind of pink metal held together links of tiny flowers, their petals every color imaginable. Even his untrained eye could see it was something special—a work of art.

"You like the bracelet?" the woman asked.

He looked up to see her standing on the other side of the counter. He nodded.

She removed it from the case and set it in front of him. "You have a good eye."

"It reminds me of someone."

"Not the classy attorney?"

He shook his head.

The woman nodded in understanding. "It's a very nice piece, one of a kind. The stones are semi-precious, set in pink gold."

"Pink gold," he murmured. He turned over the price tag and balked at the nine hundred dollar price.

"I'll let you have it for five," she said.

It was stupid to buy something for a woman who wouldn't even talk to him, who probably hated him, and rightfully so.

"I'll take it."

She smiled and disappeared with the bracelet. He wandered over to watch Chance fool around with speakers and chat up the bored guy working there. A few minutes later, the sales lady waved to him from the back.

Two small gift bags sat next to the cash register, one black and one white. He didn't have to guess which one was which. He leaned over and removed the fat wad of cash from his sock and handed it to her. She counted the bills like a teller, turning the bills face up as she thumbed through them. Without losing track, she handed the twenties and hundreds to the guy next to her, who held them up to the light and checked them with a counterfeit marking pen.

"All good," the guy said.

The woman smiled and handed Wes a receipt. "Thank you. I hope everything works out."

"So do I," he said, then stuffed the gift bags into his backpack.

When they got back in the car, Wes sighed and leaned his head back.

"You coming home with me?" Chance asked.

"Nah. I'm going home to take a shower and feed Einstein before I go see Liz."

"I'll drop you off. You working today?"

"Thanks for the reminder." He pulled out his phone and called McCormick, his boss at ASS. The man's voice mail picked up. Wes altered his voice to sound like he had the flu and wouldn't be in today—he didn't want to spread it around. After throwing in a couple of coughs to make it sound good, he ended the call.

He really didn't want to see Meg before he talked to Liz.

"How are you going to pop the question?" Chance asked.

"I thought I'd go to Liz's office and surprise her, you know, take some flowers, get down on one knee. Women love that crap."

"Sounds risky. Do you think she'll say yes?"

"I think so. She's talked before about us being a couple, going out in public and stuff. She offered to put me through college, so I could have a career and everything."

Chance nodded. "Sounds mainstream."

"It's good," Wes said, nodding. "I mean, I'm going to have a mouth to feed so I need a steady gig. I want my kid to be proud of me."

"Do you know if it's a boy or a girl?"

"Nah...I think it's probably too soon to tell."

"So, dude...what's your dad going to think if you marry his mistress?"

Wes shrugged. Anger sparked in his stomach—Randolph obviously didn't want anything to do with him. "Things have changed since he left. I'm a man now, and I'm with Liz. He'll just have to deal with it."

Chance pulled into the driveway of the townhome. "Whose car?"

Wes regarded the plain sedan and scowled. "Just some dick cop who's got a hard-on for my sister."

"Dude, who doesn't? I mean, she's smoking hot."

"Shut up." Carlotta was the other woman he didn't want to face before he talked to Liz. "Change of plans. Do you mind to drop me off at Liz's office?"

"No problem."

A few minutes later when they pulled up to the high rise building, Chance leaned forward to look out the window. "Looks like a nice place."

"Yeah." Wes had never been to her office, had only seen Liz when he was in jail or at the police station or the D.A.'s office. Or in her bed.

"What if she's not here?"

He pointed to the red Jag convertible parked in a premium spot. "She's here, that's her car."

"Sweet." Then Chance glanced over. "But dude, you stink. *I* stink, so if I can smell you, it's bad."

"I got it covered," Wes said, climbing out.

"Good luck, dude."

"Thanks."

He retrieved his bike from the trunk, then walked it to a rack and locked it. From his backpack he pulled out a courier envelope and hat he sometimes used to gain access to places when he collected for Mouse. Then he strolled in through a revolving door and nodded to the receptionist sitting behind a vase of fresh flowers.

"Hi, there," he said cheerfully, holding up the envelope. "Mail room?"

"I can take it," the woman said.

"Sorry, it requires the signature of an official mail manager. Postal code stuff, such a pain."

"In the basement," she said, pointing to the stairs.

"Thanks."

He walked down the stairs and through a door into a hallway. A couple of doors down, he found a vending machine room where he snagged a protein bar, a Coke, and a pack of breath mints.

A security guard walked in and nodded as he fed coins into a machine. "How's it going?"

"Good now," Wes said, holding up his snack. "Man, is there a bathroom down here I can use before I head back out?"

The guy pointed. "Down the hall, just past the mailroom."

"Thanks."

Wes wolfed down the food, then found the bathroom, which was, fortunately, empty. He stripped off his gray Cage the Elephant tee shirt and used hand soap and water to give himself a thirty-second wipe-down, then used paper towels to dry off. He put his shirt back on, this time with the stained emblem to the back, the plain back to the front. After wetting his hair, he held his head under the electric hand dryer for a quick, hot blast. He cracked open the breath mints and chewed a handful. Then he stowed the hat and envelope and walked back to the mailroom where he rapped on the half-door.

A handful of guys looked up from sorting bins, and one loped over. "Can I help you?"

"Yeah, man, I'm lost. I'm looking for Elizabeth Fischer's law office."

The guy thought for a few seconds. "Fifth floor."

"Thanks." Then Wes leaned in. "Listen, I'm in trouble and I'm meeting her for the first time and now I'm regretting my wardrobe choice, you know?"

The guy scanned his tee shirt and jeans. "I've seen worse."

"Still, I could really use a jacket for an hour," he said, nodding to the guy's navy blue special. "I got a twenty," he said holding up the bill. "Help me out?"

The guy shrugged. "Sure." He traded the jacket for the cash.

Wes slid into the jacket—a little loose, but not bad. "You'll have it back within the hour. Oh, by the way, when I came in the building, there was a stray kitten out front in the landscape bed. I meant to tell the receptionist, but I totally forgot. Will you call her? It sounded hungry."

"Sure," the guy said, reaching for the phone next to the door.

By the time he got back to the lobby, the receptionist was on her way out the revolving door on a mission to save a kitten. He snatched a handful of flowers from the vase on the desk, and punched the elevator call button.

On the elevator, though, he had time to think on what he was about to do. It was easy enough to say he was going to do the hard thing, but would he stick with it long-term? Through thick and thin, in sickness and in health? He swallowed.

Until death.

He wanted to think he could be someone Liz and the baby could rely on, but honestly, he didn't know. The few times Carlotta had depended on him, he'd failed spectacularly.

Maybe he was just a screw-up.

The elevator door opened onto a plush lobby and glass doors with gold lettering that spelled out "Elizabeth Fischer, Attorney at Law."

Liz would expect nice things in life—money and travel and socializing with the right people.

Could he be that guy?

The elevators doors started to close, and he put his arm out to stop them. He could only try his damnedest.

He took a deep breath and walked through the glass doors into a small waiting area. A receptionist looked up and smiled.

"May I help you?"

"Is Liz available?"

She gave the flowers a suspicious look. "Do you have an appointment?"

"No."

"Your name, please?"

"Wesley Wren."

"Just a moment."

The girl turned at an angle so he couldn't hear what she said into the phone. When she hung up, she smiled and pointed to a dark wood door. "Go right in."

His feet grew heavier with each step that carried him across the carpet. He took a deep breath, then opened the door.

Liz looked up from her desk and gestured him inside. She was on the phone and held up a finger indicating she'd be through in a minute. She arched an eyebrow at the flowers and gestured for him to have a seat.

Wes sighed. More waiting.

He decided to stand, but slid his backpack off his shoulder onto a chair. He realized this would be a good time to get the ring, and with his back turned to Liz, he pulled out the black bag. He peeked inside for reassurance, grateful the sales lady had put a bow on the jewelry case.

The jacket was feeling hot and scratchy. He ran a finger around the collar and scanned Liz's office. On her bookshelf was a picture of an older couple—her parents, he guessed. There was a lot he didn't know about her, but there was time to learn.

When he heard her wrapping up the call, his heart jumped to his throat. But this was how all men felt before they proposed, he reasoned…it was natural to be nervous.

She put down the phone and came around her desk, looking long and lean in a pencil skirt and sleeveless blouse that make her boobs look even bigger…

or maybe that was because of the baby. A matching jacket hung on the back of her chair.

"What's all this?" she asked.

"Just in the neighborhood and thought I'd stop by." He held out the flowers. His hand was shaking.

"Thank you." She took the flowers, which were, he realized, dripping a little. She found a vase on her bookshelf and put them inside. "I'm glad you came by, I was going to call you today."

"Have you talked to Dad?"

"Um…no." She turned her back for a moment and seemed to be wrestling with something. Wes decided this was as good a time as any to do it.

He retrieved the jewelry case and dipped to one knee. Too late, he realized that cutting off the blood flow to part of his body might not be a good idea. He felt lightheaded.

Liz turned around and her mouth opened. "What on earth?"

He gulped for air. "Liz, I know I don't have much to offer you right now, but I want to be here for you, and for our baby." He cracked open the jewelry case. "Will you marry me?"

Liz seemed frozen. "I…Wesley, this is so unexpected."

"Because I'm Randolph's son, you didn't think I would do the right thing?"

She shook her head. "I didn't mean it like that."

He held the jewelry box higher. "Do you like it?"

"It's very…pretty."

Something in her voice made him peek at the jewelry case. The dainty pink gold bracelet mocked him. He snapped it shut. "Sorry, wrong box." He stood and hastily retrieved the box from the white gift bag, opening it to reveal the diamond solitaire ring.

He got down on his knee again. "Now will you marry me?"

Liz's eyes swam with tears. "I can't tell you how happy this makes me."

Adrenaline pumped through his veins. She was going to say yes.

"But I can't marry you."

Abject relief flooded his body like a tsunami, quickly replaced by a wake of confusion. "Why not?"

"I was going to call you today because I went to the doctor for some more exact testing."

Concern blipped in his chest. "Is the baby okay?"

She smiled. "Yes. But I'm further along in the pregnancy than I thought."

"What does that mean?"

"It means you're not the father."

Emotions assaulted him, one after another. Shock...hurt...uncertainty... elation.

And when Meg's face popped into his head, a final emotion descended. *Misery.*

CHAPTER THIRTY-ONE

"HERE'S TO WES NOT BEING A FATHER," Carlotta said, lifting her glass.

"I'll drink to that," Hannah said with an obliging clink. She was happily back in her Goth garb, her face jewelry restored and her arm tattoos on display. "He really dodged a bullet."

"I hope he's learned something, but I have a feeling this situation wrecked his chances with the girl he likes."

"There are lots of girls out there."

"I suppose," Carlotta said. "I just hate to see him get his heart broken on the first time out, you know?"

"Like you did?"

Carlotta nodded in concession. "Yes."

"So what's the deal with Richie Rich these days?"

"He's been spending a lot of time at the hospital with the Tully family."

"How's Tracey's dad?"

"Improving, slowly."

"I guess he and your dad were close."

"At one time, I'd say they were best friends." She sipped from her drink. "But I guess friendships don't always last."

Hannah was scrutinizing the base of her glass. "People change, I suppose."

"Uh-hm."

"Have you heard from your father?"

"No. He's being held in solitary confinement."

"Solitary? That sounds extreme."

"He gets to eat with the other inmates, but it's the only privilege he has." She took another drink. "I'm not supposed to tell anyone this, but Liz said it's because a relative of one of his former clients is housed there, too."

"He's in danger?"

"I don't know if a threat has been made, but that's the general consensus." She sighed. "Wouldn't that be the cherry on top of the shit sundae if Randolph is whacked in prison before he tells us about our mother?"

Hannah shifted in her seat. "I'm sorry."

"It's not your fault—this is my crazy life." She sighed. "Speaking of which, Jack spent the night last night."

"Oh? I thought you two had made some kind of pact to keep your hands off each other."

"We tried. We failed."

"Well, how was it?"

Carlotta gave in to the warm curl of satisfaction in her stomach. "It was great, like always. But something was different...Jack was different, in a good way."

"You mean not an asshole?"

"Yeah, actually. We had breakfast this morning like normal people. I don't know, it was just...nice."

Hannah frowned. "Don't do it."

"Don't do what?"

"Fall in love with Jack Terry. There's only one way for that to end well... and thousands of ways for it not to."

Carlotta winced. "What if I said I already have?"

"Oh, Jesus. Carlotta, I get it—you two have that whole jungle sex thing going on. But..."

"What?"

Hannah sighed. "Okay, I'm just going to say this—I think because of the situation with your dad, you're always going to pick a guy who's not going to be here for you."

Hurt barbed through her chest. "That's not true...is it?"

Hannah held up her hands. "I shouldn't have said anything."

"Well, while we're on the subject, maybe you'd like to talk about why you're with a guy who worships you, and you can't wait to get away."

Hannah scoffed. "It's Chance Hollander—of course I can't wait to get away. Have you met him?"

"I think you like him."

"I do not."

"Then explain why you agreed to go out with him."

"Because he agreed to finish paying for the tattoo on my back."

"Which you and I both know you could easily afford to pay for on your own."

Hannah frowned. "Okay, I like him…he's…I don't know, he's *sweet*."

"So why are you moving out?"

"Because I don't do sweet. I do married guys who don't expect anything from me. I don't want to break the big lug's heart."

"Maybe you're protecting more than just *his* heart."

"And on that note," Hannah said, "I'm going to the crapper." She slid out of the booth and walked across the bar to the ladies' room, leather and hardware clanging. People gave her a wide berth.

Carlotta shook her head, then checked her phone, secretly hoping Jack had called. He hadn't…but Peter had sent her an email.

Here's that list you asked for, hope it helps somehow. Looking forward to our dinner Friday. I miss you. xox

She sighed. The moment when she'd rolled over this morning to find Jack in her bed had been her happiest in recent memory. With Peter, the thrill was gone. All the time she'd spent with him in his lovely home, all the meals they'd shared at his luxurious dining table, or out by his pool, hadn't given her a fraction of the pleasure of having oatmeal this morning with Jack in her dated, cramped kitchen.

She was in love with Jack, and despite what Hannah said, she believed he would be there for her. Hadn't he changed just in the time she'd known him?

She idly scrolled through the email to the list of clients Randolph had allegedly bilked. Her heart sank at the sheer number of them. Some of the names were familiar to her from the country club, and social circles her parents had once enjoyed. Even more disturbing were the foundations on the list. Stealing from people was bad enough, but stealing from charitable organizations?

"How could you, Dad?" she whispered.

Indeed, her mind pinged...*how could he*? The father she knew and loved couldn't have. If anything, seeing the names of foundations on the list made her think for the first time in a long time that maybe Randolph was innocent.

Then one name on the list stopped her cold: HAL Properties.

Carlotta's eyes watered and her vision blurred as realization washed over her. No wonder Hannah was leading a double-life around her. No wonder Hannah didn't want Carlotta to meet her family. No wonder her sister had reacted strangely when she'd heard Carlotta's name.

Hannah returned noisily and slid into the booth. "Explain to me one-ply toilet paper. I mean—hey, are you okay?"

Carlotta managed to shake her head.

"What's wrong?"

"I asked Peter to get me a list of people my father is accused of defrauding. He just sent it." She turned her phone around for Hannah to see, but since Hannah didn't look at it, it was clear she already knew.

"Please don't look at me like that. I can explain."

"I wish you would."

Hannah hesitated, then wiped her hand over her mouth. "I was still in high school when my parents lost their savings and retirement. It was a big hit to our lifestyle. I was taken out of private school, I lost all my friends, and we moved to a much smaller house. I remember the stress and my parents arguing constantly."

That all sounded familiar. "Go on."

Hannah sighed. "I don't remember when I first heard the name Randolph Wren, but I knew he was the cause of a lot of grief in my world. I was angry because I thought here my siblings and I were doing without, and his kids were probably living high...on my family's money. Years later, I was working a ritzy party in the kitchen, and I witnessed a woman being thrown out because she had a counterfeit ticket."

"Me," Carlotta said. "I remember. You let me in through the kitchen."

"I thought what you were doing was great. I hated all the rich people there because of the way they'd treated me when my family fell on hard times, and I considered it payback that someone was taking advantage of all that excess. I didn't know who you were until you told me your name."

"But you knew right away Randolph was my father?"

"Yeah. And I don't know—I guess I was a little obsessed with finding out more about you."

"And then?"

Hannah shrugged. "And then I thought you were cool...and fun. And I came to realize you and Wes were victimized by that whole situation more than anyone else."

"And so you decided not to say anything about your family's connection to my father?"

"What good would it have done? My family's business had recovered by that time and everything was fine. It seemed unnecessary to bring it up."

"What about being honest?" Carlotta said. "Wesley and I welcomed you into our home. I always thought you were kind of an outcast and didn't have much family. And now I feel as if you were role-playing when you were with us."

Hannah shook her head. "That's not true. I feel closer to you and Wes than I do to my own siblings. I was afraid if I told you, you would...hate me."

Carlotta swallowed a lump of emotion in her throat. "I couldn't hate you, Hannah...but how can I ever trust you?"

Hannah pursed her mouth and nodded. "I don't blame you. If I were in your shoes, I'd probably feel the same." She inhaled, then exhaled noisily. "Okay, I wasn't going to say anything about this, but..."

Carlotta frowned. "But what?"

"I can get you into the prison to see your dad."

CHAPTER THIRTY-TWO

CARLOTTA ADJUSTED THE SHORT WIG until it covered her ears. "So how much trouble will we be in if we're caught?"

At the sink next to her in the women's restroom at the Lendahl's Dairy Supply warehouse, Hannah was adhering a mustache. "I don't even want to think about it. The plan is to time the food delivery just as breakfast is being served. I figure you'll have twenty minutes, tops, to find your dad and have a conversation without you or him raising any alarms." She turned her head. "You know this is a longshot, right?"

"Right. It would be nice to have a layout of the prison."

"Hello? There are reasons Federal pens don't have the layout of their buildings on Wikipedia. Besides, we're going to the mess hall, and hopefully, he'll be there. If not, we're out of there. There won't be any crawling through the HVAC ducts or riding down laundry chutes, got it?"

"Got it. I didn't realize the prisons get their deliveries from local suppliers. I assumed it was all government, all contained."

"My friend's company is making dairy deliveries to the prison because of the government shutdown—until Congress passes a budget, government contracts can't be honored."

"Liz mentioned a disruption in the food service—that's why Randolph is taking his meals with everyone else instead of eating in solitary."

"Thank goodness for congressional gridlock."

"Does your friend know you're doing this?"

"Don't ask. Your only job is to look as much like—" Hannah picked up a Federal Bureau of Prisons lanyard and read the name under the picture. "—Miguel Alvarez as possible."

"I wish Miguel had a mustache, too. It would help cover the gap in my teeth."

"I would've let you be—" Hannah read from the second lanyard. "—William Henck, but he's a big guy." She walked over to stand next to Carlotta in the mirror. "How do we look?"

Carlotta nodded, impressed with the transformation to two delivery guys in white jumpsuits and billed hats. "Not bad."

Hannah checked her watch. "Time to go. We need to get out of here before any employees arrive. Leave everything in the locker. Remember, no cell phones, no money, nothing but your lanyard. And don't be surprised if you get patted down at some point."

"Boobs and butt taped down solid," Carlotta said, turning to stand in profile.

"Okay, well, let's hope between the darkness and the guards being a bit sleepy at this time of the morning, no one will give us a second look."

They walked out into the empty warehouse and climbed into the refrigerated truck that held fifty cases of eggs, fifteen dozen to a case. Carlotta reached over to touch Hannah's arm. "We can call it off now if you want. I'll be just as grateful that you offered to do this in the first place."

Hannah smiled. "I'm all in."

"Me, too."

Hannah fired up the engine and pulled forward to trigger a garage door to raise. They drove out into an industrial park that was still dark at this hour and headed across town in the direction of the United States Penitentiary, Atlanta.

"I'm sorry to exclude Wes," Hannah said, "but I was afraid the little shit would do something to get us caught."

"No, that was a good call," Carlotta said, remembering how Wes had fouled up Jack's goodwill attempt to let them have a glimpse of their father before he was transported.

"Have you decided what you're going to say to your dad if you see him?"

"All I really want to know is where to find Mother. As far as everything else is concerned, I'll let the courts handle Randolph."

Hannah looked over at her. "Are you prepared to hear...something you don't want to hear?"

"You mean that's she's dead?" Carlotta heaved a sigh. "I have to be honest, I go back and forth between hoping she's alive so I can see her again, and hoping she's not alive so I don't have to ask why she never came back. Does that sound horrible?"

"No, I get it. I just want to make sure if you see your dad, you don't run up and hug him...or slap him. And that you don't react violently to anything he might say. I know that's a lot to ask."

"I'm good," Carlotta assured her.

Hannah checked her watch. "Okay, we're about one mile out, and we're running to plan, which is a few minutes late. Hopefully, some of the prisoners will be in the mess hall eating. I'm counting on the fact that eggs will be stored somewhere nearby. You keep a lookout for your dad, and I'll keep a lookout for everything else."

"Okay," Carlotta said, trying to calm her galloping heart.

"There it is, up ahead. Put on your gloves, and don't say a word. If anyone talks to you, pretend you don't speak English."

She nodded, tamping down thoughts of everything that could go wrong, focusing instead on how it could go right. They would park the vehicle, and take as long as they could to carry in the cases of eggs.

"Here we go," Hannah said as they rolled up to the guard shack. She rolled down the window. "Egg delivery," she grunted.

"Let me see your IDs," said the guard. He was armed to the teeth and held a flashlight, which he shined over their IDs and their faces. Carlotta squinted into the beam and held her breath, but the guard seemed satisfied.

"Is the back open?" he asked.

"Yeah," Hannah said.

They sat as still as stones while he opened the back door of the truck and inspected their delivery. Then he shined a light under their truck and came around to the passenger side to pass the light over the cab and their feet.

He knocked on her window. "Out of the truck, please."

Carlotta's hand shook as she opened the door and jumped down heavily. She gave the guy a nod, then lowered her head.

"Arms up, legs open."

She did as she was told, reminding herself to stand like a man. She hoped like hell he didn't feel all the bandaging underneath her clothes to square out her figure. And she was pretty sure he could hear her heart pounding—it sounded like a bass drum in her ears.

"Have a good day," he said.

Carlotta climbed back inside on wobbly legs.

He walked around to the driver's side and put Hannah through the same scrutiny, although it seemed to take longer. Carlotta kept her eyes on the road ahead and tried to look bored.

"Pull up and wait for the gate to open," he said finally.

Hannah climbed back inside and they didn't speak until they had driven through the gate and it closed behind them.

"Still with me?" Hannah said.

"Uh-huh," was all Carlotta could manage. Everywhere she looked were walls and barbed wire and cameras. This was a far cry from party crashing. If they got caught—

She swallowed hard. Well, Jack wouldn't be able to save her this time.

They had to stop at yet another gate and endure the same scrutiny as before. By now Carlotta was sweating underneath the heavy makeup and wig.

"Stay on the right," the guard said. "Follow the letter C on the road and pull around the rear of building 4."

"C and 4, got it," Hannah mumbled.

Carlotta could tell by the faint tremor in Hannah's voice that she, too, was starting to feel the heat of what they'd gotten themselves into. Masking their voices was one thing, but passing themselves off as men unloading the truck would be something else. Her healing shoulder still pinged with pain from their practice run—she hoped it held out.

Hannah drove carefully and soon they were pulling behind a square one-story building ablaze with light. A guy on a loading dock guided her to back into a parking space next to a ramp.

"Good luck," Hannah said, then opened the door and jumped down.

Carlotta did the same and met her at the rear of the truck.

"Whatcha got?" the guy on the loading dock shouted.

"Eggs," Hannah shouted back.

"Yeah, cooks are waitin' for you. How many?"

"Fifty half cases."

"Do you need a forklift?"

"Nah, we got it—thanks, man."

They each grabbed a case of eggs. Carlotta followed Hannah up the ramp into a concrete room lined with institutional-sized stainless refrigerators. The guy from the dock was standing there waving them toward an interior door. "We need twenty-five cases in the kitchen to use now. You can put the last twenty-five in the refrigerators."

From the open door came the sounds of kitchen activity. Carlotta concentrated on not dropping the eggs. Between the exertion and the adrenaline, she was feeling a little lightheaded. But she told herself she couldn't blow this now.

They walked into a huge cafeteria with rows and rows of tables the length of the room, and identical hard plastic chairs lined up on either side. The starkness of it was sobering. They had entered near the food line, where inmates stood waiting for large pots of food to be dropped into openings to keep them warm. Behind the food line was the kitchen. She and Hannah were waved in and the cooks' helpers took the cases from them before they could set them down.

The good thing about the frantic pace was no one paid attention to them. But the bad thing was she didn't have much time to scan the inmates who were coming through line for Randolph—only a few seconds with each trip—and she was only going to get a dozen trips into the kitchen. On the fourth trip she was still optimistic...but by the ninth trip she was losing hope...and on the twelfth trip she had to concede failure.

"Anything?" Hannah whispered.

"No."

"One more case to the kitchen," the guy shouted as they walked up the ramp.

"You take it," Hannah whispered, then veered off to the refrigerators.

Carlotta threw up a prayer and veered left to take the final case into the kitchen. She slowed her step and scanned for Randolph's salt and pepper hair, his fit frame.

Nothing.

Someone took the last case from her, and as she walked out, dock guy shouted. "The rest go in the icebox."

She and Hannah met at the top of the ramp and she shook her head. They walked down together, both of them breathing from exertion. Carlotta fought back tears of frustration, and she knew Hannah was as disappointed as she was.

"Let's get this done," Hannah muttered.

The last trips took them longer because they had to climb into the truck to retrieve the cases in the back. With five cases left to carry up the ramp, the muscles in her arms were screaming.

"I'll get the rest," Hannah said.

"No," she said, not about to let her friend carry her load.

But on the next trip, her shoulder gave way and she dropped the case she was carrying on the floor in front of one of the enormous refrigerators. Instantly, yoke and white began to leak from the case.

The dock guy winced, then stepped to the door and shouted, "Cleanup!"

Hannah walked by and made a cut-off motion with her hand, indicating she'd get the rest. Carlotta didn't argue—she was bungling things.

A man emerged with an industrial size roll of paper towels. Carlotta stared at the oozing mess in dismay and thought it pretty much represented the state of her life—fragile, fractured, and out of control.

She reached for a handful of the towels, and looked straight into Randolph's blue eyes.

She inhaled sharply, but he didn't notice or recognize her, was intent on cleaning up the mess she'd made. Her pulse went haywire and her limbs froze until she remembered she only had a few seconds to pull this off. She got down on her hands and knees and put her head close to his as she wiped at the goo.

"Dad, it's me," she whispered.

Out of the corner of her eye, she saw him stiffen.

"Don't look at me." She continued to wipe.

"Carlotta, what are you doing?"

"I had to talk to you. Are you okay?"

"Yes."

"Where's Valerie?"

The guy from the dock rolled a trash can over. "Here you go. Hurry it up, Wren."

Her father stood and hefted the case of broken eggs into the trash can. She stood and dropped her towels inside. It took every ounce of restraint she had not to look at him.

"Where's Mom?" she said through gritted teeth, knowing they were running out of time.

"Here comes the mop bucket," the guy said, gesturing for them to get out of the way.

"Go home, Carlotta. Everything you're looking for is there. Don't worry about me. I have evidence stashed to exonerate me, but I can't come forward yet. I love you." He turned and walked back to the door, wiping his hands on his grey jumpsuit.

CHAPTER THIRTY-THREE

"FEELING BETTER?"

Wes looked up from the computer screen he'd been staring at for forty-five minutes. "Hm?"

His boss at ASS, Richard McCormick, was a dumpy nerd, but a genuinely nice guy. "Your bout with the flu? You're feeling better, I hope."

"Oh, yeah." Wes sat up in his chair. "Thanks."

"The flu lasts for more than a day," Meg supplied from the other side of the workstation without looking at him.

"I guess it was more of a stomach bug," Wes said.

Ravi reached for a squirt of his hand sanitizer and eyed Wes warily.

"I've even heard of the flu lasting for as long as…nine months," Meg added.

Wes pursed his mouth.

"I once had mono for six weeks," Jeff said. "It's called the kissing disease." He smiled and nodded, as if he'd gotten it from the Homecoming Queen, when he'd probably gotten it from his sister.

"Well, let's try to keep kissing to a minimum around here," McCormick said cheerfully.

Meg looked at Wes for the first time all morning. "No worries."

McCormick went on his way. Wes studied Meg, her head bent over some task. She must have callblocked him, because when he called her phone, it didn't even ring, gave him a message about the call not going through at this time. Ditto on texting—all of his bounced back as undeliverable.

"Hey, Jeff," he said. "What do you think about time travel?"

Jeff nodded. "Yeah, totally possible. I think we'll see it in our lifetime."

"If you could get in a time machine, where would you go?" He could tell Meg was listening even though she pretended not to.

Jeff twirled a Sharpie pen over his fingers. "Maybe fifty years into the future and talk to myself as an old man, get some advice."

"He'd tell you to dress better," Ravi said, eliciting laughs.

"How about you, Ravi—where would you go?" Wes asked.

"Scientists predict in twenty years, we'll be able to walk into a pharmacy and order a custom-blended antibiotic for any kind of germ or infection. I'd like to go there."

"I think the medication you need is already available," Jeff offered. "And it's not an antibiotic."

They all laughed, including Ravi.

"How about you?" Meg asked, looked at Wes. "Where would you go?'

"That's easy," he said. "I'd travel back in time one week, and do everything different."

"Ha!" Ravi said, then stopped. "Wait, that's not funny."

"Ravi," Jeff said, pushing back his chair. "Why don't we go get something to drink?"

"I'm good," Ravi said, clueless to Jeff's maneuvering.

"Then go with me to help me pick out something I want." He frowned, then jerked his head toward the hallway. Ravi got the hint and they left Meg and Wes alone.

"Walked right into that one, didn't I?" Meg said.

"Kind of. I think something's wrong with your phone."

She shook her head. "Nope."

"How am I supposed to reach you if I have something important to tell you?"

She shrugged. "I guess you're out of luck."

"The baby isn't mine."

There was a small tic of surprise in her eyes, then it disappeared. "Okay."

"I thought you'd be happy."

"Why? It doesn't affect me one way or the other."

"You said some nice things last week. I thought you meant them."

"This thing is, I didn't." She splayed her hands. "Sorry. You're not the only one who wishes they could go back in a time machine and do everything different."

Man, that hurt.

She checked her watch. "Ooh, gotta go. I have a lunch date."

Probably with that preppie architect who wore plaid. Wes packed up his stuff to get out of there, too. When he reached into his backpack, his hand touched the jewelry case he was still carrying around with him. He opened it to look at the bracelet he'd thought would be so perfect on Meg. Earlier this week he might've gotten to third base with it, or even home plate. But now...

He glanced over to her desk. Next to her lamp sat a teddy bear wearing a Georgia Tech sweatshirt. She loved that teddy bear, had named it, and would sometimes idly stroke its fur when she was deep in thought on a project.

Wes removed the bracelet from the box and looped it over the bear's neck. Nice. From a distance, no one would notice it. It might even be a while before Meg noticed it. But it made him feel better knowing it was at least near her.

He slung his backpack over his shoulder and left after waving goodbye to McCormick.

It was a nice day, and for the first time in a long time, he didn't have anything he had to do. He rode back to the pawn shop and told the lady the marriage proposal hadn't worked out. She seemed almost happy for him, but told him they didn't offer refunds, only store credits. So he put a hold on an item and said he'd be back to pick it up soon.

Then he went back to the townhouse and fed Einstein. He remembered that Carlotta was returning to work today and had plans this evening. With hours of free time on his hands, he decided it would be a good opportunity to tackle some of the drywall repairs from installing the alarm system—that would make Carlotta happy.

With a bucket of spackle and a putty knife, he filled as many superficial holes and blemishes as he could. After the spots dried, he would go back and sand them smooth. There were a couple of holes large enough to require a drywall patch, which he'd learned how to do from watching a YouTube video.

Near the bottom of the doorframe, he noticed the drywall was warped and remembered one of Mouse's guys telling him he'd have to cut it out and replace it. The guy had even left him a quarter sheet of drywall in the garage for the repair. He figured while he was at it, he might as well do that, too. In the garage he found a hand saw for the job.

He used a drill to create an opening big enough to get the saw in (more YouTube), then started hacking at it. A few minutes in he realized the wall had been repaired before because a crack appeared along a perfect square around the damaged area. He stopped sawing and used his fingers to try to pull it out. The piece of drywall was stubborn, but he put some muscle into it and it popped out so quickly, he fell back on his butt.

When he sat up, he squinted at the opaque black bag sitting between the drywall studs. He pulled out the bag and looked inside.

"Holy shit."

He reached inside and pulled out a stack of bills. All hundreds, brand new, and the currency strap around them read $5000. By his quick estimation, there had to be at least a hundred stacks...a half a million dollars?

"Holy shit!"

Had his father put it there? It made sense, but if so, why wouldn't Randolph tell them? They certainly could've used the cash over the years—he'd seen Carlotta cry over unpaid bills too many times to count.

Wes pushed his hand into his hair. Who should he tell? Carlotta, probably, although she'd go straight to Jack. Liz would turn it over to the cops, too. He couldn't tell Chance because he'd blab to cronies who would commit murder for a lot less.

He was stuck...everyone he knew was either too good or too bad to tell.

For now...it would be his secret. But one thing was certain—he needed to find a *big* poker tournament.

CHAPTER THIRTY-FOUR

"HOW WAS YOUR FIRST DAY BACK?" Lindy Russell asked Carlotta.

"Quiet," Carlotta said. "Which after the week at the Wedding World Expo, I was ready for."

Lindy smiled. "Everyone is singing your praises—Edward King, Jarold Jett...and especially Patricia."

"I'm glad it all worked out the way it did. As for me, I was just in the right place at the right time."

"That's been happening a lot lately." Lindy angled her head. "You seem to be into all kinds of things."

Thinking that Lindy was questioning her loyalty to Neiman's, Carlotta tried to recover. "But retail is my number one priority."

"I understand Jarold Jett might be trying to woo you away."

Carlotta arched an eyebrow. The last thing she wanted was for her boss to think she was shopping for another job. Lindy had given her several passes for misdeeds. "I—"

"I just want to inform you..."

She closed her eyes. *That you're suspended...that you're fired?*

"That we value you here very much, Carlotta. And I'm going to be looking for a place in our organization where you can contribute at a higher level."

She opened her eyes. "A promotion?"

Lindy nodded. "Meanwhile, I know you worked a lot of hours at the Expo, and you represented Neiman's beautifully. Why don't you take a few paid days off, and we'll talk when you get back."

"I...thank you."

"I'll call human resources and have the paid time added to your check."

When Lindy walked away, Carlotta laughed into her hand. This had to be one of the best days of her life—she was getting a promotion…her personal life seemed to be taking shape…and this morning she'd seen and spoken to her father.

It was still surreal. She'd managed to keep quiet about the encounter until Hannah had driven outside the prison grounds. Her friend had been morose, believing the escapade had been for nothing, so when Carlotta told her about the spill and her conversation with Randolph, Hannah almost ran the truck off the road.

All day Carlotta had been repeating the brief conversation in her head. Randolph hadn't answered the most basic question about their mother's whereabouts, and he'd seemed almost unconcerned about his own plight, as if he were biding his time until the timing was right. His advice to her was more philosophical than practical.

Go home, Carlotta. Everything you're looking for is there.

Like Dorothy in *The Wonderful Wizard of Oz*, whose ultimate acceptance of the mantra "There's no place like home" had transported her back to a safe place.

She was angry with him for not simply being straight with her—how long would it have taken to simply tell her if Valerie was dead or alive? And where?

It was as if he were talking in code…as if he were afraid she was wired or something. He knew the D.A. had once set up a fake funeral for her and had to know she'd been in on it. Did he still think she was working with Kelvin Lucas to bring him down?

Go home, Carlotta. Everything you're looking for is there.

Carlotta headed to the employee break room to retrieve her purse, keeping an eye on the time. Peter was supposed to pick her up at six thirty to whisk her away to an out of the way place to have dinner and catch up.

She sighed. Peter had been wonderful lately, and so patient with her while she sorted through her feelings. And although he'd been on board with her decision to hit the pause button on their relationship until the situation with Randolph was resolved, she knew he wouldn't be held at bay much longer. Which was why she'd decided to tell him tonight they could only be friends.

It would be a difficult conversation, but she knew it was the right thing to do to clear her head and heart, to see where her feelings for Jack would take her.

Go home, Carlotta. Everything you're looking for is there.

The very idea that Randolph would use the word *home* was so hypocritical. The townhouse had never felt like a home, even when he and Valerie had lived there. It was simply the place where they'd landed when they'd stopped rolling downhill. To her, home would always be the house in Buckhead where she and Wes had grown up. Which probably explained why when she'd been transported to the other place in her travel-dream, she had climbed out of her car and found herself standing in front of it...

Go home, Carlotta. Everything you're looking for is there.

And then the answer slammed into her head with amazing clarity.

Go home...the place she considered home.

Was it possible Randolph was monitoring the listening device from their old home?

She fumbled for her phone to call up an app Wes had shown her to map the distance between two points. She entered the address of their townhome, and the address of their previous home in Buckhead. The driving route was more than two miles. Randolph had been an excellent runner—he'd boasted about his seven-minute mile. But even he couldn't run two miles in the short span of time between Abrams attacking her and the time Randolph had arrived, which she estimated to be about five minutes.

She did the reverse math and, assuming his running speed had slowed with age, she calculated that in five minutes, Randolph would be able to travel about six-tenths of a mile.

Going back to the map app, Carlotta changed the route between the houses from a driving route, which was circuitous, to the pedestrian route, which was practically as the crow flies, cutting across a lawn or two. The result was seven-tenths of a mile.

Definitely runnable in five minutes.

Her hands were shaking as she pulled up Sammy Sanders's number and connected the call.

"Hello, Carlotta."

"Hi, Sammy. I need another favor."

"At five o'clock on Friday? There had better be another coupon involved."

"Absolutely. Can you look up an address and tell me the recent purchase history of the house?"

"Sure. I'm at my computer…do you have the address?"

Carlotta recited it slowly, even though her pulse was running wild.

"Oh, that's one of mine," Sammy said. "Did I mention I've been the number one agent in Buckhead for the last three years?"

"Um, yes, I think you did mention it."

"Here we go…oh yes, I remember this one. Nice place in an established neighborhood, but it sat empty for a long time. I sold it about six months ago."

She gripped the phone tighter. "What can you tell me about the buyers?"

"Well, I only met the husband. His wife is supposed to be joining him shortly."

"Do you remember their names?"

"Bill and Melanie, I think?"

"What about a last name?"

"I can't recall, but let me find the contract." There were sounds of file cabinets being opened and closed, paper shuffling. "Yes, here it is—last name… Randolph."

CHAPTER THIRTY-FIVE

RUNNING LATE, meet you at the restaurant.

Carlotta hit the send button. A few seconds later, Peter texted back. *Ok... can't wait to see you. xox*

She sat in the rental car in the driveway of the Buckhead house. *Home.* The curved flagstone walkway was the same, and the front door, with stained glass accents. But the landscaping was overgrown, a few shingles were missing, and the corners appeared to be sagging a bit.

For the fifteen minutes she'd been parked there, she'd seen no signs of activity. The house appeared to be empty.

So why was she still sitting here?

Because she was afraid of what she might find inside?

The idea that Randolph had been monitoring them from here still seemed too fantastic to believe. But there was only one way to find out.

Carlotta opened the car door and stepped out, instantly recalling details she'd forgotten, like the tiny flecks of blue glass in the pebbled driveway, and the curve of the covered entryway. She had the strangest feeling of déjà vu and realized it was because she'd acted out this very scene only a few nights ago when she'd traveled to an alternate universe.

Now she was thinking her subconscious was telling her then what she had only just figured out—that everything came back to the house where the Wrens had been a happy family.

She walked tentatively to the front door and rang the doorbell. The chime echoed inside, a familiar tone. How many times had she heard it and bounded down the stairs to greet a school friend or Peter?

With heart pounding, she stood for a while, expecting any minute for some stranger named Bill Randolph to open the door and ask what she wanted.

But he didn't.

She rang the doorbell again, and waited, but still no answer. Trying to appear casual in case a neighbor was watching, she bent over and felt along the stack stone steps until she found the loose stone where they'd kept a spare key.

And found it.

As she inserted the key into the lock of the front door, her heart was in her throat. Was she about to walk in on some poor, unsuspecting family?

Or Valerie?

She pushed open the door and walked inside. "Hello?"

Nothing.

"Hello?"

The house appeared to be empty of furniture, except for barstools in the kitchen. The electricity was on, and there was some food in the refrigerator. The milk was expired by two weeks, so the timing was right for Randolph to have been here. The garage was empty, so if he'd been using a car, it was parked elsewhere.

She soaked in the familiar details of the house, moving from room to room, looking for...she didn't know what.

On the second floor, she found it.

In the room that had been her father's den was a sleeping bag and a few men's clothes in her father's size. On one of the built-in bookshelves sat a small device that looked like a walkie-talkie...the receiver for the bug in their kitchen? It seemed likely.

There was also an accordion file of papers associated with the house contract. She scanned them for some sign of the buyer's original address, but she couldn't find one. She scanned the room for any other bits of information that might tell her where Randolph had been, and where Valerie might still be, but came up empty.

Then she went back to the clothing and was rewarded with a wadded up receipt stuffed in the corner of a shirt pocket—for a post office box...in Las Vegas, Nevada.

So her mother, it seemed, was in Vegas.

Dead or alive, she didn't know, but at least she had a place to start looking.

Carlotta sat in the floor and let the feelings of relief and wonder wash over her. What an amazing day.

And she could think of only one person she wanted to talk to. She pulled up Jack's number and connected the call, not yet sure how much she would share, but just wanting to hear his voice.

"Hi, Carlotta."

She smiled into the phone. "Hi, Jack. How was your first day back?"

"Fine. I think Detective Salyers and I will be working together some."

"That's a good thing, right?"

"Sure…Salyers is a sharp detective, and I'm happy to have the help. Tying up the loose ends of this case alone will take weeks, if not months."

"You're welcome, Jack."

"Listen, I'm glad you called," he said, lowering his voice. "I have something to tell you."

"And I have something to tell you."

"Just let me say this—"

"If it's about my dad—"

"It isn't. Liz is pregnant."

She gave a little laugh. "I know…I've known for a while. But good news—Wes isn't the father after all."

"I know," he said. "Because, well…I'm the father."

Pinpoints of bright lights sparkled and buzzed in her head, as if something in her brain was shorting out. Just when she thought she might be having a stroke, the noise stopped and the lights went out, leaving a dark emptiness. It was as if her future had just been switched off.

"Carlotta? Are you there? I'm sorry—"

She punched the "End" button on her phone. It seemed fitting.

CHAPTER THIRTY-SIX

"HI, THERE," Peter said, smiling wide.

"Hi," Carlotta said, proud of herself for sounding normal when inside, she was still reeling from her discovery...and Jack's announcement. "Sorry I'm late. Traffic snag."

"You're worth the wait."

He looked handsome and successful in slacks, a lightweight sweater, and polished accessories. Peter was always so well put together. And calming. Everything about him was stable and reassuring and dependable. She could almost feel her blood pressure coming down.

"I ordered a bottle of malbec," he said. "I hope that's okay."

She nodded and observed his body language as he filled her glass. Elegant, confident, accomplished.

"How was your day?" he asked.

She gave a little laugh. "Eventful."

He held up his glass. "Then here's to your eventful day."

She clinked his glass, humbled by his sensitivity and chivalry. When the wine flowed into her mouth, she hummed with pleasure.

"I'm glad you like it," he said, reaching across the table to clasp her hand. "I've missed you so much. I got spoiled having you around the house and being able to talk to you every day." Then he gave a little laugh. "Sorry. I promised myself I wouldn't do that."

"Do what?"

"Gush...crowd you...all those things that men aren't supposed to do. But I can't help it. I want you in my life, Carly. I went along with this idea of yours to pretend we broke up because I wanted to please you. But I don't want to do it anymore. I don't care if anyone at work questions my loyalty to the firm... all I care about is being able to tell and show everyone how much I love you."

In five minutes Peter Ashford had said everything that Jack Terry hadn't said in a year...and she'd never have to worry about Peter getting someone else pregnant.

Peter was so good, she didn't deserve him. Then she stopped herself.

Was that her problem—she thought she couldn't measure up?

Which was absurd. Hadn't she just helped the police solve a big murder case? Figured out her father's riddle? She suddenly felt empowered, as if she were about to embark on a new phase of her life.

Peter sighed. "There I go again...gushing."

"It's fine." She squeezed his hand. "In fact, it's more than fine. I've had some time to think while we were apart."

His expression was hopeful. "And?"

"And my boss gave me some paid days off, so how would you like to take that trip to Vegas we postponed?"

He grinned. "I would love it."

"So would I." And she meant it. "Just one favor?"

"Anything."

"Would you mind if Wes came along?"

"Not at all."

"Thank you." She leaned forward and kissed him on the mouth. He kissed her back with surprising passion. Maybe in Vegas they could rekindle the flame.

When she pulled back, she laughed. "This is going to be fun. Can I let Wes know?"

"Sure."

Carlotta picked up her phone, pulled up Wes's number and texted *Pack your bags, we're going to Vegas!*

-The End-

A NOTE FROM THE AUTHOR

Thank you so very much for reading 7 BRIDES FOR 7 BODIES! This book marks a personal and professional milestone for me because I'm thrilled to be able to continue a series my former publishing house lost interest in, but that I loved writing. And if not for readers like you asking for more books and spreading the word about the Body Movers gang, this wouldn't have been possible. Thank you for being so patient as I worked to make this book happen. I hope it made you laugh and groan and sigh…and want to read more! Rest assured I'll be continuing the Body Movers series—I'll keep writing as long you keep reading.

If you enjoyed 7 BRIDES FOR 7 BODIES and feel inclined to leave a review at your favorite online bookstore, I would appreciate it very much. Reviews help my books find new readers, which means I can keep writing new stories! Plus I always want to know what my readers are thinking.

And are you signed up to receive notices of my future book releases? If not, please visit www.stephaniebond.com to sign up for my mailing list. I will never share or sell your address. And you can unsubscribe at any time.

Also, although I can't count the times this book has been edited and proofed, I am human, so if you do spot a typo, please email me at stephanie@ stephaniebond.com to let me know! Thanks again for your time and interest, and for telling your friends about my books. If you'd like to know more about some of my other books, please scroll ahead to the next section.

Happy reading!
Stephanie Bond

DON'T MISS A SINGLE MOVE!

Look for all the books in the continuing *Body Movers* series:

Also, to read BODY MOVERS stories written by fans of the series (and to submit your own), go to **BodyMoversFanFiction.com**!

OTHER BOOKS BY STEPHANIE BOND

Humorous romantic mysteries:

TWO GUYS DETECTIVE AGENCY—*Even Victoria can't keep a secret from us...*
OUR HUSBAND—*Hell hath no fury like three women scorned!*
KILL THE COMPETITION—*There's only one sure way to the top.*
I THINK I LOVE YOU—*Sisters share everything in their closets...including the skeletons.*

GOT YOUR NUMBER—*You can run, but your past will eventually catch up with you.*
WHOLE LOTTA TROUBLE—*They didn't plan on getting caught...*
IN DEEP VOODOO—*A woman stabs a voodoo doll of her ex, and then he's found murdered!*
VOODOO OR DIE—*Another voodoo doll, another untimely demise...*
BUMP IN THE NIGHT—*a short mystery*

Romances:

ALMOST A FAMILY—*Fate gave them a second chance at love...*
LICENSE TO THRILL—*She's between a rock and a hard body...*
STOP THE WEDDING!—*If anyone objects to this wedding, speak now...*
THREE WISHES—*Be careful what you wish for!*
TEMPORARY ARRANGEMENT—*Friends become lovers...what could possibly go wrong?*

Nonfiction:

GET A LIFE! 8 STEPS TO CREATE YOUR OWN LIFE LIST—*a short how-to for mapping out your personal life list!*

ABOUT THE AUTHOR

 Stephanie Bond was seven years deep into a corporate career in computer programming and pursuing an MBA at night when an instructor remarked she had a flair for writing and suggested she submit material to academic journals. But Stephanie was more interested in writing fiction—more specifically, romance and mystery novels. After writing in her spare time for two years, she sold her first manuscript; after selling ten additional projects to two publishers, she left her corporate job to write fiction full-time. To-date, Stephanie has more than seventy published novels to her name, including the popular BODY MOVERS humorous mystery series. Stephanie lives in Atlanta. For more information on Stephanie's books, visit www.stephaniebond.com.

Made in the USA
San Bernardino, CA
28 October 2015